THE AWAKENED

Book One of the Magi War

Copyright © 2022 John W G Bankhead

All rights reserved

The characters and events portrayed in this book are fictitious. Any similarity to real persons, living or dead, is coincidental and not intended by the author.

No part of this book may be reproduced, or stored in a retrieval system, or transmitted in any form or by any means, electronic, mechanical, photocopying, recording, or otherwise, without express written permission of the publisher.

ISBN-13: 9781739679101

Published by: Dwing Publishing UK
Cover design by: Ambient Studios

Dedicated to MRB, who always believed.

CHAPTER 1

As the wagon entered the gates of Tarrondale, Bartack could not help but be in awe. A country boy from the South Forest near Dalleen, he had never seen such a thing before. The majestic red sandstone walls rose eighty feet into the air. Patrolling along the wall parapets and at the gate stood chain-mailed guards. Peering just above the wall ramparts, the cone shaped roofs of some high towers could be seen.

Bartack had just turned seventeen. He was fair haired, medium height and thin for his age.
He had been travelling five days now from his village to reach the city. He was heading to Tarrondale for the annual selection trials to the Royal Academy.

Luckily, on the road he had met some friendly cloth traders. They had been travelling from Mourkley to Tarrondale by wagon. The traders had allowed him to join their caravan and this reduced his journey time considerably. Not travelling on foot was a relief and had made things much safer for him. He did not have to worry about ambush from brigands or any other dangers while he was with the party. Caravans were always well protected and this one had been no different. They had several outrider scouts who had provided a look-out, and they also had guards armed with crossbows. The column of caravans drove into the imposing archway of the gate house.

A stern faced, chain-mailed guard was standing there. He indicated with his hand for the wagon to stop. The wagon master brought his team of horses to a halt. He signalled to the other teams to do the same.

'Your name, cargo and destination?' quizzed the guard.

'Master Belvore, cloth and Tarrondale docks, friend.' replied the wagon master.

The guard gave a cursory inspection, then grunted his approval and waved the wagons through the gate. Once within the walls the caravan party was greeted by a thriving, bustling city. People were carrying wares, selling things or just going about their daily business.

It was clear from the different races and dialects that Tarrondale was an important city. Bartack had never seen so many people in one place. After travelling several minutes through the city streets, they arrived at a large crossroads. The wagon master called a halt, and the four wagons immediately came to a stop.

'This is it Bartack, this is where you get off young man.'

The wagon master pointed ahead.

'That's where you are heading for lad; the barracks for the Royal trials are that way.'

'We are off to the docks which is in a different direction.'

'Just keep heading down that road to the front of us. You will come to a large square, then turn right. You should then see the entrance of the camp.' said Belvore. Bartack collected his pack and jumped down from the wagon.

'Thanks for the lift Belvore.' he replied.

'Good luck, Bartack. Perhaps we will see you again when we return to Tarrondale.'

'Maybe it will be you guarding the city gates next time we arrive. Take care of yourself.' said Belvore.

The wagon master smiled and waved goodbye to Bartack. He gave the signal for the teams to move out. The wagons began to move off in the direction of Tarrondale docks. A few of the other wagon drivers waved at Bartack as they passed. Bartack waved back in response.

Bartack watched the wagons depart until he lost sight of them down another street. He now felt much less assured than before, as he was now alone. He was just another arrival in the city, and the locals were not bothering with him. People were pushing past him as they went about their business.

In the days he had been with the caravan he had grown fond of the group. He had got to know most of the caravanners. Bartack was once again a lone traveller in a strange and unfamiliar place.

It was not long past noon. Bartack started walking down the road Belvore had indicated to him. He felt very small amongst the heaving masses of people. Sure enough, at the end of the road there was a large square. To the right of the square he could see what looked like people queuing. The queues were quite long and consisted of young men and boys.

Bartack joined the end of the queue.

'Is this for the Royal Academy trials?' he asked the youth in front of him.

'Yes.' replied the youth.

He stared Bartack up and down, as if to say why are *you* bothering.

Bartack had been queuing for some time. An hour or so had passed from when he first joined. There were now thirty or forty other people behind him. As time passed, he eventually reached the front where a dark, thick-bearded man was seated at a table. Bartack hesitated, reluctant to move.

'Quickly boy, come forward.' said the bearded man.

The bearded man impatiently gestured for Bartack to come towards his table. The boy did as he was told and approached the man.

'What's your name, boy?' asked the bearded man.

'Bartack Arimvale.' the boy replied, as the man began to take notes.

'Your age?' asked the man.

'Seventeen.' replied Bartack.

'Where are you from boy?' asked the man.

'Dalleen, the South Forest.' Bartack replied once again.

'A westerner eh? And a woodlander too! You're quite small for a westerner. Weren't they feeding you boy?' asked the bearded man, laughing.

'Which arm do you intend to serve in if selected, boy?' asked the man.

'Royal Guard.' replied Bartack with innocent sincerity.

The bearded man smiled, making a visible effort not to laugh at Bartack's answer. The boy was much too thin to be a Royal Guard, besides, the armour would be too heavy for him, thought the bearded man to himself.

'Very well boy, I'll put you down for Royal Guard selection then. With a second preference as a Royal Scout. How does that sound, boy?' asked the bearded man.

The bearded man wrote down the rest of Bartack's details on a parchment. At the section marked 'Preferred Arm' he wrote 'Royal Scouts'. The bearded man smiled knavishly to himself.

'Now remember boy, you may not get your first choice. Just be aware of that.'

The bearded man folded the parchment over, so that Bartack could not see it. He then reached out and handed the parchment over.

'OK boy, take this paper to the clerk over yonder.' The man pointed at another seated man.

'He'll instruct you on what to do from there.'

Bartack accepted the folded parchment paper from the bearded man, wishing he could have seen what was written. He then walked over to the clerk as instructed.

'Papers, boy, hand them over, *snap to it.*' said the impatient and clearly stressed clerk.

Bartack handed them over and watched patiently. The clerk began to read them, and started mumbling to himself as he read out the contents aloud. Bartack looked at him. He was a tall, dark man in his early forties. The clerk's hair was beginning to thin on the top of his head. He had an almost comical comb over to try and conceal the baldness. His complexion looked rather pale and weathered, but there was a certain sharpness in his eyes

'OK boy, join that group over there. Oh, and take this voucher. You'll need it to draw equipment from stores. *Do not* lose it.' said the impatient clerk.

Bartack took the voucher and walked over to the others. There were twelve in the group, the youngest looked no more than fifteen, the eldest twenty at most.

Two men dressed in studded leather armour approached the group. One was six feet tall, muscular and blonde. His companion was five feet six, bald, quite plump, with a puffed red drinker's nose. Both men wore the rank markings of Corporals. The fat man spoke.

'Right you lot, listen in. Follow me to the barracks. We'll assign you a room, and then we'll take you to stores for the equipment you'll need.'

The two men began to briskly walk away, the boys struggled to keep up with them. The fat man glanced back at them.

'Come on you lot, keep moving, we haven't got all day you know. If you had to retreat in a hurry you'd be left behind.' said the fat Corporal.

The group arrived at brick one storey building, there were several similar buildings nearby. Bartack concluded this must be the barracks that the fat Corporal was referring to.

'Right, I'm going to assign you all rooms. As soon as I do, pick a bed, leave your belongings in the room and be back outside straight away. No time for napping. Got that?'

'Good, now here goes.'

The fat man began to read names from a list.

Bartack listened excitedly for his name. The first three names were called and they were given a room number. Three of Bartack's group ran up the steps and into the barracks. Then the next three were called. There were now only six left. Another three names were called and they too ran in.

Bartack was left with two others; a brown haired boy and a sandy haired, muscular boy. They looked at each other.

'OK you three, room seven D.'

With that, they ran inside, and found their room easily as the number was clearly on the door. It was tiny and cramped, with barely room for the three small single beds and three foot lockers. The walls were whitewashed and the room had one window. Hanging from the ceiling was an oil lamp. The three boys each claimed a bed, left their belongings and went back outside as ordered.

'Come on you three, hurry up, there'll be nothing left by the time we get there,' said the fat Corporal.

The two men escorted the group to the stores. The quartermaster took their vouchers and issued each with a wooden sword, brown overalls and a pair of gloves.

The group was then led to a mess hall, where they were told to queue up for food. Many of the boys at the trials were clearly half starved, and wolfed down the food. For some, it really was the first meal they had in several days. The majority of those here were from the poor, hungry or desperate.

After the meal, the youngsters were led to a large hall.

There were lots of recruits already standing on the hall floor, each in their own groups.

'Right, assemble in line down there.' ordered the fat Corporal, gesturing towards another row of young recruits.

'Quickly! Quickly!' he barked.

The youngsters did as instructed; quickly the room became filled with recruits all neatly standing in silence. After a few minutes, a bald man wearing plate mail and a golden cloak entered the large hall. He was tall and had a visible scar across his left eye. He walked to the front of the hall.

'Atten-shun!' screamed a Sergeant. Everyone in the room stood to attention.

'Welcome to the Royal Academy, I am Commandant Kreer.'

'Tomorrow you will take part in our selection trials.'

'Most of you will be successful, some will fail.'

'However, I would like to wish you all best of luck for tomorrow, whatever the outcome.'

The plate mailed man began to exit the hall, his armour clanked heavily as he left the room.

A Sergeant screamed, 'Stand at ease!'
After the Commandant had left, the groups were marched back to their barracks. The fat Corporal led his group to their rooms.

'Ablutions are through there.' he said, pointing to a washroom and toilet.

'Now get your heads down, it's a dawn start tomorrow, and it won't be long coming round.'

The fat Corporal and his colleague then left the boys. Bartack and his room-mates had a wash, then got into their beds and quickly drifted off to sleep. The bed was hard, but this was the first time Bartack had slept in a real bed in many days.

The sun had barely risen when the silence of sleep was disturbed by the sound of reveille. A bugler blew on his trumpet, alerting everyone to rise. The boys yawned, rubbed their eyes, and reluctantly prepared to rouse themselves from their beds.
The fat Corporal burst into their room.

'Right you lazy oafs, get the hell up and to the mess!' he screamed at the boys.

Bartack jumped with a start. It took him a few minutes to adjust himself. The other two boys were up and getting dressed. Once dressed, they headed to the mess in column and began to queue behind the other trainees.

They were each given a metal food tray, and as they passed the serving area, a cook slopped food onto it. The boys then sat down and began to eat. The food was a type of rough porridge, some fruit and thick bacon. It wasn't the most appetising meal, Bartack thought, but at least it was free.

Once breakfast had concluded, they were told to report outside their accommodation. The boys formed up in line awaiting the arrival of the two Corporals. The fat Corporal arrived, still chewing on a roast chicken leg, accompanied by his muscular colleague.

'Right, listen up! You are to collect your issue items from your rooms and report outside immediately!' screamed the fat man.

The boys did as ordered, quickly running into their rooms and fetching their kit. They all lined up back outside again.

'Quickly, quickly, that's it!' said the fat man.

'Now we are off to the trials. Good luck, by the looks of it most of you will need it.' he said with a grin. The fat Corporal led his group to a large training field. In the field, trainees were already fighting and beginning their trials. They were being closely watched by soldiers who were keeping scores and awarding points.

The trials lasted six hours, they tested the trainees in weapons handling, horse riding, strength, agility and stamina throughout and now they were exhausted. Bartack had proved himself extremely agile, but he needed to bulk up his muscles. The melee tests had proved difficult for him, but his archery ability looked promising along with his tracking skills.

Bartack's room-mates had mixed results; one boy had proved inept, but the fair haired boy had proven to be the best archer of the group. After the trials had concluded, the testing officials tallied up the scores for each boy. The fat corporal ordered the twelve boys from his group to gather together. Bartack stood next to the two boys who shared his room.

'Listen up, I now have the list of results from today's trial. Mungar, Hardell, Jamos, Tholis, Garneer, you've passed, infantry for you.'

'Bellin, Orick, Yolli, you've passed, cavalry for you. Le Romme.' the corporal paused, 'Royal Guard officer training.' Delight appeared on the face of the inept boy who had shared Bartack's room on the previous night.

Bartack couldn't understand it, he outperformed the other boy right thorough the whole trials, yet he got selected. What's more, the boy got selected for officer training. Bartack now felt apprehensive. There were three of them left; himself, the fair haired boy and a short youngster from another room.

'Arimvale, Tuintharr, well done, Royal Scouts.'

'Argam,' the corporal paused, 'Fail.'

The short boy's head dropped. The corporal looked at him.

'Don't worry boy, there's always next year, and the year after, and another year after that.' said the fat corporal smugly.

'The Scouts trainees stay here, Le Romme, you will be sailing to Gunimore. The rest of you will join your own units. Collect your belongings from your rooms and return your loaned items to stores.'

Bartack's heart sunk, and he felt aggrieved that he failed to make the Royal Guard. The boys began to do as ordered and collected their belongings. The fat Corporal pointed at Bartack and the fair haired boy.

'You two wait in your room, you'll soon have a new room-mate and some other boys will join you in the barracks.'

Bartack and the fair haired boy walked towards their room. The other boys were exiting and wishing each other good luck as they left. Bartack sat on his bed, the other boy did likewise.

'My name is Bartack.'

'Tellan.' replied the fair haired boy.

'Where are you from?' asked Bartack.

'My family live in Garmer.' replied Tellan.

'That's quite a bit north.' replied Bartack.

'How did you end up here?' asked Bartack.

'My family were refugees from Tamola who settled in Garmer. My father lost everything, including my mother in a tusk-men raid. Times are hard in Garmer, and I needed work. What about you?'

'I'm from near Dalleen, in the South Forest near Mourkley Marsh. My father is a trapper. But trapping never appealed to me. I don't understand how I ended up in the Scouts; I volunteered for the Royal Guard with the bearded man at the desk.' said Bartack.

Tellan remained silent, nodding in understanding, he found it comforting that someone there knew where he was from. There was a timid knock at the door; both of the boys looked round. Through the door came a young male with shoulder length dark hair. He looked to be in his early twenties and he wore a cheeky grin.

'Hello, I have been assigned to this barracks, Derrin Hezzul is my name.' said the newcomer.

Bartack and Tellan introduced themselves and welcomed him into the cramped room. Derrin carried a small rucksack and began unloading its contents into his footlocker. He was careful not to reveal what items he was placing inside, making sure the lid of the footlocker acted as a shield.

He locked the footlocker and checked it a second

time ensuring it was properly secured. It was clear this fellow was cautious and untrusting.

'Where are you from, Derrin?' asked Bartack.

'Oh, Dunregal mostly.' replied Derrin.

Derrin seemed reluctant to answer, and his accent didn't remind Bartack of any Dolia easterner. The boy's brief respite was quickly brought to a crashing end, as the fat Corporal burst through the door.

'Right scum! All off you outside *now!*' he screamed with a red puffed face which matched his bulbous red nose.

CHAPTER 2

'Right you lot! Form line!' bawled the fat Corporal.

'This is our first day together so lets get acquainted eh?'

The corporal began to walk down the line of recruits, eyeing them up and down. The blonde muscular Corporal just looked on at his colleague.

'My name is Corporal Murrat, this is Corporal Breven. You will always address us as Corporal. Got that? Good.

You runts will speak only when spoken to.'

The fat corporal walked past the middle of the line and stopped, facing Derrin.

'You, you're a shifty looking little bastard, aren't yah?'

Derrin said nothing, and just stared ahead.

'How the hell did you get past the selection process then? Where are you from?' asked Murrat.

'Dunregal.' replied Derrin.

'Dunregal, *what*? Weren't you listening to me, scum?' yelled Murrat.

'Dunregal Corporal!' replied Derrin.

'Show some respect you scum when you address us!' screamed Murrat.

Derrin's thick mane of hair made the little man even more conscious of his own baldness.

'Get that hair of yours cut too, boy.' shouted Murrat.

Murrat continued to the end of the line, this time

stopping at a young blonde man.

Bartack and Derrin tried to listen; they could sense Murrat was becoming angrier with the boy than he had been with Derrin.

'You little scumbag!' Murrat screamed as he punched the recruit in the stomach.

The boy dropped to the ground and Murrat grabbed him by the scruff of his neck.

'Up scum, get up!' yelled Murrat.

The boy shakily got to his feet, as Murrat returned to the front of the line.

'You lot are a *disgrace*, I have never come across a worse shower of weaklings and imbeciles.

All of you, go to the stores. Sign for your equipment, then return here. Be quick damn you!' shouted Murrat.

The column fell out and ran quickly in the direction of the stores. Derrin was running next to Tellan and Bartack.

'That Murrat is an evil bastard. He'll kill someone if he's not careful.' said Derrin.

'I won't disagree with you there; did you see how he hit that recruit?' asked Bartack.

'Aye, and that could have been me.' laughed Derrin in relief.

'What did that boy say to him that made him so angry?' asked Tellan.

'Dunno, I didn't hear, but I'll find out later.' said Derrin with a cheeky grin.

They joined the queue at the stores and were issued with their equipment. They returned to their barracks, issued with a short sword, short bow and leather armour. They secured their items in their footlockers and formed line outside on the parade square.

Corporal Breven was the only instructor there; Murrat had finished for the day and was attending to other matters. Breven took the recruits to the training area and finished the afternoon with physical training. The recruits were exhausted and the strength training proved difficult for most of them.

After the training the boys were taken for their supper in the mess. The mood was subdued; the recruits were so tired they weren't interested in talking. When their meal was concluded they returned to their barracks, stopping first at the washroom to freshen up, then going to their rooms.

Bartack and Tellan lay on their beds. Derrin was no-where to be seen. Murrat was doing his evening rounds and burst into the room. He had a nosey around hoping to catch the trainees out, and seemed disappointed that everything was in order. Then he let off a large, loud fart beside Derrin and Tellan.

'There ya go lads, something for you to remember me by. Sweet dreams then.' said the repulsive Murrat, laughing to himself as he left.
Tellan looked at Bartack, the air in the room stank.

'He's one foul bastard.' said Tellan.
Bartack nodded in agreement.

Tellan closed his eyes, then began snoring and Bartack felt himself become sleepy. He got up and turned off the oil lamp and got back into bed. They would be woken at dawn, and his body was already sore from the exercise. Bartack too drifted off to sleep.

His slumber didn't last long, he was woken by a creaking noise. His eyes adjusted quickly to the dark and he saw a figure climb into Derrin's empty bed. Bartack couldn't help wondering what had he been up to? Everyone else had been exhausted, yet Derrin seemed to have the energy to stay up late. Bartack rolled over and quickly fell back to sleep.

Reveille sounded outside Bartack's barracks. As the boys began to wake, they could hear the sound of Corporal Murrat screaming at the recruits in a nearby room. They awaited ominously for his arrival, just then he burst through the door.

'Right scum, up, get washed, and go to the mess! You have thirty minutes!'

Bartack and his room-mates quickly complied; they had already seen enough to know Murrat shouldn't be crossed. After their meal they returned to the barracks. Breven had ordered them into their overalls. They all knew this meant more physical training. Bartack was still sore from the previous day and he hoped that he would be alright.

The session seemed much less demanding, but Bartack had noticed that Derrin was flagging in stamina. Breven passed the recruits over to Murrat who ordered them to change into their leather armour and bring along their short swords. Bartack was excited as this was the first time he had done any military training since passing the selection. Inside the training area, Murrat began to demonstrate basic attacks and parries.

Murrat then selected one boy as a volunteer.

'Defend yourself!' said Murrat as he lunged at the boy.

Murrat's blade struck the boy on the arm and the youngster screamed in agony. Although the cut wasn't deep, the boy's blood streamed down his arm. Murrat smirked, clearly taking great pleasure in injuring the young recruit.

'Fall into line boy, you'll live. *This time.*' said Murrat in a menacing manner.

'Next volunteer!' he said pointing at Derrin. Derrin walked forwards from the line and turned to face Murrat. Instantly and without warning, Murrat lunged at Derrin with his sword. Derrin anticipated the attack and parried it. Murrat continued the attack, but Derrin parried easily and attempted to riposte. This forced Murrat back and took him by surprise. Murrat attempted a feint attack but once again Derrin was ready for him. Derrin reposted and caught Murrat across the hand.

Corporal Murrat was enraged by this and charged Derrin, wrestling him to the floor. Murrat punched Derrin in the face with a glancing blow, using his sword's hand guard. Derrin fell flat on his back clutching his nose, his face was now covered in blood. Murrat hadn't finished with him, and pummelled him continually on the ground. Derrin lay motionless, forcing Breven to intervene. He pulled Murrat off the youngster, and managed to subdue him.

'Adam, calm down, forget it!' exclaimed Breven.

Murrat shrugged away Breven's grip, then stormed off in a steaming rage. His face once again, red and flushed with blood.

Breven called for the healers and dismissed the boys to their barracks. Bartack and Tellan were in shock and looked concerned as Derrin had not moved.

'All of you, return to barracks!' yelled Breven.
The healers crouched over Derrin and began casting symbols over him. Derrin was *still* not moving.

Bartack and Tellan made their way back to their room, still shocked and transfixed on what they just had witnessed.

'Murrat nearly killed Derrin.' said Tellan.

'He *would* have killed him, if Breven hadn't stopped him.' said Bartack.

'I hope he's alright.' said Tellan.

'The healers will do their best for him, I'm sure he will be fine.' said Bartack trying to reassure his roommate.

'I never knew Derrin was that handy with a sword, he was quite good.' said Tellan.

'Yes, he kept that secret quiet.' said Bartack wondering what else Derrin had been concealing.

'Hopefully he will be back tomorrow.' said Tellan.

'Yes, we'll see tomorrow.' said Bartack.
The two boys rolled over on their beds and fell asleep.

After some time had passed, Derrin awoke and his eyes began to adjust to the light. He looked around and he was now lying in the infirmary. He noticed one of the healers who was busy sorting bottles of elixir on a cabinet. The healer looked around at Derrin.

'Ah, you are conscious again. How is your head?' asked the healer.

Derrin rubbed his head and replied, 'A bit tender.'

The healer came over to him and inspected him.

'I used some purple weed root poultice. That should take away the swelling and ease the pain.'

'Thanks.' replied Derrin.

'You can go back to your barracks.' said the healer. Derrin slowly eased himself up and shakily left the infirmary, heading back to his room. As he entered Tellan and Bartack were already in the room. They were pleased to see him.

'Derrin, are you OK?' asked Bartack.

'How are you, we feared the worst.' said Tellan.

'I'm OK, but sore.' replied Derrin.

He walked over to his bed and lay down.

'I knew Murrat was dangerous, and he *will* end up killing someone.'

Derrin was worried about the following day, he didn't want to have to face Murrat again. The boy felt nauseous at the thought.

'I don't think I can deal with Murrat.' said Derrin.

'Don't worry. We have good news on Murrat, he's been shifted to another squad. He has been replaced by a Corporal Rowan. He seems a lot nicer.' said Tellan.

'Yes, the healers reported what happened to Commandant Kreer and he went furious. He had Murrat removed elsewhere. Apparently this wasn't the first time Murrat has been in trouble. He had previously been reprimanded for aggressive behaviour. Breven is still here, but he's a lot calmer without Murrat.' said

Bartack.

Derrin sighed with relief, at least that was one less thing to worry about. 'Kreer may have dealt with Murrat, but had Murrat finished with me?', wondered Derrin to himself.

It was close to eleven o'clock. The room was dark and Tellan was already sleeping. Derrin looked at Bartack to check if he was awake, and he too seemed to be asleep. Derrin slowly crept out of his bed, quietly dressed and stealthily crept out of the room. The floorboard let out a slight creak. Derrin thought to himself he would need to avoid that part of the floor. He left the room and quietly closed the door behind him.

Bartack had been watching. He rose and dressed and decided to see where Derrin was going. Bartack was afraid that Derrin was planning on absconding from the Scouts. If he did, he and his room-mates would equally be in trouble. He left the room and peered out. He quickly caught a glance of Derrin heading to one of the back walls, and start to climb over.

Bartack followed, carefully making sure he wasn't spotted. Derrin climbed over the top of the wall and was soon out of sight. Bartack then began to climb the area of the wall where Derrin had just been. As he got to the top he looked and saw Derrin heading in the direction of the market square.

Bartack jumped over and landed on his feet, he then began following Derrin in the shadows. Occasionally he would have to duck for cover, as Derrin would periodically stop and look around. Derrin then made his way to the Stone Giant Inn, then entered the building.

Bartack was puzzled. What was Derrin doing in there? Was this where he had been the other night, he wondered? It didn't look like he was running off, so Bartack decided to head back. Derrin had returned just after mid-night last time. He decided he would wait up and see if he came back. Bartack carefully followed the route he had taken, returned to the wall and climbed over. He had noticed that a few bricks had been missing on the outside, and these provided a foothold. Bartack reached the top of the wall, checked if anyone was near and dropped down into the camp side. He then quietly made his way back to the room. He removed his clothes and quietly got into bed.

Bartack stayed awake, but facing the opposite direction from Derrin's bed. He waited, fighting the urge to sleep, then sure enough he heard a click at the door, and someone moving in the room. This time there was no floorboard creak, but he heard a person remove their clothes and the cover move on a bed behind him. Derrin had returned, but from doing what Bartack wondered, and what would happen if he had been caught?

The following day the training began early again, this time the class was take by Corporal Rowan, with Breven assisting him. The lesson involved more sword training, dagger handling and finally, they were introduced to archery. The last session was a run, by the end they were exhausted. The group looked at Rowan, who barely had broken a sweat.

'Remember we are Scouts, not infantry, we rely on tracking, speed, stamina, stealth and use hit and run tactics. And we have to be good at all.' said Rowan.

'If you want to hack your way in a line of troops, or charge head first, the infantry are more for you.' said Rowan.

'Scouts don't charge in. We observe. We track. Then we kill our enemies.'

The Corporal cast an eye over the exhausted recruits.

'Some of you may be thinking; why the running? Stamina is important, just as much as strength. Stamina can save you too, just as much as a weapon.' said Rowan.

This training regime continued daily, and the boys began to get fitter, stronger and more adept with the weapons. Rowan was an excellent teacher. They practised regularly with the long bow, and cross bow. They also began training on horse riding and climbing.

Bartack noticed that Derrin left the barracks at night at the same time every few days. He hadn't confronted him yet but was curious as to what he was up to.

Several weeks went by, with the same routine drummed into the recruits. They had become adept at their weapons. Tellan was by far the best archer, Derrin was a clever, nimble swordsman and Bartack was the best tracker.

CHAPTER 3

Six weeks of training had flown by and the boys were looking forward to their first weekend of leave.

Bartack suspected Derrin would be staying at the Stone Giant Inn. He had never confronted him about his night time visits. How he had never been caught amazed him. Tellan was going to visit his uncle in Little Dale. As Dalleen was too far away, Bartack decided he would book himself into the Stone Giant Inn.

Friday evening found the Scout trainees on parade and stood to attention. Commandant Kreer addressed them.

'Congratulations so far, you have all come a long way from when I first spoke to you. Enjoy your weekend pass.'

The Commandant left the parade and the Scouts were dismissed. There was much chatting and excitement from them.

Corporal Rowan spoke to his Scouts.

'Enjoy your weekend boys. Stay out of trouble, watch the booze and stay safe. Make sure you are back to camp by no later than seven at night on the Sunday. Remember, you are Royal Scouts, not infantry. Behave like Scouts. Dismissed.'

The trainee Scouts all rushed back to their barracks to collect their bags. They were desperate to set off on their separate ways. Tellan bade his roommates goodbye, and headed off for Little Dale. Derrin collected his bag, then sheepishly said 'Goodbye' to Bartack.

'See you around.' replied Bartack.

Derrin made his way to the main gates and headed off into the city.

Bartack continued to pack his bags, once he had finished he set off for the inn. The streets were busy with traders moving their wares into Tarrondale in preparation for the large Saturday market. The city centre was just the same as when he first arrived with the cloth merchants six weeks earlier.

Outside the Stone Giant Inn soldiers were drinking and cheering. Bartack walked past them and they eyed him suspiciously. They whispered amongst themselves, pointed, then began laughing at Bartack. Bartack remembered what Rowan had said and, ignoring their mockery, entered the inn.

The inn was already busy, visitors were dining, singing and drinking merrily. Bartack walked over to the bar and approached the innkeeper.

'Hello.' said Bartack nervously.

'Hello, young sir. What can I do for you?' asked the friendly innkeeper.

'Can I have a room? I'll need it for two days.' said Bartack.

'Of course, now what type of room do you need?' said the innkeeper, appraising Bartack's finances.

'Just a simple, private room. Not too expensive.' said Bartack.

'We have such a room, five copper pieces per night.' replied the innkeeper.

Bartack opened his purse and handed the man ten

copper pieces. The innkeeper took the coins, turned around and collected a small iron key from under the counter. He handed the key to Bartack.

'Room fifteen, upstairs.' said the innkeeper pointing in the direction of some wooden stairs.

Bartack nodded his head, and walked towards the stairs. A red haired serving girl made eye contact with him and smiled. Bartack returned the smile and the girl carried on serving inn customers who were dining. He climbed the stairs and went looking for the room. It was at the end of a corridor, and he unlocked the door and entered.

The room was basically furnished, with a wardrobe, wooden bed and a mirrored wash-hand basin with water jug. The toilets were shared on the same floor. The room had a small oil lamp on the wall. Bartack unpacked his belongings and hung his spare clothes inside the wardrobe. The floor was wooden and there was an odd musty smell from the wood. The room was indeed simple, but it was clean. Once he had unpacked he went back downstairs, locking his door.

Bartack was ready to eat, and sat down at one of the tables waiting to be served. Soon the red haired serving girl approached him.

'Hello, what would you like to order?' asked the girl.

Bartack, just looked around at the other diners' food plates, and then pointed to one he liked the look of.

'I'll have whatever that is.' he said.

'And to drink?' asked the girl.

'An ale.' replied Bartack, trying to sound experienced.

'That will be two coppers.' said the girl.

Bartack paid her and she went off. She soon returned with a bowl, a spoon, a tankard, bread and some cheese.

'The cheese is a bit extra, just for you.' the girl winked as she spoke. 'Enjoy.' She smiled and went to another customer who was wanting service.

Bartack looked at the bowl's contents, and saw it contained a stew of some sort. He tasted it and it was very delicious. He broke off some bread and dipped it into the stew. He began to eat it hungrily. The cheese was also a pleasant, mature cheddar with a mild nutty taste. The ale was refreshing, especially as he hadn't had a drink in some time. Once he finished his meal he went over to the innkeeper.

'I'm looking for a friend of mine, his name is Derrin.' said Bartack.

'Derrin! Yes I know Derrin, he comes here often. Well he's staying here now.' laughed the innkeeper.

'He's here *now*?' asked Bartack.

'He's rented a room here for nearly two months now.' said the innkeeper.

Bartack was intrigued; why would Derrin be renting a room and living at the barracks at the same time?

'Which room is he staying in? I'll say hello.' said Bartack.

'Room twenty eight, it's on the second floor.' replied the innkeeper.

Bartack went upstairs and up to the second floor. The décor on this floor seemed more expensive than that on the floor below. He approached Derrin's room and stopped at the door. He took a deep breath and knocked on the door, not sure what to expect.

He heard the door unlock from the inside. The door opened and a stunning blonde girl in a blue dress answered the door. She had very high cheekbones, and her blonde hair was long and in curls.

'Yes, what do you want?' asked the girl suspiciously, eyeing Bartack.

'I'm looking for Derrin, I'm a friend of his. Is he here?' asked Bartack.

'Well yes,' said the girl, 'Derrin, there's someone here for you.'

Derrin approached the door and gasped when he saw Bartack. It was clear from his expression he had not expected any visitors.

'What? How did you know?' said Derrin.

'I think we need to talk Derrin.' said Bartack.

'I'm Marie.' said the girl smiling.

'I'm Bartack, apologies for my lack of introduction.' he replied..

'Come in.' said Derrin.

Derrin ushered Bartack into the room, closing the door behind him. Bartack noticed it was a much more pleasant room than his own. It had a double bed, a wardrobe, a chest of drawers and the room had a bathroom annex. In one corner was a small table and three stools. Bartack sat down beside Marie and Derrin joined him.

'So this is where you slip off to every other night?' asked Bartack.

'Yes, I'm sorry. I know you and Tellan could have got into trouble, but I had to come.' said Derrin.

'Bartack is one of your room-mates you spoke of?' asked Marie.

'Yes,' replied Derrin.

'Let me explain, Bartack. Marie is my fiancé. We left Dunregal together. There was no future for us there. My father was a miner from Aramorr, not far from your Dalleen. He worked hard and died in a mining accident and by default lost his share of a claim.'

'My mother received twenty gold coins, just twenty as compensation. If my father had lived, his share would have been two hundred times that amount.'

'The mine owner was a dwarf from Port-hareesh, Ogbar Thunderhall.'

'Thunderhall didn't even have to give her anything, but felt guilty for his part in the accident.'

'So, with no income, my mother took myself and my brother to Morrack looking for work.'

'No-one wanted to know a widow with two boys to raise, and the money soon ran out. We were forced to move to Churzey, working in the fields for a pittance, then eventually in the mills of Dunregal.'

'My brother Karim fell into bad company, the Thieves' Guild. He was a lucky thief, and then his luck ran out.'

'He and some of his friends were hired to rob a manor house. Unfortunately in revenge, the owner took out a contract with the Assassin's Guild against the thieves who robbed him.'

'My brother and his friends were tracked down and murdered in an ambush.'

'My mother had never really recovered from my father's death, but with Karim's death after all her sacrifice and struggles...well it broke her.'

'My mother passed away three months ago. My brother took the easy route and it cost him. I didn't want to follow that path. I knew the Royal trials were soon in Tarrondale. The military was my best chance to make a future for myself and Marie away from that place.'

'Believe me, I wanted to tell you and Tellan about Marie. But after Murrat took a dislike to me, I knew I had to keep quiet.'

'I can take a beating and remain silent. However it wouldn't be fair to share my secret with either of you and then you having to take a beating in order to keep that secret safe.'

'If Murrat had found out about Marie, there's no telling what he could have done. He's crazy, he would have hurt her just to hurt me.' explained Derrin.

The sight of Derrin opening his heart to Bartack brought a tear to Marie's eye. She placed her hand on his wrist to add her support.

Bartack understood his friend's logic and felt guilty. If Tellan or himself had accidentally spoken about Marie she could have been at risk. Especially as the inn was not located that far from the barracks.

'Look its OK,' said Bartack. 'You are right about Murrat.'

'Bartack, I want to add that Derrin speaks highly of you and Tellan, he said you are like extended family. Part of his silence is my fault too. When he came to see me after his beating I was so afraid. I'm sorry for any trouble it has caused you.' said Marie.

'It's no trouble. I understand.' replied Bartack.

'I want you and Marie to know, I have your backs.' said Bartack.

'We should head downstairs for the evening, the entertainment is normally very good here.' said Marie.

Bartack and Derrin eagerly agreed and the three went into the bar-room. The inn was busy with a diverse set of customers. Sailors, soldiers, traders and locals mixed in the inn. Bartack ordered three ales and they drank and enjoyed each others company.

Bartack noticed the red haired serving girl flirting with a tanned, pony tailed sailor. At one point she deliberately made eye contact with him again. Bartack pretended not to notice. At the end of the evening they agreed to go exploring around Tarrondale the following morning. Bartack returned to his room, and Derrin and Marie returned to theirs.

After a good night's sleep the three friends met downstairs. Bartack was already at breakfast. Derrin was not surprised, as his friend was usually the first to the mess hall at the barracks, followed by Tellan and then himself always last.

'Good morning.' said Bartack busy eating a slice of bacon.

'Wow.' said Derrin, whose eyes lit up at the sight of the meal.

Once Marie and Derrin had finished their breakfast, the trio left the inn and began to explore Tarrondale. The Saturday market was famous in the area and traders came to Tarrondale's docks from all over Dolia to sell their wares. The market stalls were a mixed multitude of products; vegetables, exotic fruit, clothes, furs, rugs, jewellery, pots, pans, armour, weapons and even animals for sale.

'Keep an eye on your purse.' said Derrin to Bartack.

'How come?' asked Bartack.

'There's a boy following you, wearing a brown leather jacket, a street urchin looking for easy pickings I'd guess. Just make eye contact with him, he'll move on.' advised Derrin.

Bartack turned around and walking ten feet behind him was the boy Derrin described. He looked no more than ten years old. Bartack made eye contact with him. The boy was aware Bartack was looking at him and he became nervous. He tried to pretend that he was just going about his business.

The street urchin then ran off through a group of people who were haggling with a stall trader. Bartack turned to Derrin.

'How did you know he was after my purse?' asked Bartack.

'A rough childhood in Churzey. Besides, you're not really a city boy.' laughed Derrin.

Marie looked at Derrin and laughed.

'You're right there, give me the countryside any time.' replied Bartack.

The three companions continued walking through the crowds. As they went about their way they weaved in and out of the crowds. Bartack had become more observant about whom was around him. He smiled, the street urchin would never dare to come near him again, he thought.

CHAPTER 4

Later in the afternoon they decided to return to their inn. All three were very tired and they didn't realise just how big Tarrondale was. They were in the docks warehouse region of the city. As they walked in the direction to their destination, from an alley three men appeared. They were wearing brown leather clothes, they had dark long curly hair and all had unkempt beards.

'Well, well, what have we here.' said the nearest man who wore a bright red salamander earring.

'Are we lost?' said the man beside him in a sarcastic tone.

'Hand yer purses over.' said the earring man.

'Why don't you come and get them?' said Bartack in response.

The man with the red earring pulled a dagger from inside his jacket, then advanced towards Bartack. Derrin pushed Marie behind him indicating for her to stay back. The other two men watched their companion attack.

The earring man lunged at Bartack with his dagger. Bartack easily dodged. The attacker slashed out again at Bartack with the dagger in a sweeping motion. Once again, Bartack anticipated the attack and easily dodged.

Bartack realised his Royal Scout training had taken over. He was appraising his opponent for weakness and also predicting his attack. The earring man closed in on Bartack and swung downwards in a stabbing motion. Bartack neatly sidestepped and grabbed the attackers wrist, pulling him downwards onto his knees with his own momentum. Bartack twisted his wrist and the thief dropped his dagger. Bartack kicked him over with a push kick, causing him to fall face down on the ground, knocking him clean out.

Meanwhile Derrin began to approach the attacker's companions. The men had seen enough, and turned tails and fled. Both ran off in separate directions, abandoning their leader to his fate.

Bartack lifted the dagger from the ground and pocketed it.

Marie ran over to Derrin in relief, grabbing him around the waist.

'Thieves Guild.' said Derrin looking at the unconscious man.

'How can you tell?' asked Bartack.

'His earring, the red salamander. My brother used to wear something similar.' replied Derrin.

'Well, we better get out of here.' said Bartack.

'Agreed. Where you find thieves, you can bet there will be more about.
We had better get back to a main road.' replied Derrin.

The three friends quickly left the warehouse area and joined the main road from the docks. This led to the centre of the city, and the large market area.

'Are you *OK*, Bartack?' asked Derrin.

'Yes, just a bit of a fright.' replied Bartack.

With the excitement over he began to realise

just how dangerous the situation had been. His Scout training instinct had taken over, and this had saved him. Up to that point he had never appreciated just how far he had come. From being a weak boy he had now become a skilled soldier, in a very short space of time.

'You did well, Rowan would have been proud to see that.' said Derrin.

'Well you'd better not tell him, we don't need any *more* trouble.' laughed Bartack.

Derrin smiled, and slapped his friend on the back in a congratulatory way.

They arrived back at the inn and sat down at a table. The day had been more eventful than they had imagined. As it got towards the evening both Derrin and Bartack were sad. They would have to return to their barracks, but they knew their training was nearly completed, only two weeks remained.

'Bartack, I need to make sure that Marie will be quartered by the military. That will only happen if we are married. So tomorrow, well, I need you to be my best man. We have the service arranged for ten in the morning at the temple nearby.' said Derrin.

Bartack felt proud that his friend had asked him.

'Of course, but don't we need another witness?' asked Bartack.

'Yes, but who can we ask?' replied Derrin.

'I have the very person in mind, wait here.' replied Bartack.

Bartack looked around the inn, then noticed the red haired girl. He approached her.

'My friend is getting married tomorrow morning, we need another witness. Would you be *OK* being that witness?' asked Bartack.

The girl blushed, 'I don't even know you.' replied the girl.

'My name is Bartack, my friends are Derrin and Marie.' he replied pointing to his two seated companions.

The girl immediately recognised Marie and Derrin.

'They are *your* friends?' asked the girl.

'Yes, but will you help?' asked Bartack.

'As they are regulars, as it were, of course.'

'Go with Marie in the morning, the service is at ten. Oh, and your name is?' asked Bartack.

'Suzanne, my name's Suzanne.

Bartack shook her hand and they both smiled.

The following morning they arrived at the temple. Bartack and Derrin went to meet the priest and were awaiting Marie's arrival. Derrin handed Bartack a gold ring.

'You'll need to give that back in a bit. At least I know no-one will steal it from you.' said Derrin laughing.

Shortly before ten, Marie arrived accompanied by Suzanne. Marie was dressed in a beautiful gold coloured dress and a veil.

The service was emotional, and Derrin kissed his bride. Suzanne was emotional too.

'We had better leave the happy couple to themselves.' said Bartack to Suzanne. She smiled and nodded.

'Derrin, we're off. Congratulations to you both. I'm going to head back to the barracks. Don't forget to be back by seven.' said Bartack.

'Bartack, thanks. And I promise I won't slip away at night again.' said Derrin.

Bartack smiled, and waved his friends goodbye. He returned to the inn accompanied by Suzanne.

'Thank-you for helping.' said Bartack.

'You are welcome.' said Suzanne. She reached over and kissed Bartack on the cheek, then returned to her duties behind the bar.

Bartack went to his room and collected his belongings, returned his key to the innkeeper, then set off back to the camp.

At the gates other trainees were already arriving back at the camp. He went to his barracks and back to his room. The door was already open. Tellan was the first of the three to return.

'Hey Bartack, did you have a good few days.' asked Tellan.

'Well it was certainly interesting, and a lot happened.' said Bartack. He then started to explain the situation with Derrin, and the events of the last two days.

'You certainly had a more exciting time than I, but I had a nice relaxing weekend at Little Dale. If you get a chance you should visit it some time.' said Tellan.

Later in the evening Derrin returned to the barracks. He looked so happy and his room-mates congratulated him. They knew they would have to prepare themselves for the morning, as Rowan would have an impromptu parade to make sure everyone had returned. Derrin would also have to notify Rowan that he was now married. This meant he would no longer be quartered with the single men in future and Marie would now come under the responsibility of the military. The three companions went to bed early, as they expected a busy day.

Reveille was sounded early and they were greeted by Corporals Rowan and Breven outside the barracks.

'Fall in!' shouted Rowan, and the trainees formed up.

Rowan began a roll call, making sure that all his troops had returned.

'Good, at least you are all back, and in one piece.' said Rowan satisfied.

'We still have two weeks to go, and I expect maximum effort. And before you think you are home and dry, you can still fail, even now.' added Breven.

The training continued and for the recruits it was almost like second nature. Bartack had used his combat skills for real and he had become more confident as a result. They trained at night, in both navigation and tracking. Faster, stronger, smarter; they were no longer recognisable as the timid boys who first arrived on the camp.

The days flew by and graduation day arrived. The trainees were on parade for the last time. Commandant Kreer addressed them and gave his congratulations and wished them well in their careers. The parade broke up and the newly graduated Royal Scouts returned outside their barracks to await their transportation orders.

Corporal Rowan walked to the administrative building and was issued with posting notifications for his men. He then then returned to the barracks and joined his troops waiting outside.

'Bartack, Derrin, you are assigned to Ormsby Keep.'

'As Ormsby is a forward post your wife will be quartered at Dollan. She will travel there separately' said Rowan to Derrin. Derrin gave a sigh at this news. Rowan issued each man with their personal orders.

'Don't worry, that's not too far from Ormsby.' Rowan added. Derrin felt more upbeat at this comment.

'Tellan, you are assigned to Westerly Watchtower.' said Rowan, handing Tellan his papers. Tellan looked at the papers then felt sadness as he would now be separated from his friends.

Once all the men had been issued their orders, Rowan stood to the front of the group.

'Take your belongings and go to the wagon assembly area, then join the wagon that is travelling to your new post. Good luck all of you.' said Rowan as he waved them farewell.

The three boys did as instructed. Tellan felt anxious, as he knew no-one at that location and would have to make new friends there. He found the wagon assigned to travel to Westerly; there was one other Scout already on the wagon, along with a Corporal.

'Well, this is goodbye then.' said Tellan to Derrin and Bartack.

'Not goodbye Tellan, just farewell.' said Derrin.

'Farewell it is then.' replied Tellan.

Bartack gave Tellan a hug, then Derrin did likewise.

'Stay safe.' said Bartack.

Tellan loaded his belongings onto the back of the wagon, then climbed up. He waved to his two friends as the wagon driver flicked the reins of his team of horses. The wagon left the main gates, turned, and was soon out of sight. The two boys wondered if they would ever see Tellan again.

Derrin and Bartack then found the wagon that was travelling to Ormsby Keep. There were eight new Scouts already on the wagon. Derrin and Bartack loaded their belongings and jumped into the wagon. Checking his manifest and satisfied that all his cargo was accounted for, the wagon driver ordered his horses to move.

The wagon drove out of the camp gates. As it passed the Stone Giant Inn, Derrin longingly looked at the second floor window, just in the hope that he would catch a brief glimpse of Marie. Bartack smiled and also thought of Suzanne.

The wagon ride to Ormsby Keep took four hours and passed the outskirts of the city of Morrack to the west. Their final destination was then due north of the city. Luckily the road from Tarrondale to Morrack was a well maintained traders route. The road was mostly cobble, but there were some stretches which were bare stone. The road only became a track once they reached the north side of Morrack.

Ormsby Keep was a large, daunting white stone

keep, its silhouette cut across the skyline to the north. Its red stone roof reflected the sunlight, and from each of the four corner towers large flags flew in the wind. The tower itself was protected by a dry moat. Scattered outside the tower, the land housed many small wooden cabins. It was clear that a small village had grown within the shadow of the keep, dedicated to servicing the tower itself.

The wagon was driven down a track leading to the entrance of the keep. The track, for it only consisted of mud, was now a main street of sorts. At the side of the track were a general store, blacksmiths shop, a herbalist and a mixture of residential cabins. It was clear that there had been no consideration of planning and some of the cabins looked out of place.

The driver stopped his horses at the front of the keep. Bartack and Derrin now fully appreciated the size of the building, as it towered one hundred and fifty feet above them. The width of the tower was one hundred feet wide on each side. The main heavy wooden doors were defended by a pair of imposing iron portcullises.

The building was clearly large enough to house many men, but there was no warmth or homeliness radiating from it. It was a symbol of might and power. The keep was there because of its strategic location, to protect the road east, and support the northern watchtowers. The boys found it hard to believe that this would be their new home, and compared to Tarrondale it seemed really remote.

Unlike Tarrondale there didn't seem to be much entertainment either; they thought it must be boring for the soldiers based here. The village outside the keep seemed bland and plain and there was no luxury.

The village population was not like the brisk diversity they had encountered in the city. The buildings were practical, created from the plentiful supply of wood found readily in the local area.

The keep on the other hand was made from chiselled stone blocks. The material would have to have been transported here, and
that had proved extremely expensive.
Expense in this case had no cost. The keep, and the route that it guarded showed that the location was of very strategic significance.

CHAPTER 5

From their official orders, Derrin and Bartack had been assigned to Ormsby Keep. Derrin's orders stated that he was married and his spouse quartered at Dollan. An old sergeant approached the wagon.

'Right you lot, off. Except you, you and you.' he said, pointing in turn to Bartack, Derrin and another boy.

'Off to the guardroom, and have your orders ready, quickly!' he shouted to the other Scouts.

The Scouts on the wagon grabbed their belongings in a hurry and leapt onto the ground. The sergeant pointed them in the direction of the guardroom and they ran, happy to have arrived at their destination. The wagon driver had finished his shift too and followed the troops inside after unharnessing his team of horses, leading them to some stabling.

'Sergeant, where are we assigned to? Aren't we stationed here?' asked Derrin.

'You *were*, but you are now needed at High Peak watchtower. We supply that post, with troops too if required.' replied the Sergeant.

One of the first lessons Derrin had learned was don't ask too many questions, so he didn't respond to the Sergeant. Derrin looked at the other young Scout seated opposite him, his name was Markus. He had seen him in training and the mess hall, but he had been assigned to a different team of instructors.

'High Peak watchtower, where or what is that?'

Derrin asked aloud.

'That's one of the watch towers bordering on the High Peak Mountains, there's loads of them along there. We're done for.' replied Markus. This had been the first time the boy had spoken the entire journey.

'What do you mean by *done for*?' asked Derrin.

'It's dangerous up there, one of those places people don't volunteer to go.' replied Markus. Bartack just looked at Derrin in surprise. For Derrin this meant he was even further away from Marie.

Several soldiers began loading supplies into the back of the wagon; grain bags, sacks and four large barrels. The vacated wagon had ample space now for the supplies.

From the guardroom approached a dark haired, bearded Sergeant. He was short, stocky with noticeably muscular arms. He was carrying a backpack and armed with a sword and dagger attached to his belt. He threw his pack into the back of the wagon and then sat down between Derrin and Markus. He smelled strongly of pipe tobacco.

'First tour then boys?' asked the Sergeant appraising the three boys on the wagon.

'Yes Sergeant!' replied Derrin, Bartack and Markus simultaneously.

'Cut that out boys. O'Rourke is the name, Barran O'Rourke. What's yer names then?' asked Sergeant O'Rourke.

The three boys introduced themselves.

A new wagon driver approached leading two fresh horses with him. He began securing the horses to the wagon and jumped up onto his seat holding the reins. He glanced round at the wagon occupants, and only recognised one.

'Hey Barran, you volunteering again for the High Peaks?' asked the driver.

'Aye Michael. Lost a stripe a few weeks back, thanks to a snot nosed young Ensign. Little bastard had connections it seems. So, if I do a tour in the mountains, I'll get it back. They were needing a Sergeant anyway.' replied Barran in an acquiescent tone. The wagon driver laughed at his comment.

'Yahaa!' exclaimed the driver. The two cart horses began pulling. Derrin and Markus fell back slightly and were not prepared for the sudden movement. Bartack had already braced himself, familiar from his previous travel to Tarrondale by wagon. The wagon trundled off, bumping and shaking as it ran over uneven, muddy tracks.

'We are heading straight to High Peak tower, not going into Glyvale. The garrison commander needs that oil desperately, and replacements too. I then have to supply Beanoch Tower on my way back.' said the driver, pointing to the supplies and looking at Derrin, Bartack and Markus.

O'Rourke groaned at the news, and rubbed his hand down his face.

'Not going to Glyvale.' repeated O'Rourke, and he gave a loud puff.

After an hour's travel, Markus fell asleep and was quickly followed by O'Rourke, who began snoring loudly. Bartack drifted off too. Derrin was unable to sleep and just watched the countryside as the wagon travelled the road.

He noticed more and more fir trees, and it began to become quite hilly and noticeably colder. In the distance he could see high mountains, capped with snow and blanketed by mist.
The wagon driver looked around at Derrin.

'That's the start of the High Peak mountains yonder, you can just about see the Great High Peak.' The driver pointed ahead.

'Every time I see this view I'm always impressed, and I've seen it many times.' said the driver.
Derrin looked, it was indeed impressive, but also daunting and worrying. He had never been this far north, having spent most of his young life within the cities.

'What's the garrison like up there? At High Peak tower I mean?' asked Derrin.

'It's a small garrison, a stone high tower. It's cold mostly, snowy, very snowy too. And remote. There is a row of watch towers all along there, every two miles apart. You can see the beacons lit sometimes.' replied the driver.
The horses began to whinny.

'Easy girls, easy,' said the driver in response.

'What's wrong?' asked Derrin who began to feel apprehensive.

'Don't know, but the horses smelt something. Something spooked them. We better get going a bit faster.' said the driver, as he shook the reins.

The wagon began to pick up speed. Derrin was

looking around, trying to see if anything was about. Dusk was approaching, and the long shadows created by the trees made spotting things more difficult.

Derrin couldn't see anything, and certainly the driver no longer seemed to be concerned. This reassured Derrin slightly, and he slowly became relaxed. As the wagon drove higher into the peaks, more and more snow lay on the ground. Soon only snow covered fir trees and exposed rock were the only scenery. A low, cold mist began to fall.

The driver stopped the wagon.

'We need some light, hand me two of those torches.' said the driver, pointing.

Derrin lifted the torches as ordered and handed them to the driver. The driver began to position the two torches in tall holders on either side of the driver's seat and lit them.

The torches began radiating light around the wagon. Michael urged the horses to move and the wagon rumbled off once again. Any mist that came into contact with the flames dissipated.

'Good,' said the driver. 'At least that will keep the trolls away now.' he said jokingly.

Derrin gulped at the comment.

'*Trolls*. What do you mean?' asked a concerned Derrin.

Michael the driver laughed.

'Trolls lad, aye. That's why the towers are here. That's why *you* are here. Someone has to protect the kingdom.' said Michael grinning at the boy's surprised face.

'Have you seen any...trolls?' asked Derrin.

'Aye, one once, and once was enough. Seen a man torn in half and his horse decapitated with him. Took six men to bring it down, they burnt it with oil bottles. Them trolls don't like fire, terrified of it.' said Michael.

'What did it look like?' asked Derrin.

'Big, white, and hairy, lots of teeth.' said Michael shivering at the very memory.

'Trust me lad, if you see one, my best advice is run. Run for your life.'

The wagon pressed ahead at pace. O'Rourke, Bartack and Markus were still fast asleep. O'Rourke's snoring was still as loud as it had ever been. Despite the road being bumpy, the snorts were undeterred. As the wagon rocked, Derrin began to feel tired and the snores seemed to fade. Derrin struggled to keep his eyes open. Eventually he could no longer resist sleeps embrace and soon drifted off into slumber. He began to dream.

'Wake up, we're here!' cried Michael the driver. Markus and Bartack woke with a start. Derrin was woken just at the best part of his dream. O'Rourke groaned and snorted. It was pitch black now and only the wagon's torches provided illumination. Ahead they could see torch lights and the outline of a large stone tower. At the top, torches were alight and there were some men looking down.

As the wagon moved closer, Derrin could see that the base of the tower was defended by wooden stakes all along the bottom. There was also a trench around the base, and the only access was across a small drawbridge with a pair of heavy wooden doors behind it.

The drawbridge began to lower and the doors behind it opened. Torch light appeared and standing in the doorway were three people, each carrying lit torches. The drawbridge finally reached the ground and the three people approached the wagon.

'Hallo!' cried Michael to the men.

'Hey Michael, glad to see you, hope you have our supplies?' asked one of the men.

'All here Captain, and your four replacements too.' replied Michael.

The other two men began unloading the oil barrels and rolled them inside the watch tower. They also started removing the other supplies from the wagon.

O'Rourke jumped off the wagon with his backpack and saluted the Captain.

'Well, well, Barran O'Rourke again. What did you do this time?' asked the Captain.

O'Rourke laughed. 'Long story, Captain Burke.'
The Captain then shifted his gaze to Markus, Bartack and Derrin.

'OK you three, out, get your gear and report to Quartermaster Tyerose inside.' ordered Burke.
Derrin, Bartack and Markus did as ordered and walked across the drawbridge towards the open doors of the tower. Meanwhile Michael was unreining the wagon horses and began to lead them over the drawbridge into the tower.

The three boys entered the main gates and looked around them. In the lower level of the tower was the area where they stabled horses. There was also a small forge in one corner. To the right were wooden stairs leading up to the next level. There was one man hammering away at a sword on the forge. Nearby him, feeding the horses, was a young man and standing alongside him was a senior Sergeant. The Sergeant glanced around and approached Derrin and Markus.

'Ah, you must be our replacements. Give me your orders.' asked the Quartermaster.

The three boys each handed over their orders to the Sergeant. He opened them up and began reading them. Derrin could tell from the expression on his face the Sergeant wasn't entirely impressed with what he had read.

'All of you straight out of training?' said the Quartermaster shaking his head in disbelief. 'I just don't know why they keep doing this.'

'Toby,' called the Quartermaster to the young man beside the horses.

'Yes sir.' replied the young man.

'Get these three equipped, billeted and fed.' said the Quartermaster.

Michael led his two horses over to the others and secured them. He then collected food and two water buckets for them, then fed his animals. Toby walked over to where Derrin, Bartack and Markus stood.

'I'm Toby, come with me and I'll get you some equipment.'

Toby led them up the wooden stairs to the next level, this was clearly used as a guardroom. A metal grill gate was beside the stairwell and could be used to seal off the top of the stairs if required. Toby walked over to a large chest and opened it. He removed three short swords and three daggers and issued one of each to the three boys.

'There you go, you'll need these. You will get issued bows if needed later. Follow me.' said Toby.

Toby walked up another set of wooden steps onto the next level. The three boys followed him. This part of the tower was a lower bedroom and kitchen area. It was also used for food storage. In the corner opposite the kitchen were six basic wooden beds with footlockers at the bottom.

'This is where I sleep,' Toby indicated one of the beds which had a wooden barrel alongside used as a bedside cabinet.

'You can choose any of the other beds here. The level above is the main hall where we dine. The ablutions are also there too. The floors above are the bedrooms for the senior soldiers, Sergeants and the Captain's quarters. The top floor is the beacon and main watch point.'

The three boys thanked Toby and then choose a bed each. The room was at least dry thanks to the vicinity and regular use of the kitchen fire. In terms of privacy there was very little, as any person wanting to go up or downstairs would pass through this area. Toby had moved some crates in front of the bed in an attempt to create a crude partition.

Markus placed his weapons and belongings into the footlocker, then collapsed on top of his bed. Derrin too was exhausted, he watched as Toby sat on his bed.

Toby wasn't that much older than himself, he was athletic in build, fair haired with very green eyes. His face had a much older look, almost as if he had aged before his body. Bartack choose the bed adjacent to Derrin.

'My name is Derrin, he's Bartack and that's Markus.' said Derrin to Toby, pointing to his two companions.

Toby looked up and smiled.

'Yes, we never really had time to be introduced properly.' replied Toby

'I guess by the looks of it you are just out of training?' asked Toby.

'Yes, just finished. I had been assigned to Ormsby Keep, but they ended up sending me here instead,' replied Derrin.

'How long have you been here Toby?' asked Derrin.

'I've been here two months now. Just another four months to go,' said Toby, in a tone of relief.

'They keep you here six months, then send you on a new assignment elsewhere. The officers stay a year though.'

Derrin was relived that the tour was only six months, then horrified that he would be stuck here.

Toby got up and walked into the kitchen, then brought three plates back. He handed one to Derrin, the other to Bartack and placed the other by the now asleep Markus.

Derrin looked at the plate and thanked him. There was some bread, cheese and an apple. Derrin and Bartack began to eat hungrily. It had been some time since he had last eaten. For some reason the food reminded Bartack of the red haired girl in the Stone Giant Inn. The cheese he thought, tasted similar.

As the boys were savouring the taste of their food, from downstairs came a loud clank. The drawbridge was pulled up and the heavy doors closed and bolted. Derrin heard footsteps and Sergeant O'Rourke, Captain Burke, Quartermaster Tyerose and Michael climbed the stairs onto the floor. The Quartermaster approached Derrin and Bartack, then spoke.

'Early start tomorrow, rise at sunrise, parade, then eat. Then we assign duties for the day. Get some rest. It will be morning soon.'

Burke, O'Rourke and Tyerose then left the room, taking the stairs up to the next level. Only Michael the driver was left. He went over to the spare bed and sat down.

'Well lads looks like you are settling in.' said Michael cheerfully.

'Are you staying Michael? I thought you had to do a delivery to Beanoch Tower?' asked Derrin.

Michael let out a laugh.

'Not at night lad! That would be suicidal around these parts. Especially on your own. *Far* too dangerous. I'll be staying here until sunrise, then heading off. Besides there's a big snowstorm brewing outside, this makes navigating a wagon even more dangerous.' explained Michael as he undressed himself for bed.

At that, Michael lay down, then rolled over onto his side and quickly he was fast asleep. Toby had already gone to sleep.

'Goodnight Derrin.' said a tired Bartack.

'Goodnight.' responded Derrin.

Now only Derrin was awake. He laid back on his bed and stared at the ceiling. He wondered what exactly he had got himself into and what would happen tomorrow. At last the realisation struck him that he was alone, this wasn't training any-more, this was real.

He wondered how Marie was and if she was OK. Derrin longingly breathed deeply and rolled over on his bed, closing his eyes. He knew his dreams could take him elsewhere, but when he woke up he would still be in this location.

He started to wonder had he made a massive mistake in joining the Royal Scouts.

CHAPTER 6

The following morning Derrin was awakened by lots of noise and activity from upstairs. Toby was already awake, and Markus was rising. Bartack was out of his bed trying to sort out his locker. A Corporal came down the stairs onto their floor and shouted, 'Wakey, wakey you lot, get cleaned up. Parade in twenty minutes outside.'

Derrin, Bartack, Toby and Markus grabbed their wash bags and went upstairs to the ablutions. There were already Scouts coming out washed, heading back to their rooms to get dressed. The boys quickly washed themselves, then went back to their floor and began to dress.

As they dressed, other Scouts were already ready and heading outside for the parade. The boys hurriedly put on their uniforms, then went downstairs into the stable area and outside. The main doors to the tower were already open and the drawbridge lowered.

As they walked outside they could see the Scouts were already lined up in two ranks behind each other.

'We need to join the parade ranks.' said Toby.
The boys followed Toby over and then fell in at the end of the row. Minutes later O'Rourke appeared and formed up. There were thirty men in all, standing in two rows of fifteen. Quartermaster Tyerose walked out of the tower and stood facing the parade. Captain Burke then joined the parade.

'Atten-shun!' shouted Tyerose.

The parade stood to attention as the Captain arrived. Tyerose saluted and Burke returned the salute.

'Stand at ease! Stand easy!' yelled Tyerose.

The men in the parade relaxed. Burke accompanied by Tyerose began inspecting the troops. They were looking at their equipment and general appearance. Burke finally arrived at Derrin, Bartack and Markus.

'Welcome to our little garrison, I'm Captain Evan Burke, garrison commander. I'll speak to you three later.' said Burke, as he turned and nodded at Tyerose with satisfaction. There was a slight smile on the Captain's face.

Burke walked back towards the watchtower and disappeared inside the door.

Tyerose turned and faced the parade.

'Parade dismissed.' he yelled.

The soldiers began breaking up and went about their business, some went to breakfast, others took the opportunity for a quick smoke.

The boys passed Michael the wagon driver, leaving with fresh horses.

'Good morning lads, that's me off now, have my next supply delivery.' said Michael, waving to the lads. 'Remember what I told you.' said Michael to Derrin.

'Goodbye Michael, and thanks.' replied Derrin.

'Yes, thanks.' said Bartack.

Derrin, Bartack and Markus started to make their way upstairs to the dining hall, it was the floor above their bedroom. The smell of cooking came from their own room, Toby was busy in the kitchen side of the room under the direction of a portly Scout who was cooking.

The boys plated up and then sat down to eat. They had eggs, bacon and fried bread, and it tasted good. Much better than the food served in the training camp.

After breakfast, the boys were approached by a tall, ginger Corporal with a scar on his left cheek.

'I'm Corporal Haynes, I need you to assist me. Follow me.' said Haynes sharply.

The three boys followed as instructed and they headed to the stable area. Haynes handed each of them a shovel. Derrin immediately thought here we go, shit shovelling in the stables.

'Burial detail.' said Haynes.

Derrin gulped, his eyes open wide with surprise.

Haynes pointed to a cloth coffin in the corner.

'Two of you carry the remains, the other can carry the shovels and the wooden headstone. Follow me.' said Haynes coldly.

Derrin picked up the top of the cloth coffin and Bartack lifted the bottom half. There was definitely something inside but it wasn't that heavy. Markus carried the shovels and headstone, and followed Haynes out and away from the tower.

He led them over a small hill about four hundred yards away. Once they reached the top of the hill there were well over thirty graves. Haynes picked a suitable spot and then ordered the boys to begin digging. They buried the man's remains and hammered in the wooden headstone marker. Haynes stood silently to attention as a mark of respect, then mumbled a prayer.

'What happened to him?' asked Markus.

Haynes looked at him. From his expression Markus

immediately felt he had said something wrong.

Initially Haynes didn't respond, but then said 'Scout Tenby was his name. He died of his wounds, he was a member of my patrol.'

The boys could see Haynes was noticeably upset, but doing his best not to show it.

'You should return to the tower, and take your shovels back with you. The Captain wants to see you' said Haynes, 'And thank you for your help.'

The boys walked off and headed back to the watchtower, and then reported to Captain Burke's quarters. Burke waved them in, and the boys saluted.

'Sit down.' said Burke. The boys sat as instructed.

'I like to keep things informal. From your orders I can see you were meant to have been based at Ormsby Keep, but you ended up here.' Burke surveyed each of his newest recruits in turn.

'There are only four types of people who come to a location such as this. Those that seek guaranteed advancement, those that are desperate, those running away from their past and those that have no idea what awaits them.

I know which group I belong to. I don't know which you fall under, *yet*.'

'But I suspect one of the latter groups.' said Burke knowingly.

'This is one of the most dangerous assignments in the kingdom, and I have rules. Strict rules to keep us alive.

Rule one, you never go anywhere alone.

Rule two, never get caught outside at night.

Rule three, if you get caught outside at night, go to ground until dawn.

Rule four, don't become complacent.

Rule five, learn from the experienced soldiers, that will help you survive.

Rule six, remember all these rules.' Burke paused to allow the Scouts to absorb his words. He could see the raw recruits wondering what they had got themselves into.

'Normally in these outpost watchtowers you would expect to lose between four to five men every two weeks.

So far, I have managed to reduce this to every two months.' Derrin shifted uneasily in his chair.

'The tower itself is protected by a dry moat, and as you probably noticed wooden spikes.

The moat is dry because it is also a fire pit, we pour oil into the pit, then it can be lit if we need an additional defence.

At the top of the watchtower is a beacon, we light that in an emergency. The other watchtowers will then know we are in trouble and come to our aid.'

Burke paused again, weighed up the boys with an appraising glance once more. He felt they could cope, then continued.

'Another thing, I'm sure you have heard your training Corporals boast about fighting trolls single handed.

It's a fool's tale, they never did. When you see a troll, and you *will* at some point, you'll do well not to fill your trousers gentlemen.

Your best chance, probably only chance, is using fire. Trolls are terrified of it.
But it's not just trolls, the environment here can kill you just as quickly.
The good news is that the length of tour here is only six months.
Stay safe, remember the rules and best of luck. Dismissed.'
The boys saluted in unison and left the Captain's quarters. Corporal Hayes assigned the boys their duties. Markus was selected for tower guard duty that night and stood down until the evening. Bartack was placed on guard duty around the stockade. Derrin was selected for a morning patrol. This was his first, and he felt apprehensive. Derrin had an uncomfortable sleep that night.

At dawn Markus had been relieved from his watch duty, he had heard some distant howls in the night, but had seen nothing. It had begun to snow during the night and the biting cold had almost frozen his fingers. He remembered what Captain Burke had said about the environment. He returned to his room and Toby, Bartack and Derrin were not there. Markus collapsed on his bed and went to sleep exhausted.

Derrin had collected his weapons, he was saddling his horse in the stable and attaching his quiver and securing his long bow. The patrol was being led by Corporal Haynes, and with him was a Scout called Banner, Derrin was accompanying them. Derrin led his horse outside, where Haynes and Banner waited.

'Ready to go?' asked Corporal Haynes.

'Yes Corporal.' replied Derrin.

'We do a sweep of the area. Make sure you watch around you and behind. Try and keep as quiet as possible. Any questions?' said Haynes.

Derrin shook his head in the negative. He climbed onto his horse and trotted behind Banner. Bartack was on guard outside and waved Derrin goodbye. He was grateful to be beside the tower, and concerned for his departing friend.

The Scouts slowly rode off towards the north. The ground was thick with snow and the three riders were in a column formation. Derrin was at the rear, with Haynes up front and Banner in the middle.

The forest started to become thicker, and the visibility was much less as the snow began to fall. The sun was bright in the sky, but it was still a biting cold, with very little breeze. They had been riding for several hours and nothing of significance happened. They had found a few troll and wolf tracks, but nothing else. Satisfied with the patrol, they then returned to the watchtower by early afternoon.

'Easy isn't it?' Haynes said.

Derrin nodded, he had been on edge the whole time, and was relieved to be back in one piece. Haynes told him he was scheduled for a patrol tomorrow afternoon. 'Was it always going to be like this?' Wondered Derrin to himself. 'Markus hadn't even left the tower, and Bartack had gone no further than the stockade'.

****

Timmis smiled satisfied to himself as he brushed the dirt off the stone hatch. The old map he had been given by a hooded man in the Thieves Guild in Morrack had proved accurate. At first he had thought this had been a prank or a fool's errand.

The price of the map had been the recovery of a willow wand and talisman. That had been all the hooded man had requested in return. Checking along the seals for signs of any traps and content there were none, the thief retrieved a crowbar from his pack. He began to prise open the hatch, slowly at first until he was able to get a grip of the edge with his hand. He pushed the hatch to one side; beneath it darkness welcomed him with a musty pungent odour filling his nostrils. He coughed as the dust caught the back of his throat.

Reaching again into his pack, the rogue retrieved a fire lighting kit and a wooden torch. Preparing some dry birch bark on the ground, he struck his flint which began to spark. Soon a few smoking embers ignited into a small flame. He fed the fire with more bark and then lit his torch.

Replacing the equipment into his pack and then using the torch he peered into the hole; it was a small shaft just wide enough for a man. The shaft dropped no more than ten feet and at the bottom the thief could just make out a corridor with stone walls. The floor of the corridor was earth and it appeared to be damp, his torch light danced against the walls of the shaft as he looked around.

He dropped the torch to the floor, it landed with a thud but stayed alight. Nothing happened. Satisfied, Timmis took a small, coiled rope from the side of his pack and tied one end around a toppled stone pillar. The other end he tied to his pack. He lowered his pack into the hole, carefully avoiding the burning torch. Climbing down the rope, he found the shaft rather tight, but he quickly reached the floor. He wiped the sweat from his brow, and a troublesome spiders web that had attached itself to his balding silver hair. Timmis was short, and his appearance belied his superb dexterity.

He picked up his torch and stared ahead into the dark corridor. There was no sound. Collecting his pack he checked the earth floor; there were no tracks and more importantly, no signs of traps. Judging by the condition of the corridor this area had been undisturbed for many, many years. Timmis began to slowly walk down the corridor, regularly checking both the floor and the walls.

The corridor terminated at a wall, in front of which a rectangular stone door stood. Carved into the door was a series of glyphs and what appeared to be writing. Timmis didn't understand it, but it appeared similar to elvish.

Timmis was now growing impatient. He quickly began to check the door edges for traps and finding none began to prise the door from the wall. The stone door began to shift, and as the seal opened there was a hiss of air from within. He greedily pushed the door away; it fell to one side against the wall. There was enough room for him to climb through the door. He shone his torch into the room and clambered through. The door concealed another chamber. Inside the room were six sarcophagi, and on the far wall an arched door lead to another room.

Timmis laughed, breaking the deadly silence. The Thieves' Guild in Morrack had continually mocked him. Now he would have the last laugh, he had been brave enough to enter the Stone City and he would receive his just rewards of the plunder. The room had more glyphs painted on the wall, and each of the sarcophagi had the stone image of the human occupant carved onto the lid. Two depicted warriors, one a bard carrying a flute, the other three depicted hooded figures.

Timmis walked past the sarcophagi towards the arched doorway, attracted by a blue light that appeared to emanate from within. He cautiously approached the arch and peered through. Inside the room stood another, bigger sarcophagus on a high plinth. Placed on the lid lay a clear quartz crystal the length of Timmis' forearm that shimmered with a dark blue light. The thief laughed, he never realised just how lucrative this trip would be. He had to take the items of most value, and quickly too.

He knew that when he started to sell the plunder word would quickly get round wondering where he'd been. If he came back here for a second haul he would surely be followed, and probably end up murdered. This was a one time trip. Besides, the Stone City was not a safe place to be loitering in. It was common to encounter wolves or even trolls here. He did not want to bump into either.

He would steal what he could and be gone before the afternoon, pass Beanoch watchtower and then arrive in Hander by early afternoon to meet a contact. He had an ally at Beanoch who would turn a blind eye for the right price.

The thief walked towards the crystal and lifted it, appraising its value as he did so. It was clear there was more to this object than a common crystal, why it shone with an inner light he had no idea. Perhaps the Thieves' Guild in Morrack would have more knowledge about the crystal or its origin. As he placed it into his rucksack he noticed the crystal's light changed from dark blue to a sky blue.

His attention now fixed on the sarcophagi. He removed his crowbar from his pack and he began to prise open the lid. Unlike the others, this lid had no representation of the occupant below. The lid moved easily, Timmis slid it over the side. Inside lay a preserved man wearing a red robe, his flesh was dry and withered. His cheekbones protruded from his face and his eyes were closed.

The thief checked the corpse, and removed a ruby encrusted gold signet ring from its left hand. He broke the little finger in his desperation to remove it. The corpse was holding a hazel wand in his right hand and a wore a gold talisman, which he removed. Timmis knew the wand and talisman were the items described by the hooded man.

Carved into the wand's base was more elvish style writing. The thief carefully slipped all the items into his pack. He then walked into the other room containing the six sarcophagi and began opening the bard's lid. Inside, the male occupant was dressed in a scarlet robe with a black hood, attached to which was a full length black cape. He was handsome, with shoulder length brown hair. Timmis was slightly startled; the corpse looked newly preserved. This couldn't be, he thought, after all the chamber had been sealed for such a long time.

He quickly checked the body, casting aside a plain wooden piccolo the corpse had held and removing a small leather purse. The rogue smiled as he gave the purse a little shake.

'Not bad.' he said out loud.

He tucked the purse inside his jacket and moved onto the next sarcophagus which depicted a warrior. He prised the lid with his crowbar, and it slid to the ground. Inside was a tall plate mail armoured knight, a broadsword and dagger were resting on his chest. The blades of each were marked with strange glyphs. Timmis grabbed the dagger and tucked it into his belt.

Suddenly he felt a slight tremor from the ground, dust fell from the ceiling. Fearing the collapse of the room, he dashed to the exit and into the stone corridor. The tremor got stronger under his feet and he ran to where his rope dangled in the corridor. He quickly tied the end of the rope to his pack. The thief quickly climbed the rope to the surface.

He then pulled up his pack behind him. The

tremor was now strong and there was an audible rumble. Untying his pack he put it on, leaving the rope attached to the pillar. The ground was shaking beneath him. He ran to his horse, untied its reins and mounted it. The thief galloped off, terrified that everything was going to collapse beneath him.

Gorath Marr's eyes flicked open. He had finally awoken from his slumber, and his bony hands began to move. He raised himself up; the thief had damaged his finger and stolen his possessions, he would not tolerate this, but he had more important work first.

He chanted some ancient words and a light orb appeared in his right hand. The corpse walked into the adjoining room and inspected the sarcophagi, stopping beside the bard's opened tomb.

'Mareck, Mareck, awaken my servant, we are now free once again and I have need of you.' said the lich.

The bard's eyes flicked open, and he raised himself from his sarcophagus. This had been the first time he had heard his master's voice in centuries.
He stood up and made has way over to his master's side. Mareck could see that Gorath Marr was angry.

'Yes master.' said Mareck.

'Awaken the others.' rasped Gorath Marr.
Mareck did as commanded, and began to wake the other sleeping disciples of Marr.

Mareck could see that the binding stone which had trapped them was gone, and the person who had entered the crypt had now escaped.

****

Timmis arrived at Beanoch watchtower, Captain Darnley was waiting for him and approached him. One of the Corporals began to walk suspiciously towards Timmis.

'It's OK Corporal, stand down.' said Darnley waving him away.

Darnley walked up to the thief who was still on horseback.

'Well Timmis, have you been out collecting once again? Any luck?' asked Darnley.

Timmis nodded and said 'Your usual fee, Captain?

Darnley smiled and laughed, 'Well I class it as my retirement savings.'

It was a good thing the Captain was rotten to the core, thought Timmis. He had been useful for moving undetected across the frontier quite a few times now. Timmis handed over a small emerald and two gold coins to the Captain that had been in the leather pouch he had robbed from the sarcophagus.

Darnley greedily inspected the items and had a satisfied expression on his face. He quickly pocketed them into his purse.

'A pleasure doing business once again.' said Darnley.

'I'll be off on my journey Captain.' replied Timmis.

'Where are you heading to?' asked the Captain.

'Hander, I have a buyer there who deals in antique items,' said Timmis, lying.

'Goodbye for now Captain.' and at that he rode off.

Darnley waved farewell, and Timmis rode south in the direction of Glyvale. It was probably the last time he would have any dealings with Darnley. His one year tour was close to the end and whoever replaced him might not be so understanding or cooperative. Timmis could sell some of the items in Glyvale, but would need to go to the guild at Morrack if he wanted a bigger price. The Thieves Guild had experts there who could identify, value and even find buyers for the items. Timmis couldn't wait to see their faces when he showed them the loot.

The wand and talisman though were the items he had been commissioned to find by the man who had given him the old map. He had been promised a large reward for it. Any other items found were a bonus. Timmis had arranged to meet a contact in Hander who would introduce him to a client in Glyvale.

His horse was now tired, and he stopped at the Iron Hammer Inn in Hander village where he had arranged to meet his contact. Timmis walked in and over to the bar. The innkeeper recognised him from previous visits, when he had told the innkeeper that he was a trapper and trader from Glyvale.

'Hello sir, what can I get you?' asked the innkeeper.

'An ale, can you also send your stable boy to feed and water my horse?' replied Timmis. He handed a silver piece to the innkeeper.

The innkeeper nodded and responded 'At once.' He went off to instruct the stable boy. Timmis went and sat down in his favourite corner seat, then glanced around the inn. The fire was blazing in the hearth. There were four others there; two men seated together, from their fur clothing, they looked like trappers, and a blonde woman, who was sweeping the floor.

In the other corner Timmis noticed a grey bearded man, whose gaze was transfixed on him. He recognised him from Morrack, and nodded to him. The grey bearded man nodded back, and started walking towards Timmis. The innkeeper watched as the bearded man walked past him to the opposite corner of the room towards where Timmis sat.

'The air is sweet with the smell of mountain lavender is it not?' said the grey bearded man to Timmis.

'But not as sweet as the morning dawn.' replied Timmis.
The two men knew that both were members of the Thieves' Guild.

'I have a buyer for you in Glyvale, specialises in ancient elven artefacts, of course with an introduction fee.' smiled the bearded man in expectation.
Timmis nodded in approval of the deal.

'Of course I have to view the wares beforehand,' said the man.
Timmis removed the small leather purse from his pocket and handed it to the grey bearded man. The man opened the purse and a broad smile ran across his face.

'*Excellent*, my client will be happy to buy these items.' said the man.

'Now of course, the fee. I will take one of these elven gold coins, part set up fee, and part guild fee.'

'Agreed,' said Timmis. 'Now whom do I deliver this to?'

The grey bearded man removed a gold coin from the purse, then handed the purse back to Timmis.

'You need to visit a man by the name of Bonna. You'll recognise him when you see him, he's bald and has a tattooed head. Tell him Amarra sent you. His address is the Fine Wares store, Red Oak place, in Glyvale.' said the man.

He stood up, bowed, and left Timmis, returning to his own table to dine.

Timmis finished his drink, then the innkeeper approached him.

'Your horse has been fed and watered sir.' said the innkeeper.

'Thank you. I'll be on my way now.' said Timmis.

Timmis got up and went to collect his horse from the stable, then checked everything was in place and nothing stolen. Satisfied, he mounted his horse and rode off. He began to travel on the Glyvale road and knew his destination was none too distant. He would be relieved to make his first sale on the items he found, and pressed his horse eagerly onwards in anticipation.

****

Gorath Marr continued to rage. For over one thousand years he had been trapped here by the magic of the Elf King, but somehow a greedy thief had freed him and his followers.

His revenge upon the elves would be swift and

furious. To reach his full power he would need his wand, ring and talisman returned. The ring stored spirit energy to help him cast spells. His wand acted as a conduit for his energy. The talisman, though, was the most important item. It enabled him to become a daywalker, protecting him and his followers from the purifying light of the sun. Otherwise he could only travel in the open by night. The talisman also allowed him to appear as a mortal man, for without this his true, ghastly form could not be concealed.

Marr walked silently into the main chamber. Standing awaiting his command were his devoted followers. Two armoured knights - the dark paladins Hazak and Randarr - the three hooded priests, Drusilla, Amera, Yandora and his bard Mareck.

Night had fallen and Gorath Marr left the chamber through the doors followed by his disciples. As he walked past the stone door he noticed the elvish writing. Marr's bony fingers touched the words which read, "Let he who sleeps eternally, never be awakened."

Marr's withered lips twisted a grotesque smile, the words amused him. The roof of the corridor had collapsed and an exit was easy thanks to this. Gorath Marr felt the cold night air embrace his face as he gazed at the stars in the sky for the first time in centuries. Marr wandered through the stone city. This once fine place was now ruined and in decay, but would make a wonderful new capital. The elves had long since gone. How apt, Marr thought, that his new necropolis, would be built in the former home of his enemies. He looked at the snow covered mountains that lay around the city.

A grey troll heard the footsteps of Marr and his party, the troll sniffed the air. It followed the scent and standing in the open, it saw seven figures. The troll let out a roar and leapt towards them. Mareck raised his piccolo to his lips and began playing a tune. The troll began to scream, covering its ears and falling upon the ground writhing in agony. It started shaking violently, then lay still.

Hearing its cries, two other trolls approached, and once again Mareck played his tune and both trolls collapsed clutching their ears, then became rigid. Mareck pounced on the first troll and sank his fangs into its flesh and began to drink. Marr stood watching as his bard tasted his first fresh blood after such a long, long time.

'Mareck.' said Marr.
The bard walked over to his master wiping away the troll's blood from his lips.

'Yes master.' replied the bard.

'Find the thief, and recover my belongings. Take Randarr with you, he will prove useful.' said Marr.
The lich made a circular motion with his right hand over his left open palm, and a yellow orb appeared. He peered into the orb and began scrying.

'The thief I seek went south-west, to a tower. There a man will help you find the answer.'

'Master, how will I know which man?' asked Mareck.

Marr reached into his pocket, and produced a small yellow crystal. He began to chant as he held it in his hand, then a green light appeared within it. Marr handed the crystal to Mareck.

'The crystal will glow when you find whom you seek.' said Marr.

Mareck bowed to his master and beckoned Randarr to follow him, they made their way south-west.

Gorath Marr addressed his other four disciples and pointed at the dead trolls.

'These...creatures, these animals, they defile the city. Destroy them, drive them out!' roared Marr.

The three hooded figures bowed, as did the remaining armoured knight and they set off into the city ruins in different directions.

CHAPTER 7

Derrin prepared for his next patrol. This time he was accompanying Lance-Scout Anders, again with Scout Banner. As it was already afternoon they would arrive back much later to the tower. This patrol would take them north-east towards the Great High Peak. The area was covered in fir trees thick with snow. The weather had changed for the worse and the snow started to fall heavily. They had found many troll tracks, and what appeared to be cart tracks towards the steppe cliffs.

'We'll follow these cart tracks, could be illegal trappers, but we need to investigate. We need to get a move on in case the snow covers everything.' said Anders.

As the snow fell harder the tracks began to become covered. Anders knew that a quick pace wasn't the best idea. Visibility became difficult as the snow frequently blew into the faces of the men.

As they continued their patrol, Anders noticed an overturned wagon ahead. As they approached the wagon they could see no sign of any team of horses, and the cargo was strewn onto the ground.

They dismounted, then began looking for tracks, but there were none. Lying on the ground were troll and animal traps, furs and several crates of provisions.

'Illegal trappers by the looks of it,' said Anders. 'As I suspected.'

Illegal trapping had become a problem, mainly because it reduced the food supply for creatures such as wolves and trolls. This provoked the animals and also forced them to hunt food in the low lands; raiding farms and attacking villages. The trappers though would make lots of money from the pelts.

'What happened here?' Derrin asked Banner.

'Don't know, the trappers are gone, including their horses, they must have rolled their wagon in the snow. But they left in a hurry leaving their stuff.' replied Banner.

Anders began rifling through the abandoned belongings, and began pocketing items.

'Lance-Scout, shouldn't we be moving on, its getting late?' asked Banner.

'Not yet, there's stuff here worth taking. Mind your own business Banner and keep watch.' said Anders in a greedy tone.

Banner knew that it was dangerous to loiter too long. He gave a concerned look at Derrin and said to him, 'Keep alert Derrin, he's stealing loot for himself.'

After ten minutes of rifling through the trapper's belongings, Anders was satisfied and mounted his horse. Derrin and Banner got onto their horses too. Derrin noticed the horses had become very agitated, as if they were sensing something.

From nowhere, a tree trunk came spinning through the air striking Anders off his mount, killing his horse instantly. Anders' decapitated body struck a nearby tree. The snow was splashed red with blood.

Derrin and Banner's horses began to panic, rearing up and throwing the riders onto the ground. The animals bolted southwards and Derrin and Banner got shakily to their feet and drew their swords. They began looking all around in desperation. A fearsome growl sounded, the noise scared Derrin. His knees became weak with fear.

'Troll!' screamed Banner.

Their torches and equipment had gone with the horses. Banner then ran over to Anders' dead horse, and grabbed a torch. He took out a fire lighter and desperately began to try and light the torch. It was damp from the snow and he struck the flint in vain.

The growl became louder and Derrin could hear heavy footsteps approaching. The thickness of the fir trees and snow fall made it difficult to see. Suddenly, bursting through a clump of trees charging towards Banner was an eight foot humanoid, covered in shaggy white fur. It had a distinct grey mane around its neck, its mouth was open and inside were rows of sharp white teeth. Derrin felt petrified, he had never seen such a creature. His stomach wretched with fear.

'Banner, look out!' screamed Derrin.

The creature covered the ground in huge bounds very quickly. Banner turned round and screamed as the troll lunged towards him. It swung at him with its hand clawing him with long grey nails. Banner was knocked to the ground and was cut across his back by three parallel claw marks. Banner desperately reached for his dagger in his belt, but fumbled and dropped it as the pain and shock took hold.

Derrin was frozen to the spot, he looked on in terror as the troll grabbed Banner by the leg and began dragging him towards a clump of fir trees. For a second the troll let go of Banner and disappeared through the clump.

Banner was now screaming in both fear and agony, he looked over at Derrin.

'Run, boy, *run!*' screamed Banner, his face ashen with terror.

A huge hand grabbed Banner's leg once again and dragged him completely into the clump of trees.

Derrin panicked and began to run, he made off as quickly as he could in the opposite direction. His heart was pumping and felt like it would burst. All of his training could never have prepared him for such a scene as that he had just witnessed. Behind him he could hear Banner's screams, then there was another chilling roar, and the screaming ended.

Deathly silence returned. Derrin sprinted as fast as he could. From behind him he heard the noise of footsteps crushing the snow, coming his direction. He ran and ran, the trees began to thin out and rock was exposed from the blanket of snow. In front of him was now the edge of a ravine.

Derrin looked over the edge, but he couldn't see how far the drop was, there was a layer of thick mist just below, but the rocks were dusted with snow. The footsteps became louder, and Derrin forced himself to look around. Fast approaching him was the troll, its mouth and fur stained red with Banner's blood.

The troll roared and closed in. Derrin thought of Marie and longed to be back with her. He prayed the end would be quick, then jumped. He closed his eyes as he fell through the layer of mist.

Less than a second later the troll's claw swiped the air where Derrin's head had just been. The troll roared in anger as its prey had been denied it, and it looked down, giving another frustrated roar towards the mist.

****

It was late evening at the High Peak watchtower, the patrol was now long overdue. The sun had gone down and Corporal Haynes reported the missing patrol to Quartermaster Tyerose.

'They haven't come back sir.' said Haynes.

'How many?' asked Tyerose.

'Three of them, Anders, Banner and young Derrin.' replied Haynes.

'We should report this to Captain Burke.' said Tyerose

The two men went upstairs and went to the Captain's quarters.

'Sir, our afternoon patrol failed to come back, three men in total.' said Tyerose.

'We will send out a search party in the morning. Ask O'Rourke to lead it, and you go with them, Haynes. Take young Bartack, his tracking skills will be useful, and he'll probably want to help find his friend.' said Burke.

Haynes and Tyerose saluted and left the Captain.

'Approaching horses!' came a shout from the watchtower lookout.

Haynes ran up to the top of the tower, as two galloping, riderless horses came to a stop close to the drawbridge.

Two guards outside the tower took hold of the horses' reins, and calmed them. Haynes rushed downstairs, through the stable and outside.

'Corporal, these are two of the horses from the missing patrol.' said the guard.

Haynes inspected the animals and confirmed they were. He noticed the bows and equipment were still attached to the saddles.

'Take them in and feed the animals.' ordered Haynes.

'Yes Corporal!' replied the guard.

Haynes knew the horses would make finding the lost patrol much easier. Following the horse's tracks would lead them right to their position. He hoped that the weather would not conceal the tracks and they would still be visible in the morning.

Haynes breathed slowly and took a deep breath, they would head out at first light. He went to see O'Rourke and informed him of the situation.

'Don't worry Haynes, we'll find them.' said O'Rourke hopefully.

Haynes gave the order to secure the tower for the night. The torches were lit outside, the drawbridge lifted and main doors closed. Haynes knew the prospect of finding them alive was very low.

****

The Sun finally broke over the High Peaks, the rays trying desperately to heat the ice cold earth. As the temperature warmed, the mist lifted.

The warmth touched Derrin's cold skin, and his

eyes flicked opened. His fall had been broken by a thick layer of fresh snow on a ledge. The edge of the ravine was about thirty feet above. If he had fallen just eight feet to either side or front then he would now be lying dead at the ravine's bottom.

Derrin's body was in agony as he tried to lift himself, his muscles strained across his body. Derrin was cold and shivering, but he knew he would have to move. Staying here was not an option, if he remained here he would die of exposure. He managed to get himself to his feet and hobbled to the face of the ravine.

His sword was gone but his dagger was still tucked into his belt. Derrin looked at the cliff despairingly; it was quite a moderate climb, but in his fragile condition it would be more difficult, he would have to be very careful.

****

O'Rourke, Haynes, Bartack and three other Scouts departed the watchtower. The horses' tracks were still visible due to the weight of the animals load and the speed they had been travelling. Bartack immediately picked up the trail. He led the column, with O'Rourke beside him and Haynes and the other three men behind.

Bartack could smell a strong scent of pine coming from O'Rourke.

'Pine oil?' asked Bartack looking at O'Rourke.

'Yes, me father swore by it. Hides yer scent, and yer horse's scent too.' replied O'Rourke.

Haynes overheard this and laughed, shaking his head.

'Its an old woodman's trick, my father used it too.' Bartack responded.

'Do yea want some? I have a spare bottle?' asked O'Rourke.

'Thanks, I might use it later.' said Bartack.
O'Rourke reached into his side pocket and handed Bartack a small bottle. Bartack tucked the bottle carefully into his saddle bag.

The journey was slow, as periodically the tracks had been covered by drifting snow. The sun had also began to melt some of the top layers.

They had noticed that there had been an unusual numbers of troll tracks, all heading southwards. Eventually they reached their destination and saw ahead an overturned wagon. As they got closer they saw the remains of Anders' horse, the broken body of its rider, and bloody drag marks heading towards a clump of fir trees.

The Scouts dismounted, and then started investigating. Haynes followed the trail marks with one of the Scouts. Very soon they found the decapitated remains of Scout Banner, next to him lay a large, dead, great grey troll. The animal was dead, and someone or something had killed it during its meal. There were no signs of sword marks nor arrows. Haynes was puzzled by this, but more puzzled by the grey troll. It was well know that great greys never came this far from the Stone City.

Grey trolls were much larger and stronger than normal mountain trolls.

'We found Banner!' shouted Haynes.

Bartack began looking for signs of Derrin. At least he was still unaccounted for, he thought. He found tracks heading off in the opposite direction from the wagon site, and there were troll tracks beside them too. He could tell both were travelling at pace.

'Sergeant O'Rourke, I think I have a track, it leads this way.' said Bartack pointing ahead.

O'Rourke ran over to him and started following the track. The remaining Scouts began tending to Anders' remains, and recovering his equipment from the horse.

Bartack pushed on, and saw he was approaching the edge of a ravine.

'Oh no! You don't think...?' said Bartack.

O'Rourke looked concerned. From the trail Bartack realised that a troll had chased Derrin towards the ravine edge. He feared the worst.

He carefully stepped towards the edge and peered over. On a ledge, about thirty feet below him he could see Derrin.

'Derrin!' shouted Bartack in joy.

Derrin slowly looked up and with difficulty waved a hand.

'Sergeant, I found Derrin, he's alive!' Bartack exclaimed.

O'Rourke came over beside him.

'Well bless me lad. Ye did, ye did! I need to get a rope, I'll let Haynes know!' said O'Rourke, as he walked back to the wagon site.

O'Rourke returned shortly after with Haynes and a Scout.

'Derrin, can ye tie this around yer waist?' shouted

down O'Rourke.

Derrin nodded and O'Rourke threw the rope down to him. He began to tie it around his waist, his body ached.

'We'll pull you up lad, just keep hold as you need'. O'Rourke, Haynes, Bartack and the Scout began pulling Derrin up. As they heaved, Derrin tried to climb up too. He lost his footing and slipped.

'Woah, easy there lad.' exclaimed O'Rourke.

They continued to pull and at last Derrin reached the top of the cliff face. Haynes and Bartack grabbed him by the arms and helped him up. Absolute relief was etched upon his face as he reached the top of the ravine. Derrin was limping and was heavily bruised. O'Rourke and Bartack assisted Derrin while he walked. They took him back to the wagon site and helped him onto Bartack's horse.

'We'll have to bury Anders and Banner here.' said Haynes regretfully. Haynes and the Scouts dug the graves and marked them with their swords and helmets.

'We need to head back to the watchtower, Derrin needs treatment and rest.' said O'Rourke.

The party mounted their horses, and Bartack doubled up with Haynes. They left the area quickly and headed back to the tower. After a few hours they arrived back. The watchtower lookout called out to them. Haynes waved back in acknowledgement to the guard.

They arrived at the front of the tower and dismounted, Burke met them outside along with several other Scouts.

'What is your report, Sergeant?' asked Burke.

'Anders and Banner are dead sir, killed by a troll. Derrin is injured.' replied O'Rourke.

'Get Derrin to his bed and ask Toby to tend to his wounds.' said Burke.

The party walked their horses into the stables and then returned to their rooms, except Haynes who went to visit Derrin.

'Derrin how are you feeling?' asked Haynes.

'Better Corporal, and certainly a lot warmer.' replied Derrin in considerable discomfort but still smiling.

Haynes smiled.

'Derrin we found a troll next to Banner, it was dead, it was a grey troll, do you know who killed it? asked Haynes.

'No, the last I saw of it was when I jumped, the others were already dead. Banner told me to run, so I did.' explained Derrin.

'Keep resting, Toby will take good care of you.' added Haynes.

Markus arrived in the room and eagerly came over to see how Derrin was. At that point Corporal Haynes took his leave, and went to see Captain Burke.

'Sir, the patrol was attacked by a great grey troll. We found the troll dead, and Derrin confirmed it hadn't been killed by them. Something killed it.' said Haynes.

'Grey trolls are only found right at the very High Peaks around Stone City, they don't come down this far.' said Burke.

'Clearly that's no longer the case. We found unusual numbers of troll's tracks too, perhaps they *are* moving south?' said Haynes.

'If you're right Corporal, we are in real trouble. We will have to report this to Ormsby Keep immediately.' said Burke.

He started to write a report letter, signed it, then placed it in an envelope and sealed it with wax.

'Corporal, send one of the Scouts to Ormsby Keep with the letter. It needs to be delivered to the garrison commander. Also let them know we need two replacements, one Lance-Scout and a Scout.' said Burke.

Haynes saluted then issued the letter with instructions to a Scout. The Scout galloped off immediately to Ormsby Keep, quickly disappearing out of sight.

'I hope he gets there quickly.' said Haynes out loud.

Haynes turned and then returned towards the watchtower entrance, then entered the stables area. He stood alone and took a quiet moment to himself, stroking the mane of his horse. The loss of two more of his comrades began to take its toll on him.

CHAPTER 8

As night fell the tower raised the drawbridge and sealed the main doors. Markus was on guard duty at the top of the tower. The icy wind picked up, and snow once again began to fall. The top of the tower was badly exposed to the weather, and a blizzard was beginning. Markus had quickly learned you need to wrap up well for this duty.

Throughout the night shift he sometimes heard howls. At first they disturbed him, but he had grown accustomed to the sounds.

The shift had gone untroubled, but then just after one o'clock a flash in the distance caught his eye. It was the Beanoch watchtower beacon! It was lit! Markus immediately ran to notify the watch officer, Quartermaster Tyerose.

'Sir, the emergency beacon at Beanoch has been lit!' said Markus barely believing what he had just witnessed.

'I'll awaken the Captain and notify him. Go back to your duty post,' said Tyerose.

Markus left and returned to the top of the tower. The Quartermaster went to the Captain's quarters and knocked on the door.

'Sir, the emergency beacon at Beanoch has been lit.'

Burke woke with a start, and then began to comprehend what the Quartermaster had just told him.

'They must be in trouble. We head there at first light. Double all our guards and place an extra two men on the watchtower. Also add oil to the moat, if we need to light up we'll be ready to go.' ordered Burke.

Tyerose saluted, 'Right away sir.'

High Peak Watchtower was now on full alert. Tyerose knew that Westerly watchtower would also have seen the beacon. With luck they too would be sending men to aid Beanoch.

The tower guards continued to observe Beanoch. A mere thirty minutes after being lit the beacon went completely out. The watch officer was informed. Tyerose began to wonder if the beacon had been lit by accident. However, that would have no bearing on going to the tower's aid. Standing orders were if the beacon was lit the surrounding towers would come to help.

****

The attack on the Beanoch watchtower had been brutal. Overpowered by Mareck's bard magic, the defenders had become paralysed as they had no mage or priest to counter it. Mareck removed Marr's crystal from his pocket and watched. With no glow apparent yet, Mareck directed Randarr to cut through the defenceless men.

Those higher in the tower could hear the screams of their fellow soldiers in the lower levels below. This enhanced both their fear and their feelings of complete helplessness. Mareck and the merciless Randarr continued to sweep through the tower, killing everyone in their path.

At last the only place left was the top of the watchtower itself. The only defenders remaining were Captain Darnley and three others. Facing certain death, two of the soldiers jumped from the tower to escape. One impaled himself on a wooden stockade spike; the other broke his neck impacting the frozen ground at the bottom of the moat.

Mareck's crystal began to glow as it neared Darnley, and he signalled Randarr to dispose of the last soldier, lopping his head from his shoulders with one huge sweep of his broadsword. Randarr grabbed Darnley like a toy doll and raised the Captain upside down by his ankle. A gold coin fell from his pocket onto the floor, Mareck recognised it and picked it up. Mareck lowered himself to face the Captain.

'This coin, who gave it to you, and where did they go?'

Randarr raised Darnley higher and began to crush his ankle. He screamed in agony.

'I'll ask you again Captain, and for your sake I suggest you answer swiftly.' responded Mareck in an intimidating manner.

Darnley's resolve began to shatter, and he just wanted the pain to end.

'T...Tiimmisss..Timmis is who you want...he went to...to...H...Hander.'

Mareck smiled, he now had the name of the thief, and the location. He would head to Hander and find this Timmis.

'I'm going to give you a gift Captain, I know it

would be a jolly to see your friends' reaction when they arrive to rescue you.' said Mareck to the trembling, broken Darnley.

Mareck lunged at Darnley and bit into his neck. The Captain screamed and Mareck began to drink, his eyes glowed red as he savoured every drop of blood. As he drank he saw a vision of Timmis talking to Darnley and giving him the coin. When he had finished feeding, Randarr dropped Darnley to the floor in a heap.

'Oh, one thing Captain, avoid the sunlight, and if you become hungry, well, you will quickly work that out for yourself.' sneered Mareck.
Mareck and Randarr made their way out of the tower with great haste. They would have to arrive in Hander before dawn, and there seek cover until nightfall.

****

Timmis arrived in Glyvale, a large market town. It was still dark and the streets were empty apart from a few singing drunks returning from the local inn, staggering their way home supporting one another.

He found the Fine Wares store easily, and could see that a light was on downstairs. Timmis knocked loudly at the door, but there was no answer. He knocked once again, and could have sworn he saw a shadow move at one of the upper windows.

After a few minutes he heard several locks unbolting and the door to the store partly opened. A bald, tattooed man peered through the gap in the door.

'What do you want? asked the man, pretending to be surprised by the visitor.

'I'm looking for Bonna. Amarra sent me.' replied Timmis.

At this, the bald man's demeanour seemed more relaxed. He fully opened the door.

'Come in.' said Bonna, beckoning Timmis inside.

Timmis entered the store. It contained a mixture of old antiques and more modern finery. For a thief, this location would be a goldmine and Timmis automatically started scanning for loot. However, as Bonna had been an introduction, he was protected by the Thieves Guild itself. He might even be a member of the guild too. Timmis quickly retired any thoughts of plunder.

Bonna peered outside once again, checking that Timmis had not been followed. Satisfied, he closed the heavy wooden door and bolted it.

Bonna walked over to Timmis and said, 'Come with me.'

Bonna was smaller than he had appeared at the door, and was dressed in a green robe. The robe itself was trimmed with gold cloth and it looked both expensive and impressive.

Bonna led Timmis to an upstairs room, and offered him a seat at a table. The room was decorated beautifully, and reflected its owner's love of opulence. Timmis sat down and Bonna sat opposite him on red velvet high backed chair.

'Amarra told me that you may have some wares that I'm interested in. So show me.' said Bonna expectantly.

Timmis removed the small leather purse and the

ruby encrusted signet ring from his pocket and handed them to Bonna.

Bonna opened the purse and removed the gold elven coins and began to examine each of them. He then examined the ring and appraised the rubies on the ring.

'I'll give you two hundred gold pieces for the lot.' said Bonna.

Timmis said, 'I would be looking for a lot more.'

'OK, three hundred, and that's my last offer. These type of coins are hard to shift.' replied Bonna.

Timmis knew selling such unusual coins direct would draw unnecessary attention to him. He decided to cut his losses; the gold coins would be hard to get rid of. It would be safer for him that someone else would be selling them.

'OK, deal.' said Timmis regretfully.

'Good.' said the smiling Bonna, who got up and removed a medium sized pouch from a side board. He started to remove gold coins and began counting them. Once he counted to three hundred, he handed them to Timmis, along with a leather purse.

'The purse is a bonus, on me.' said Bonna smiling smugly. He knew he could sell all of the items for twenty times that amount to the right buyer.

'Do you have any other items to sell?' asked Bonna.

'Yes, but I'll sell these at Morrack and I have a buyer already for two of those pieces.' replied Timmis.

Timmis placed the leather purse into his cloak pocket, and then made his way downstairs.

'I'll show you out, nice doing business.' said Bonna continuing to smile.

He began to unlock his front door and saw Timmis out.

'Where are you off to now then my friend?' asked Bonna.

'Morrack, I have some debts to pay off there.' replied Timmis.

'Ahhh, Morrack, off to the Guild then. Say hello to Osumain for me if you see him.' said Bonna.

Bonna closed the door and Timmis returned to his horse, then tucked the leather purse into his saddle bag. He mounted his horse and set off on the road to Morrack. If Bonna knew Osumain, he *must* be a member of the Guild, thought Timmis.

****

Burke, Haynes, O'Rourke, Bartack and ten other Scouts had set off to Beanoch Tower at first light. In the distance they could see the top of the watchtower.

'Riders to our front!' exclaimed one of the Scouts. Just coming into a clearing were ten riders in a column. They noticed Burke's group and stopped. One of the riders left the group and rode in a trot to Burke's party. As he got closer, Burke could see the man was wearing the uniform of the Royal Scouts, his tabard showed he was a Lieutenant.

Burke urged his horse to turn and move towards the Lieutenant.

'Lieutenant Marshall at your service sir.' said the man, as he saluted Burke.

'Captain Burke, garrison commander at High Peak watchtower.' replied Burke returning the salute.

'I'm the garrison commander at Westerly watchtower sir. We saw the beacon fire last night from Beanoch.' said Marshall.

'Well I'm glad we crossed paths, that gives us more numbers. Can you kindly ask your troops to fall into our column?' asked Burke.

'Right away sir!' said Marshall, as he began to give hand signals to his men. His troops rode over and joined the others. Bartack watched as they rode over, then he noticed a familiar face amongst Marshall's men.

'Tellan!' said Bartack.

Tellan looked over and could not believe his eyes. The last time he had seen his friend was back at the training camp. He had missed him and had much catching up to do.

'Good to see you, Bartack.' said Tellan.

'Yes, we have much to discuss, but later.' replied Bartack.

Tellan nodded in agreement and he fell in behind Bartack's horse.

The column got closer to the Beanoch tower. There was no sign of anyone at the top of the watchtower, nor outside. The drawbridge was down and the doors both open.

'Form line.' said Burke, and the column of riders smoothly changed formation to a line facing the tower. As they rode closer, they began to see the carnage that awaited them. They spotted a soldier impaled on the stockade stake. The Scouts dismounted and drew their swords. Two of the Scouts kept hold of the others' mounts, the others led by Burke made their way to the tower entrance. As they crossed the drawbridge they saw a dead soldier lying at the bottom of the moat. The front doors, though open, showed no sign of a forced entry.

Burke ordered ten Scouts to go inside, accompanied by Lieutenant Marshall. Bartack and Tellan were amongst them. The remaining troops were ordered to search and secure the area outside the tower. From their faces, you could see the Scouts were apprehensive as to what they would find.

They entered the main doors, the stable area was empty apart from the garrison horses. Two Scouts rushed up the stairs to start searching. Thirty seconds later there was a scream as one of the Scouts fell back down the stairs clutching his bloodied throat and tumbling to the ground. Bartack and the others rushed up the stairs. On the ground the other Scout lay twitching, as a man in a Scout officer's uniform lay over him.

Captain Darnley turned to face Bartack and the others. His eyes were red like glowing embers and from his bloodied lips protruded two noticeable fangs. Darnley hissed at them evilly, his fingernails now appeared sharp and claw like. He began to advance towards them. Bartack's heart began to race rapidly, he could feel it pound within his chest. Tellan's face became pale and colourless. One of the Scouts muttered 'By the gods.' The Scout charged at Darnley with his sword and lashed at him. Darnley responded by swiping him with his claw. The impact knocked the Scout over and his body struck against the wall with some force.

Another Scout slashed at Darnley but he managed to dodge each attack with unnatural ease. Bartack then joined the fray and lashed at Darnley also; causing him to stumble backwards. Darnley clawed back at Bartack in a counter attack, just missing his face by a mere inch. Bartack felt his heart skip a beat.

Tellan realised the room was now too crowded for melee weapons, so he reached for his crossbow that was strapped to his back and quickly loaded a bolt. Bartack lashed at Darnley again, this time he struck his arm cutting him. The other Scout swung his sword, but Darnley dodged the attack with ease, then clawing upwards catching the Scout on the face. He dropped his sword which clattered to the floor then clasped his bleeding eyes in agony.

Darnley lunged at Bartack, who pushed him to one side, and again just missed a claw attack. Tellan aimed his bow and fired. The bolt struck Darnley in the neck. He was knocked back by the impact, but then hissed, gave a screech and pulled out the bolt with defiance. Tellan reloaded. One of the other Scouts now joined the fight. Darnley lashed at the blinded Scout, striking his chest and knocking him to the ground.

Bartack attacked Darnley once again, feigning an attack, then delivering another cut to Darnley's torso. Darnley leapt through the air, claws outstretched towards Bartack. Bartack rolled to his right, then attempted a reverse cut with his sword but missed.

Lieutenant Marshall, hearing the struggle, arrived upstairs and was shocked by what he was witnessing. Marshall stared in disbelief as he observed Tellan trying to aim his crossbow, and the malevolent Darnley attacking the other Scout. Tellan fired, this time his bolt struck Darnley on the forehead. He fell backwards and onto his back.

Despite the wound, Darnley was still hissing and eyeing all his attackers. Marshall advanced then swung at Darnley with a downward attack. Darnley rolled over swiftly, knocking both Marshall and the other Scout off their feet. Ignoring the embedded bolt, like a wild animal, Darnley bit into Marshall's leg, tearing his artery. Marshall screamed in agony, as Darnley began to gorge himself. Darnley's earlier wounds began to visibly heal themselves.

Darnley was preoccupied briefly with feeding. Bartack swung with a side cut, separating Darnley's head from his torso. The body fell to the ground, but grotesquely, Darnley's head was still attached to Marshall's leg with his fangs. Bartack pulled the head off the Lieutenant, which made him wince even more in pain, and threw it to the floor.

Darnley's eye were no longer glowing. The blood began to flow in spurts from the Lieutenant's wound. Bartack fell to his knees exhausted. Tellan began to administer first aid to his commander, doing his best to stem the flow of blood but to no avail.

Marshall began to go quiet, and stopped moving, Tellan bowed his head, then whispered a prayer. He got up and went over to attend to the blinded Scout.

'You'll be OK Bill.' he said, attempting to reassure him.

Bartack told one of the Scouts to fetch Captain Burke and Sergeant O'Rourke. He ran off immediately to report what had just happened.

The Captain ran into the tower along with O'Rourke, they saw the now dead Scout at the foot of the stairs, then went up to the next level. There they found Bartack sitting on the floor, Tellan tending to his comrade, and another Scout slowly getting to his feet. On the floor lay the dead bodies of one Scout, Lieutenant Marshall and the headless body of Captain Darnley.

'What the hell happened here?' asked Burke.

'Two Scouts went ahead of us upstairs. One man fell back down the stairs with a throat wound. We ran up here and found the Captain biting the other Scout on the floor. He turned round and attacked us, eyes blazing. He injured several off us, and bit the Lieutenant on the leg. Tellan even hit him with a crossbow bolt twice and it made no difference. I ended up having to cut off his head.' explained Bartack.

'What do you mean by "eyes blazing"?' asked Burke.

'His eyes glowed red sir, like they were on fire. He hissed, and his finger nails were sharp like claws.' Bartack said.

The Captain could see that all of the men who witnessed everything were visibly shaken. He walked over to Darnley's body and examined the head. The irises were indeed red and he could see the protruding fangs. A crossbow bolt had struck Darnley on the forehead.

The Scout who had been attacked on the floor was also dead, and had been completely drained of blood.

'What's your orders sir?' asked O'Rourke.

'Advice Sergeant?' said Burke.

'Well sir, I've never seen anything like that, and I've been a Scout over twenty years. We need to warn Ormsby Keep. There's forces at work here we don't understand. I'd burn the lot, but send that head to a cleric in Ormsby for an answer.' said O'Rourke.

'You are right Sergeant. We need to burn the lot, and warn Ormsby right away. The whole garrison at Beanoch is dead, we lost four men today; two Scouts, and also the garrison commanders of Beanoch and Westerly watchtowers.' said Burke.

'I'm thinking sir, ye might want to bring the message to Ormsby yourself. Beanoch is now impossible to hold and we have weakened both our own and Westerly watchtowers with these men being here.' said O'Rourke.

'OK, I'll head to Ormsby Keep right away. Bartack, you and your friend will accompany me. You saw what happened.'

Bartack and Tellan got to their feet.

'O'Rourke, get every body here cremated, every last one. Take all of the tower's spare horses with you, and send everyone back to their respective watchtowers.' said Burke.

'Will do sir!' said O'Rourke.

'Oh, don't forget to let tell the Westerly Scouts to brief their watch officer on what happened.' said Burke. Burke lifted Darnley's severed head by the crossbow bolt and placed it inside an old sack and tied off the top. O'Rourke saluted Burke, then got straight to work. They began collecting the bodies of the dead and carried them outside.

The Scouts began to collect wood for a funeral pyre and started placing the logs carefully. When the Scouts carried Darnley and his three victims' bodies outside they immediately dissolved to dust in the sunlight. The men were shocked by this, and reported this to the Captain and O'Rourke, who barely believed them.

'There's somethin' very wrong here.' said O'Rourke to Burke, as he blessed himself.

'Burn *every* body right away!' ordered Burke to the Scout.

'Yes sir!' replied the Scout, who then returned to working on the pyre.

'Have you ever seen…' uttered Burke.

'Never sir. Nothing like this in all me days.' replied O'Rourke interrupting Burke's sentence. The Captain looked at him and the veteran Sergeant looked dumbfounded

'Sure, I've seen watchtowers attacked by trolls, but I have never seen one fall, *ever*.'

'They didn't even have time, or even attempt to ignite the moat to defend themselves.' added O'Rourke.

Burke knew that the Sergeant was right, the moat

had not been lit. This meant that whatever attacked them happened at an alarming speed.

The Scouts busied themselves, pouring oil on the remains, and then lit the oil. The fire quickly took hold and the bodies of the dead soldiers started to burn.

CHAPTER 9

Captain Burke tied the sack to his saddle, then set off accompanied by Bartack and Tellan. Behind them the funeral pyre was already well ablaze, the smoke having a strange smell.

Burke was disturbed by the slaughter at Beanoch, but he knew the attack was conducted by neither trolls nor wolves. He began to wonder if the appearance of great grey trolls had a connection to the attack.

Burke wasn't looking forward to giving his report at Ormsby Keep. He was a senior Captain, and this tour was his last opportunity for promotion to Major. For an officer commanding a watchtower garrison promotion was usually guaranteed soon after. If the command was a failure promotion was gone.

'How have you been, Tellan?' asked Bartack.

'OK, I've seen wolves and all sorts here, but nothing like that thing today.' replied Tellan.

'Derrin is at the watchtower too. He's currently recovering after surviving a troll attack.' said Bartack.

'He's lucky to be alive.' said Tellan, knowing how dangerous trolls were.

'Yes, he is. He ended up having to jump off a cliff. We managed to find him, but the other two people with him were killed by the troll.' said Bartack.

'Captain?' asked Bartack.

'Yes, what is it?' replied Burke.

'What do you think happened at Beanoch?' asked Bartack.

'I don't know, it made no sense. Some of the people in the tower were killed by a sword. But that creature, or whatever it was, that's what worries me most.' said the Captain.
Bartack and Tellan looked at Burke. They could see real concern etched on the Captain's face.

****

Mareck and Randarr arrived in Hander under cover of darkness. As they walked along the main street, to their right was an old church with an attached graveyard. Mareck smiled to himself. Stone houses were on either side of the street and in the village square was a red painted water pump. Just behind, to the back of the square, was the Iron Hammer Inn.

Mareck skipped towards the inn's doors and entered followed by Randarr. Inside, the inn was of medium size, with six customers; four busy playing cards and two drinking and dining at a wooden table.

The innkeeper was busy trying to tend to an open fire that kept going out much to his annoyance. The fire finally took hold and it blazed up, illuminating the entire room. The gamblers noticed the oddly dressed minstrel standing in the doorway, their eyes fixed on him and his armoured companion. Mareck grinned at them and closed the door behind him.

Mareck and Randarr approached the bar, where the innkeeper was now busy tidying up.

'May I enquire do you have a room that is free?' said Mareck bowing graciously.
The innkeeper was startled, as he had never even heard

them open the front door.

'Errr, yes we have a room.' said the startled innkeeper, who looked at Randarr and quickly glanced away.

Mareck handed the innkeeper a gold coin.

'It's not *that* much, it's...' said the innkeeper.

Mareck interrupted him, '*No*, it's fine. Keep the difference my good man. I do need a favour though. I'm looking for a traveller who came through these parts. Short, balding with silver hair, and would have passed this way no more than a day or so ago. Calls himself Timmis. Do you know such a man.' quizzed the bard.

'Yes, I know someone like that, a trapper, he comes by this way from time to time, but I never caught his name. Amarra knows him I think, or at least I saw them speak.' said the innkeeper, who was clearly shaken.

'Amarra you say, where would I find *Amarra*?' asked Mareck staring at the innkeeper.

'He lives in the cottage across the square, it has a yellow door.' said the scared innkeeper.

Mareck bowed, 'Thank you for that. I'm a bard by the way, I will happily hold a little concert here tonight if you like.'

'Well, we...I'm not sure we can afford your fee.' said the innkeeper.

A blonde serving woman came out from the backroom and stood to the side of the innkeeper.

'No, there is no fee. I haven't played to an audience in a while. This is free, and will attract you some custom. Just spread the word around the village.

We shall begin at eight o'clock tonight.' replied the bard.
The innkeeper was unsure whether to take the offer.
The blonde woman then said, 'Oh, how wonderful, we haven't had a bard play here for so long.'
The innkeeper reluctantly nodded his head in agreement.

'Excellent, we shall see you at eight o'clock tonight.' said Mareck bowing.

'Oh, and just one other thing, innkeeper; I cannot be disturbed. I…need time alone in preparation for my performance.' Mareck added, eyeing the woman and innkeeper both.
The innkeeper reluctantly handed Mareck a room key, his hand visibly shaking.

'Room eight.' said the innkeeper.
Mareck bowed once again, and left the pair, heading up the stairs followed by Randarr.

'My, he's a handsome one, but his friend with him is scary.' said the blonde woman.

'Hhmm…back to your work Rebekah.' said the innkeeper, unimpressed.

'While you are at it, get the stable boy to send word around the village of the concert tonight.'

Mareck unlocked the room, and the door opened inwards. It was a simple, but adequate room. Randarr drew the curtains, then dragged a wardrobe across the window, further darkening the room. Mareck pushed the bed across the door.

The room was now as secure as possible, Randarr would act as guard while Mareck slept and they would then pay Amarra a visit later once the sun had set.

****

O'Rourke arrived back at High Peak watchtower with his men. As he crossed the drawbridge he was greeted by Corporal Haynes and Quartermaster Tyerose. Both looked and noticed Captain Burke was absent.

'You're in command, sir.' said O'Rourke to the Quartermaster.

'Where's the Captain?' asked Tyerose with concern.

'He's gone to Ormsby Keep, took the lad Bartack and another lad from Westerly with him.' replied O'Rourke.

'What of Beanoch?' asked Haynes.

'Gone, everyone dead, and it wasn't no troll did it either. The garrison commander of Westerly was killed too.' replied O'Rourke.

'Who attacked it?' said a shocked Haynes.

'They were all dead when we got there. The garrison commander of Beanoch was the only survivor. He went mad, killed two Scouts and the Lieutenant. He was killed, but his eyes were red and he was biting people.' Tyerose could see from the look on O'Rourke's face that this was not one of the Sergeant's jokes.

'We burnt the lot to be on the safe side, and abandoned the tower.' said O'Rourke with regret.

'Anyway, the Captain took the head of the deranged officer with him to Ormsby. The head had fangs and red eyes as I said.'

Tyerose and Haynes looked amazed at this.

'And he drank the blood of one man, and he bit the Lieutenant too.' added O'Rourke. The story sounded unbelievable to his listeners.

O'Rourke went inside the watchtower, headed upstairs and walked into Derrin's room. He was sitting up on his bed.

'Ahh, you are up lad. Feeling better now are you?' asked O'Rourke.

Derrin looked at the Sergeant and smiled.

'You made it back from the tower safely? Where is Bartack?' asked Derrin.

'He's safe, gone to Ormsby Keep with the Captain. He bumped into your friend Tellan too while there.'

'Tellan!' exclaimed Derrin.

'Yes, he's well too, how do you know him?' asked O'Rourke.

'Bartack, Tellan and myself were room-mates in training together.' replied Derrin.

'Ahh.' said O'Rourke.

'Was Beanoch tower OK?' enquired Derrin.

'Well, it's a long story for another time, just get yerself back to normal.' said O'Rourke.

A Scout came up the stairs and interrupted the conversation.

'Sarge, our messenger has arrived back from Ormsby along with the replacements for Anders and Banner.'

'Thanks, I'll let the Quartermaster know, and he'll come down and meet them.' replied O'Rourke to the Scout.

Sergeant O'Rourke left Derrin and went upstairs,

leaving Derrin to his thoughts.

'Sir, our messenger is back from Ormsby, along with the replacements for Anders and Banner.' reported O'Rourke to Tyerose.

Tyerose went to meet the messenger and the two new arrivals. He walked over to the messenger first.

'Did we receive any orders from Ormsby?'

'No sir. Just continue to report any unusual occurrences.' replied the Scout.

Tyerose gave a laugh, '*Unusual occurrences*, just wait till the Captain gets there with his report. Thank you, carry on.' replied Tyerose.

The messenger Scout then left and went inside the tower.

Tyerose walked over to the two waiting replacements.

'Orders!' said Tyerose, and the two men handed over their papers. Tyerose inspected the first man, he was tall and had a distinct white braided beard.

'Orlek sir! Scout Orlek reporting.' shouted the man.

Tyerose then moved towards the other man, who was a short, fat Lance-Scout. The man stood to attention.

'Murrat sir! Lance-Scout Murrat.' shouted the man.

'Well, welcome to High Peak watchtower.' replied Tyerose.

****

The sun had finally set, and Mareck awoke. Randarr was still dutifully guarding his companion. They removed the bed which blocked the door and crept out the back of the inn. The innkeeper's description of the cottage was correct, and it was the only one with a yellow door.

Mareck signalled to Randarr, who slipped silently away into the dark. For such a big, heavily armoured man Randarr could move without a sound when needed. Mareck skipped up to the front door, and could see clearly that there was a light coming from inside. Mareck knocked on the door, then again with more force, but there was no answer.

Inside Amarra heard a knock, then another, which startled the thief. He drew his dagger, as he had no expectation of any visitor tonight. The knocking ceased and Amarra stealthily made his way to the back door, quickly glancing to see if the coast was clear. Satisfied, he opened the door quietly, and slowly edged it open little by little. Once the space was big enough to do so he crept out the doorway into the darkness. He turned around for a second to close the door.

Suddenly, a metal gauntleted hand grabbed him firmly by the neck. The hand flung him forwards through the door and back into the house. Amarra landed in a stunned heap on the floor. He turned to get up, but found he was being dragged by a plate-mailed warrior into the living room. The warrior's strength was overpowering and Amarra was pinned to the floor.

Mareck entered the rear of the cottage and skipped into the living room. On the floor was the struggling Amarra.

'Ah, you must be Amarra.' said Mareck. Amarra began sobbing as the pressure exerted by

Randarr became painful.

'I'm looking for a person, and you may know him; balding, silver hair, Timmis is his name and you spoke to him recently.' said Mareck in a threatening tone.

'I don't know any Timmis, I don't know what you are talking about.' screamed Amarra, attempting to lie.

Mareck sighed deeply, in a bored tiresome way, then nodded at Randarr. The powerful warrior stomped the full force of his metal boot onto the back of Amarra's knee, crushing the knee cap and splintering the bone. Amarra screamed in agony, and almost passed out from the pain, tears rolled from his eyes.

'Now that that I have your *full* attention, let's try again shall we? Timmis, where is he?' asked Mareck.
The blubbering Amarra pointed to a leather purse that lay on the sideboard. Mareck snatched it up and opened it. Inside was an ancient elven coin, the very coin that Timmis had stolen from Mareck himself. Amarra's fate was now sealed.

'Where is Timmis? asked Mareck, his face beginning to twist in a grotesque mask of fury.

'Glyvale, he went to Glyvale, to the Fine Wares store. Bonna, yes, ask Bonna!' screamed Amarra, hoping this would placate his captors.
Mareck satisfied, departed the cottage. Amarra continued to scream. He felt Randarr lift his foot from the crushed kneecap, and Amarra breathed a short, quick, breath of relief. But this was fleeting, as the metal gauntlet once more seized Amarra by the neck.

Randarr twisted his hand, breaking Amarra's neck,

killing him instantly. Mareck walked into the cemetery followed by Randarr and began playing his piccolo, the tune was sweet and sad. The sound seemed to penetrate the very earth beneath his feet, when he finished he smiled.

'Awaken my pretties.' whispered Mareck. At that, the graves began to stir.

Mareck returned to the inn, and bade Randarr guard the rear of the building.

By now the majority of the villagers of Hander had gathered in anticipation for the evening show. It was not often that a bard came through their village and over forty people crowded into the inn. Indeed it had been over a year since any bard had entertained in the Iron Hammer Inn.

Mareck took to the stage and the audience quietened down in anticipation. He removed his piccolo from his robe and began playing. The sound was seductive and intoxicating. The villagers could feel every note and the sound seemed to caress them at will.

It was clear to the audience that this minstrel had a mastery of this instrument and was an exceptional bard. They had never heard his equal, and the music mesmerised them more and more. Mareck's tune shifted, and it suddenly flowed into a melancholy lament. The audience were bewitched and could only stare as he played.

Suddenly, there was a thump, thump, thump, from the front door as if someone was knocking to be let in. Few of the audience were aware of the sound. The innkeeper looked at the door briefly, almost thinking that he had just imagined it, then his vision fell back to Mareck.

Once again, from the door came, a thump, thump, thump. The innkeeper now realised that someone was trying to get in. He walked towards the door.

'OK, *OK*, I'm coming, wait a moment' said the innkeeper.

He was impatient and did not want to miss the show, or any customers looking to buy beer. Tonight was a rare opportunity for a large profit, and he did not want to miss it.

As the innkeeper opened the door, from outside a decayed hand reached forward dragging him into the street. He began to scream, but no-one seemed to take notice. Through the door poured decaying corpses who began to attack and consume the people inside. Mareck stopped playing and the people's trance suddenly ceased.

Then screaming began, as people now realised what was happening. Some of the audience even recognised recently deceased family members, but unfortunately the recognition was not mutual. The zombies only recognised food, and their hunger for fresh flesh was ravenous. As the horde began to burst through the inn doors, they spread out.

They started chasing after the closest targets to them that they could find. Two men and a woman dashed past the loose zombie group and tried desperately to run out of the front door to escape.

One of the fleeing men was pulled over and he was sent crashing into a table, falling onto the floor, where several zombies dived onto the screaming man.

The man and woman continued to run. The man used the woman as a human shield, and pushed her towards the horde, trying to buy himself an opportunity for escape. The zombies grabbed the screaming woman and began chewing on her.

The cowardly man then made it outside the inn, but a look of horror crossed his face as he realised there were more undead outside than in. He screamed and was quickly overwhelmed by grasping, decaying hands, and their gnawing hungry teeth.

Inside the inn, a man tried to fight the zombies with a stool. He bashed a few zombies, knocking them over, but they slowly got to their feet. His attacks proved fruitless, as the undead clawed and bit him; blood poured from his open wounds and he was pulled to the ground.

Many of the victims were already too inebriated to defend themselves with any success. One man managed to escape by the back of the inn and was concentrating only on escape. He ran and failed to notice Randarr. The man was swiftly cut down by the flash of a broadsword.

Trapped in the inn, the unarmed villagers were quickly overcome. Outside, people tried to flee from their homes into the woods, but they too were overcome. Soon the crying and the screaming stopped, and a deathly silence descended on the village, broken only by the sound of the dead feeding.

With the dead distracted by their hunger, one woman who had hidden, seized her only opportunity. With her child clasped firmly to her, she ran as fast as she could and managed to reach the woods unnoticed. The woman disappeared into the night, her heart racing, panic and fear her only companions.

The minstrel looked around at the carnage and laughed. Just as he had predicted, the villagers had all come to see his show in the inn.

Mareck danced and twirled amongst the bodies, his cape extending in the breeze. He skipped past the corpses, humming to himself a tune that existed only in his mind. From his belt pouch he once again produced his wooden piccolo.

The minstrel began to play a haunting tune. In turn, the zombies ignored their meals and began a gasping groan in unison that seemed to echo from everywhere in reply.
He played for several minutes and danced amongst his undead choir. His melody ceased, and just as quickly, the zombies fell silent and returned once again to their bloody feast.

'Well my children, you enjoyed my little tune it seems.
The living will arrive soon to try and take this place from you.
Embrace them with death.' said Mareck to his undead minions.

Mareck then went to the stables located behind the inn and chose two horses, bringing one to Randarr. They mounted their steeds and Mareck began to laugh manically. His laughter filled the cold night air. The minstrel then smiled wickedly.

'The Master will be so pleased, we will soon find the thief who stole from him…and me.' said the bard to his companion.

Mareck and Randarr set off for Glyvale disappearing into the darkness. Behind him, Hander was now the village of the dead. Only the feeding groans of the zombies broke the still silence of the night air.

CHAPTER 10

Captain Burke, Bartack and Tellan arrived at Ormsby Keep. The tower looked just as imposing to Bartack as it previously had. There was now a thin layer of snow across the keep's battlements, and the once muddy track of the main street was now concealed by a white blanket of snow.

Outside the keep, twenty soldiers sat on horseback, awaiting to depart on a patrol. Each man had a rounded helmet and a shiny, steel cuirass, indicating that they were from a light cavalry regiment. Accompanying them were two mounted soldiers wearing light leather armour, the uniform of the Royal Scouts.

Burke, Tellan and Bartack dismounted and secured their horses to a wooden post. Burke removed the sack and carried it with him, carefully trying to keep the item and its gruesome contents at arm's reach. At the open doors of the keep, two soldiers guarded the entrance. They were wearing chain mail armour, with chain coifs upon their heads.

As Captain Burke approached, the two mail armoured infantrymen stood to attention. Burke saluted in response, and the two men then stood at ease.

'I need to speak to the commander of the garrison urgently.' said Burke to one of the soldiers.

'The commander is Lord Garlan sir, but you will need to speak to either Sergeant-at-Arms Roe or the Adjutant, Knight-Captain Harbill first.' replied the soldier.

'Their rooms are through that entrance yonder sir.' said the soldier, pointing to a set of stone stairs that lay under an archway on the opposite side of the keep's inner courtyard.

Burke nodded in thanks and they swiftly made their way up the stairs. They arrived on the floor above, a large stone walled room decorated by beautiful tapestries. In the centre of the room was a long wooden table, and behind this was a large fireplace, which contained a blazing warm fire.

Standing in conversation beside the fireplace were two soldiers, one man wore the rank of a Master-at-Arms, a Sergeant-Major. He was a balding, muscular man, and looked in his late forties. The other soldier wore the uniform of a knight, he had a gaunt thin chiselled face, and Burke estimated him to be aged in his late twenties.

Burke approached them, followed by Tellan and Bartack behind. The knight ceased his conversation, having glanced round and noticed Burke's approach. The Master-at-Arms did likewise.

'Yes, can I help you?' asked the knight.

'Captain Evan Burke, garrison commander at High Peak watchtower.' said Burke, formally introducing himself.

'Good evening Captain, I am *Knight*-Captain Darian Harbill.' replied the man, clearly overemphasising the word 'knight'.

Burke said nothing in response, a typical cavalry

officer, he thought to himself, trying to create an air of superiority. The 'knight' part in fact meant nothing to Burke, as in reality they were both of equal rank. The Royal Scouts, just like their infantry counterparts, did not address their officers as knights.

'Master-at-Arms Roe sir.' said the Sergeant-Major, bringing himself to attention.

Captain Burke nodded his head in recognition, and Roe stood at ease once more.

'So Captain, how can we assist you?' asked Harbill.

'I assume you received my previous report from my messenger.' said Burke.

'Ah, yes, we did, and the Knight-Marshal was *most* upset by the news.' replied Harbill.

'Perhaps the Knight-Marshal may be allowed to decide *himself* whether he is upset or not, *Knight-Captain*.' said a grey haired older man standing in a doorway behind Harbill, lightly mocking the previous overemphasis of his rank. He had obviously been listening to the conversation from the beginning.

'Yes sir!' said Harbill, embarrassed by this in front of the newcomers.

Knight-Marshal Lord Garlan entered the room and approached Burke. Captain Burke stood to attention with Bartack and Tellan following suit.

'Please.' said Garlan, motioning the men to relax with his hand.

'Now Captain Burke, I did receive your report, and you stated that a great grey troll attacked your men in the vicinity of High Peak tower?' added Garlan.

'Yes sir, we have never had grey trolls in that area

before. The amount of troll tracks has also increased significantly.' said Burke.

Lord Garlan began slowly nodding his head absorbing the information.

'I also have to report that Beanoch tower was attacked and the garrison destroyed.' said Burke reluctantly.

Garlan looked at him and said, 'Destroyed you say, explain!'

'Well sir, after we found the troll dead and one survivor from the missing patrol, that night our lookout spotted the beacon at Beanoch lit. At first light we set out to come to their aid. En route we encountered an aid party that had been dispatched from Westerly watchtower. This young man was a member of that group.' said Burke, gesturing to Tellan.

'The Westerly group was led by Lieutenant Marshall, their garrison commander. We combined the two parties and then approached the tower. All the men there were dead, there were no survivors, except one, if indeed you could describe him as a survivor.' said Burke.

'Go on.' said Garlan.

'The area was literally dead, we had the building searched, then there was a disturbance inside the tower. My Scouts were attacked by the Beanoch garrison commander who seemed to have gone insane. He injured one man, and killed two others, and bit the Lieutenant. These Scouts accompanying me witnessed the whole incident.

Darnley was finally killed during his attack upon the

Lieutenant, who subsequently died from his injuries.' said Burke.

'I then ordered the Lieutenant and the other victims of the garrison commander cremated, but they dissolved to dust when the bodies were taken outside of the tower.'

Garlan walked over to Bartack and Tellan.

'And you witnessed this?' asked Garlan.

'We did sir.' said Tellan.

'He fought with me sir, his fingers were like claws and his eyes were red and glowing. Like the embers in that fire sir.' said Bartack, pointing to the huge fireplace in front of him.

'I was the one who laid the final blow.' added Bartack.

'It's true sir, I shot him twice with my crossbow, and one of those hit his head but he kept coming.' said Tellan.

In the background, Knight-Captain Harbill gave a chortle at the young Scouts comments. Garlan heard this and looked back at Burke.

'The Knight-Captain here does have a point. The story does sound somewhat far-fetched.' said Garlan.

'I may need more than the word of a couple of young boys Captain Burke.' added Garlan.

'I understand sir, hopefully this will be sufficient proof.' replied Burke, as he began to untie the sealed sack he had been carrying and placed the head of Captain Darnley upon the long wooden table to the shock of those in the room.

Roe and Garlan gasped with astonishment

and Harbill almost wretched at the hideous sight. Now lying before them they truly appreciated the monstrosity that Bartack and Tellan had witnessed. The tips of sharp fangs still protruded from Darnley's lips and the irises of his eyes were red, but no longer did they have a fiery glow. The crossbow bolt was still embedded within his skull.

'By the gods!' exclaimed Garlan.
The old Knight-Marshal had never seen such a thing before.

'Allun, can you ask Brother Oram to come to to these quarters immediately?' requested Garlan.

'Sir.' said Roe, and the Master-at-Arms swiftly departed the room.

'Let us see what Oram can make of this.' said Garlan.

The group stood waiting, then footsteps approached. Returning to the room was Roe, and he was followed by a short, brown robed monk. The monk stopped in front of Garlan.

'My Lord, you requested my presence.' said the monk bowing.

'Brother Oram, can you examine this...item, on the table.' said Garlan.

The monk gasped slightly, muttering something quietly to himself, as he had not expected to behold such a surprise. He quickly composed himself and began to examine the head in detail. He opened the mouth, appraising the fangs and then looking closely at the red eyes.

From a belt pouch Oram removed a small quartz

crystal. He began to chant, and when he had finished his incantation the crystal had an orange glow. Oram moved the crystal closer to the head and the orange glow became noticeably brighter. The crystal's glow then decreased the further he took it away from the head.

Oram turned to face Lord Garlan.

'I can't tell you exactly what that was, but I can tell what it wasn't. This thing was not living, nor was it dead either, it was undead.' said Oram.

'*What?*' Harbill said with a start.

'I infused a prayer incantation into the crystal that causes a reaction in the presence of undead. The last time I saw this happen was when I assisted in a search for a ghoul that was lurking and attacking travellers in and around Mourkley Marsh.
Before that, I had used this incantation to find a spectre that was haunting an old house in Snowvael.' said Oram.

'By the gods, this is more serious than we first thought.' said Garlan.

'What type of undead this is I don't know, I will have to consult with Abbot Jenna at the Temple of Zella in Morrack.' said the monk.

'The real question is how did the Captain of the garrison end up like this, and what *did* attack the watchtower?' said Garlan.

'This thing was feeding on its victims, and the daylight did seem to react with its victims' remains.' said Burke.

'My Lord, I'll need to take the remains of this

creature with me to the temple in Morrack, the abbot will wish to examine it.' said Oram.

'Of course, take it with you.' said Garlan.
Brother Oram placed the head into the sack and sealed it.

'I'll leave for there at once. When I discover more I will send a carrier pigeon to contact you my Lord.' said Oram bowing as he left the room.

'Oh and Captain, you can have this.' said Oram, tossing the crystal he had used towards Burke, who caught it immediately.

'Knight-Captain Harbill, take three detachments of cavalry, two detachments of infantry and one Royal Scout detachment to reinforce Beanoch and the wider area, long patrols if possible, and keep in contact by carrier pigeon if needed.' said Garlan.

'Yes sir. And the replacement garrison commander at Westerly sir?' asked Harbill.

'Any suggestions Knight-Captain?' replied Garlan.

'Yes sir, we have a new Royal Guard Ensign, Sebastian Le Romme. He recently completed officer training at Gunimore. He's from a good Ronnestone family; I served with his brother Adam at Garmer, nice chap.' said Harbill.

Bartack recognised the name from his time at Tarrondale. Surely that wasn't the same incompetent fellow that he encountered during the royal trials for Guard selection, he thought to himself?

'Very well, prepare Ensign Le Romme's orders. Also send Master-at-Arms Zill along with him. Should your boy get into difficulty he'll need a good Sergeant Major to help him out.' said Garlan to Harbill.

The Knight-Marshal's remark brought a smile to Roe's face. Harbill didn't notice and he left the room pleased with himself.

'What of ourselves sir? Shall we return to High Peak and young Tellan return to Westerly?' asked Burke.

'No, you and your men are to remain at Ormsby Keep for the time being. I will have to notify Sir Jeffrey Rolland, and advise King Tarnus of what has happened. We may also hear back from Brother Oram soon.' replied Garlan.

'Thank you gentlemen, dismissed.' added Garlan and the Knight-Marshal retired to his private quarters. Apart from Burke, Bartack and Tellan, Roe was now the only person remaining in the long table room.

'Sir, I'll get one of my Corporals to get your lads quartered and fed. The officers' mess is in the other wing, I'll escort you there.' said Roe.

'Thank you Sergeant Major.' said Burke as he followed Roe from the room. Ten minutes later a Corporal arrived.

'Are you two lads from the watchtowers?' he asked.

'Yes Corporal.' the boys replied.

'Come along then, lets get ya' fed and a bed.' the Corporal said. Bartack and Tellan followed him out of the room and down the stairs.

****

Randarr and Mareck arrived at the outskirts of town early in the morning. Glyvale used to be the main trading route to the mines of the Brokenlands, thanks mostly to its bridge and proximity to Ormsby Keep.

A great deal of agricultural produce from the farmlands of Churzey travelled in the other direction to feed the army of miners. With precious minerals and gems exchanging hands in Glyvale, a significant jewellery economy was created.

Unfortunately, that same economy attracted the attention of the Thieves' Guild, drawn by rich plunder, a black market and smuggling of illicit goods. Beside the archway of the town gate, a chain mailed soldier was chatting to a whore who was trying desperately to drum up some trade. She noticed Mareck and Randarr.

'Hello gents, are you looking for some company?' asked the whore.
Mareck looked at the woman.

'Good evening, no, but I seek an establishment called, Fine Wares, do you know of such a place?' asked Mareck.

'Fine Wares, aye that's in the jewellery quarter. But it won't be open now.' replied the woman.

'And how would one find it?' asked Mareck.

'Easy, follow this street to the second crossroads, go left and that takes you down to the quarter, its on the left a bit down there.' answered the soldier.
The soldier then drew his attention back to the woman.

'I've changed me mind, maybe we can come to an arrangement.' said the guard. The woman giggled then began to flirt with him again.

Mareck bowed, and continued following the directions that the soldier had given him. The streets were still busy, as the inn drunkards struggled to make their way home. As they left the central part of town they reached the second crossroads. It was considerably darker than the other streets. This of course was no issue to Mareck, who could see clearly. From the shadows two masked men approached them.

'Going somewhere this time of night?' asked the first man.

'And what business, pray, is it of yours?' replied Mareck.

The first man laughed at this.

'You're a cheeky bugger, ain't ya?' said the man.

'Tam, teach this bugger some manners.' said the first man.

His large accomplice approached Marek grabbing his horse's reins. Mareck reached over with unnatural speed, grabbed the man's hand and twisted his wrist back, instantly snapping the bone.

The man screamed in agony, and tried to support his broken limb with his other hand. Witnessing this, the first man drew a dagger, and began running towards Mareck. The man never even noticed Randarr, as the warrior cut down forcefully with his broadsword, cutting the man's head in half, his lifeless body falling to the ground.

Panic set in, and the big man began to run for his life. Injured, he stumbled and staggered trying desperately to ignore the pain and the shock. Behind him Randarr dismounted and swiftly approached the panicking man. The dark paladin's blade tip pierced the big man's back. The big man looked down at his torso, as a sword tip appeared from out of his belly. He gasped and stopped moving. Randarr withdrew his blade, and the man's lifeless body fell to the ground.

Mareck found the whole incident somewhat inconveniencing, but it had rather amused him. Randarr was a man of few words, but his actions more than made up for this, thought Mareck.

Randarr climbed onto his horse, and he and Mareck continued to follow the given directions, leaving the two rogues' bodies lying where they fell.

They reached the jewellery quarter and as directed, the store was down a little on the left. The outer door was extremely sturdy, and although Randarr would eventually gain access, Mareck opted for a stealthier approach. Randarr hammered at the front door, and Mareck went to the back of the building, climbing a drain pipe to access the roof and then across the top to the rear of the building. Bonna heard the hammering, and peered behind the curtain of the front room on the first floor.

Whoever was hammering had now gone, and he returned to his bedroom at the rear. As he walked into his bedroom at the far end of the room he saw a pair of flame red eyes staring at him. Terror set in, and Bonna's heart raced as he stumbled backwards bumping into a metal object behind him. He glanced around and right beside him was a tall plate mailed knight. Bonna tried to scream, but a metal gauntleted hand covered his mouth and he passed out.

Bonna awoke inside his bedroom, he was lying on his bed and he assumed that he had just had a horrible nightmare. He got out of bed and felt different, then he realised that his vision was perfectly clear in the darkness. It was still night, yet he could still see. He also felt stronger, and the long term pain he had from his back was now gone.

He walked to the front room, and peered out the window into the street. He could see, so clearly, even the areas with the darkest shadow. Now a hunger took him, and he felt a deep cramp come from his stomach. Bonna fell to his knees, and rubbed his abdomen. As he raised his head, before him stood the figure that he saw earlier, it hadn't been a dream.

'Fear not Bonna.' said Mareck.

'I have given you a gift, you will no longer age, and you are stronger and faster than you ever were. But you can no longer walk in the daylight, for that will destroy you. And you must also feed, the blood of others will sustain you and heal you.' Mareck towered over Bonna as he cowered on the floor.

'You have a ruby ring sold to you by a man named Timmis. That ring belongs to both my and your new master, Gorath Marr. Be loyal to our master and he will reward you with all that you desire. Betray him, and he will destroy you. Now give me the ring.' said Mareck.

Bonna stood up and walked over to a dresser, opened a drawer and lifted out a ruby encrusted ring. He handed it to Mareck without a word.

Mareck's hand closed around the ring tightly, and he could feel the power and energy of his master radiating from within it.

'Thank you. Now the man Timmis stole other items from Gorath Marr. A wand and a talisman. Did you see these items?' asked Mareck.

'No, but Timmis said that he already had a buyer for one of these and would sell the other in the Thieves' Guild of Morrack.' said Bonna.

'We need to find the these things. You have a contact in the guild there?' asked Mareck.

'Yes, Osumain is a member there.' said Bonna.

'You will need allies, and we will need foot soldiers. You can share your gift with others, and they will be completely loyal to you. It's time to expand into the surrounding towns. Now, dawn will arrive soon and we need to rest until sunset.' said Mareck.

'I have a basement.' replied Bonna.

'Perfect.' and Randarr will ensure our rest is not disturbed.' replied Mareck.

'Won't the sunlight harm him?' enquired Bonna.

'No. He is...well...different to us. But before you rest you must feed. Head out into the street and find your meal, then return.' said Mareck.

Bonna left the shop and started walking down the street. Mareck smiled, the idiot Darnley was expendable, but Bonna was clever and would prove a useful minion. Mareck laughed, if Bonna did not do as asked, Gorath Marr would be merciless.

Mareck judged that Bonna was a man who was driven by personal wealth and greed. He could tell that from the finery and items which adorned his shop. Such a person would be ruthless, perhaps even more ruthless than Mareck, but easy to control.

Mareck lay down on the floor of the basement and composed himself to sleep. Randarr said nothing but stood faithfully guarding the basement door, awaiting Bonna's return. Thirty minutes later, Bonna returned to the shop just as the sun began to rise. He returned to the basement entrance, and there standing at the door was Randarr.

'Mareck was right, *I am* stronger and faster than before.' said a smiling, gleeful, Bonna to Randarr.
The dark paladin said nothing in response to this, but just stared at Bonna as he walked past and entered the basement. Mareck was already asleep, and Bonna looked at him lying on the floor. He copied Marek's repose, then closed his eyes.

CHAPTER 11

Derrin was feeling much better. He heard footsteps on the stairs to his floor and saw the head of Tyerose as he reached the top of the stairs. Tyerose continued onto the stairs of the next floor and disappeared out of sight.

Following behind the Quartermaster was a Scout with a white braided beard and behind him was Corporal Murrat!

'*Hell!*' exclaimed Derrin. He began to feel nauseous, but that feeling was quickly replaced by anger and then fear. Derrin had hoped and prayed that he would *never* see this man again, but here he was, and here Derrin was.

Murrat had failed to notice Derrin, but he knew at some point their paths would cross.
He thought back to Tarrondale when Murrat had almost killed him, only Breven's intervention had stopped him. Derrin then noticed Toby returning to his bed space, searching for something in his footlocker.

'Did you see that new Corporal?' asked Derrin.

'No.' replied Toby.

'I know him from Tarrondale, he was my and Bartack's instructor and he almost killed me. Beat me to a pulp.' explained Derrin.
Toby had a look of shock, and looking at Derrin he could see his friend was genuinely afraid.

'I'm going to have to watch my back, he had a real genuine hatred for me.' said Derrin.

'Eventually your paths will cross, this is a small

place. Then what will you do?' said Toby.
Derrin nodded in agreement.

'Don't know, but I will think of something.' he replied.

Much later, in the main mess upstairs, a meal was being served to the Scouts. Derrin collected his food and sat down to eat. Murrat entered the room and glanced around, then collected his food. He sat by himself at a table then began to look at everyone who was in the room in the hope of seeing a former comrade. He didn't recognise any of the other Scouts.

His eyes moved to the rear of the room and he locked onto Derrin. Derrin looked up and could almost feel Murrat's icy stare. Derrin kept his head down and tried to ignore him. Murrat quickly wolfed down his food then deliberately passed Derrin on his way out.

'Well, well, if it isn't the little scum. Healed up then? You and your little friends cost me a stripe.' said the snarling Murrat pointing to his missing rank marking on his sleeve.
Derrin looked up, and could now see Murrat had the rank of Lance-Scout and he had indeed been demoted. The vague outline of a missing stripe was still visible on his uniform.

'And now I have to do six months here in this shit hole to get it back.' said Murrat angrily.
Corporal Haynes entered the room, and there was a brief silence as he looked at both men. Haynes sensed that something was up, but wasn't sure what.

'You know each other?' asked Haynes.

'Aye, young Derrin here knows me well, ain't

that right?' replied Murrat, his demeanour completely changed from earlier.

Derrin remained silent and barely acknowledged the comment.

'I need another Scout for a patrol, do you feel up to it yet Derrin?' asked Haynes.

Derrin quickly realised that this would give him a chance to stay as far away from Murrat as possible. He knew deep down Murrat was a coward and a bully, and would avoid danger whenever and wherever possible. He would also look to take on the easiest duties for himself and leave the dangerous ones to others.

Murrat only had six months to do to reclaim his lost stripe, and he would lie low, letting others take the risks. Derrin knew his plan of a cat and mouse avoidance was dangerous, as he would be the one putting himself voluntarily in danger. But he had no choice at this point and time and seized the opportunity offered by Haynes.

'Yes Corporal Haynes, I'm feeling a lot better now.' replied Derrin.

'Good, we leave in twenty minutes, wide patrol, get your gear and horse ready, and bring a bow. I'll see you outside then.' said Haynes.

Haynes walked back downstairs, and Derrin rose from his seat and began to approach the steps.

Murrat smugly laughed behind him and said, 'Careful out there now.'

Derrin departed the room, glad to be out of the presence of Murrat's open contempt, and readied his equipment. In a way he was content to be back on patrol, as his fear of the unknown was gone. The worst had already happened to him thanks to the troll, so for him now anything else would never be as bad.

Derrin mounted his horse and joined Haynes' patrol, and they rode off.

****

The woman carried her child to the gates of Glyvale, she was terrified and shaking, the only living survivors she knew of from Hander village. Her face was covered in dirt and her clothes ripped and dirty. The child was crying and she struggled to make her way to the gate. One of the town guards noticed her and concerned by her behaviour approached her to investigate.

'Help. Help me!' cried the woman to the guard.
The guard turned and signalled to one of his colleagues, and another guard approached.

'Take them to the Constable.' said the guard. The guard led the woman down the street, clutching her child. The guard approached a flat, low stone building, and then climbed the steps to the door.

'The Constable's office.' said the guard pointing at the building, as they entered.

Inside there were drunks who had been detained, now sober, people who had been brawling, now peaceful, and others still chained up for various transgressions the previous night. A chain mailed soldier wearing a royal blue tabard approached.

'What happened here, guard? Who is this woman?' asked the man.

'She arrived at the main gate asking for help. It looks like she has been attacked sir.' he replied.

'Well, woman, what happened?' asked the Constable.

The woman was hysterical, and clearly had been traumatised.

'They...they killed everyone, ripped them apart.' said the woman struggling to get the words out.

'Who? Where? Speak up woman.' said the Constable impatiently.

'In Hander, they attacked us. It was that bard's fault, all of it!' she screamed.

'Soldier, get them to the healer and clean them up. I'll report this to the Captain.'

The Constable then went off to see his superior to give him the news.

It had been a busy night in Glyvale; two known rogues had been found murdered, one decapitated the other stabbed and then a woman's body was discovered later with bite marks and a broken neck. Murder was not uncommon in Glyvale, but the style of the attack and the ferocity had been most brutal.

The Captain thanked the Constable, and then began to draft a courier report. He would begin an investigation into the killings in Glyvale, but Hander fell under the jurisdiction of Ormsby Keep, and it would be up to the authorities there to look into that.

The Captain marked his report with his seal, and then began to fold the report into a tiny roll. He placed it into a carrier pigeon pouch, then entered another room which had several wicker baskets containing pigeons. He opened the door flap, and removed one of the birds, checking its condition. He tied the pouch to the pigeon's foot, then released the bird from the window. The pigeon flew off northwards, its wings beating furiously, as it picked up speed.

****

Brother Oram entered the Temple of Zella carrying the sack he had received at Ormsby Keep. The Temple was a beautiful, peaceful building, and the stain glass windows reflected colours onto the stone floors inside, as the daylight shone through them.

He blessed himself, then approached the front of the temple which had a shrine containing a huge statue of the goddess Zella. He approached a monk who was walking past the shrine and bowed. The monk bowed back at Oram.

'Brother, I need to speak to the Abbot as a matter of urgency. I am Brother Oram, assigned to Lord Garlan at Ormsby Keep.' said Oram to the monk.

'Of course, please follow me brother.' replied the monk. Oram bowed once again.
The monk led Oram past some cloisters, and into the living quarters for the monks of the temple. He brought him to the Abbot's private quarters, then stopped.

'Please wait here.' said the monk bowing to Brother Oram, and he went to the door, knocking on it twice.

'Come in.' said a voice from inside, and the monk disappeared through the door.

A few moments later the door opened and the monk reappeared.

'The Abbot will see you now brother.' and the monk beckoned him inside.

Oram entered the Abbot's room, and the other monk bowed then left the room, closing the door behind him. At a wooden writing desk sat the Abbot, he was dressed in a white robe which had brown edging. Irwin Jenna was an elderly man and completely bald. Oram thought that he must be well over seventy years of age. The room was a study, and the walls contained shelves holding vast volumes of tomes, books and scroll holders, all stacked together.
Oram walked forward to the Abbot and bowed.

'I am Brother Oram, I am assigned to Ormsby Keep and in service to Lord Garlan. We have a matter which requires your guidance.' said Oram.
The Abbot smiled and said, 'Welcome to our temple Brother Oram. I am Abbot Jenna, how may I help you?'
Oram explained to the Abbot what they had encountered, and also spoke about what he had discovered about the head.

'Show me the head brother?' asked the Abbot.
Oram untied the sack and removed Darnley's remains. The Abbot instinctively made a gesture of protection.

'In the name of Zella.' said the Abbott.
The Abbot got up from his chair and then started to look through the tomes, many were dusty and eventually he said, 'Aaahh, this is the tome.'
The Abbott blew dust off the book and brought it over to Oram, and opened it on his table. The monk was not

sure what to expect.

'This is the Tome of the Undying. An old text and depicts all manner of the unholy ever encountered in Dolia.' said the Abbott.

The book was extremely old and contained hand drawings of different entities. Under each, was a description, which gave a detailed account of the habits, nature, means to identify, how to protect oneself and how to destroy them. The Abbot flicked through the volume and came to the section on corporeal undead. He swiftly read the description for each, and then began to nod his head in agreement with the text.

'Ahh. From what you have told me, the creature is a thing called a vampera.'

'A vampera?' repeated Oram.

'Yes, they feed from the blood of the living, are unnaturally quick, and have an aversion to daylight.' said the Abbot.

The Abbot turned the tome around on the table to show it to the monk. The picture depicted a figure that looked human, but they had two prominent fangs, and the eyes of the creature had been coloured in red ink.

'This *could* be it Abbott.' said the monk nodding in agreement.

The Abbott turned the book around again and began reading the rest of the text, then continued.

'Now, according to the tome there is another simple test to perform. We need to place a drop of liquid light potion onto the head.'

'If it is a vampera, the liquid light will react

immediately with its skin. Now, we do have some at the temple.'

'Wait here Brother Oram, I will return shortly, I am just going to speak to our apothecary.'

The Abbott left the study, leaving Oram alone with the tome and the head. He studied the picture once again, comparing it to Darnley's remains, and there was a resemblance. Five minutes passed and the Abbot returned carrying a small, yellow phial of liquid which was capped with a dropper.

'Here we are, now lets see what happens.' said the Abbot. The Abbot unscrewed the lid, and squeezed the dropper, some of the yellow liquid was drawn upwards. The Abbott then carefully held the dropper near Darnley's forehead and squeezed. A solitary drop of the liquid landed on the forehead and instantly reacted with a hiss. The impact location ignited briefly and the skin became dark, burnt and discoloured.

'Well, that's it then, exactly as the tome described.' said the Abbot.

Brother Oram was aghast.'But these vampera, these were legendary creatures only, surely? I have never heard of these existing today.'

'They are able to infect others with their condition, and this is how they can spread.'
Oram looked at the Abbot in surprise.

'Abbot, how do we destroy them and protect ourselves?' asked Oram with a concerned tone.

'Well, daylight will destroy them, both fire and liquid light potion will damage them severely. They also cannot enter a blessed circle. If they do not feed, they enter a torpor and become incapacitated.' said the Abbot.

'They can spread, you say?' asked Oram.

'Indeed they can, their victims must be burned utterly, lest they will rise as vampera and prey on others.'

'And the potion of liquid light?' asked Oram.

'A mixture of blessed water, sun root and sky flower. The recipe is contained in the book.' said the Abbot.

'I need to warn Lord Garlan, this is more serious than we first expected.' said Oram.

The Abbot handed the Tome of the Undying and the remains of the phial to Brother Oram.

Oram was surprised by the kind gesture.

'Take these, you will have more use of these items than us now I fear, my son. Besides, we will have another volume somewhere and our apothecary can make more phials of liquid light if needed. We will transport the remains of this creature to our High Abbott on the Isle of Zella. May Zella's light protect you Brother Oram on your mission.' said the Abbot, casting the symbols of a blessing and then bowing to Oram.

'Thank you for all that you have done.' said Oram, and he bowed to the Abbot and departed the temple carrying the tome and the phial.

Brother Oram then made his way to the local infantry garrison, introducing himself to the Captain there. He would now need to send a carrier message to Ormsby Keep.

'Captain, I need to send a message of great

urgency to Lord Garlan at Ormsby.' said Oram.

The Captain was preoccupied reading a newspaper and uninterested. He just waved and said, 'Fine, fine. The boy there will help you.' Pointing to a small boy who was seated at the end of the room.

The boy took Oram to the garrison aviary, and provided him with paper, a quill and ink. Oram began scribbling a message to Lord Garlan. Once completed he folded the note and handed it to the boy, who then placed it into the pouch on the pigeon's foot.

'And this bird will reach Ormsby Keep?' Oram asked the boy.

'Yes, sir, this here bird is the Mighty White Wing, she's a good 'un.' promised the boy.

The pigeon had distinct white wing tips and appeared both strong and lively. The bird made a cooing noise and did a circular dance. The boy then lifted the bird, releasing it through an open window and it flew off immediately. Oram blessed the feathered messenger with a safe flight, and the bird soon flew out of sight into the distance. Oram then returned to his horse, tucking the tome and phial securely into his saddle bag. He set off on the road to Ormsby Keep, urging his mount to move quickly. Oram knew that the pigeon would arrive long before himself, delivering the bad news. He imagined the look that would be on Lord Garlan's face when he read the letter.

CHAPTER 12

Knight-Captain Harbill's detachment arrived at Beanoch watchtower, and the troops were ordered to secure the tower and carry out repairs where needed. There were too many men to be accommodated in the tower itself, and they began pitching tents adjacent to the drawbridge and the stockade.

There was a certain apprehension and fear amongst the troops, as they knew they were returning to the scene of a massacre. Worse still, the reason for that massacre had not been found. Rumours had begun to circulate amongst the men that the post was haunted or cursed, and many believed it.

Harbill set straight to work, and began to plan the patrols. He divided the detachment of Royal Scouts amongst the two cavalry detachments. One half of the force were sent north in the direction of the High Peaks. The other half were sent southwards to patrol the area around Hander.

The northern patrol found large numbers of troll, wolf and animal tracks exiting the peaks. The southern patrol found several troll tracks that led into the woods north of Hander. Both patrols returned and reported their findings. Harbill decided they would investigate the woods the following day. If trolls *were* there, the danger was obvious and they could attack Hander or even Glyvale if unchecked.

Harbill's fear was the coming night, not just for the soldiers outside the tower, but for those within.

The tower's walls and defences had not saved Darnley and his men. It may well have even trapped them, and sealed their fate. He would make sure that there were ample torches ready to light in the area, and there would be adequate men allocated to picket duty to protect the others while they slept.

He was determined that the fate of the previous occupants would not befall his own men.

****

The aviary master at Ormsby Keep received two unexpected visitors in the afternoon. The first was a bird from Glyvale, and it belonged to the office of the town Constabulary. The letter was officially stamped by the regulator Captain and carried a report requesting an investigation into a woman's allegation of killings in Hander.

As a civil matter, this would be issued to the Provost Marshal for further consideration. The aviary master had the message delivered to the Provost. This was not uncommon, and thinking nothing of it the Provost then ordered two of his regulators to travel to Hander to look into the allegation.

The second visitor was a pigeon with white wing tips, which had been sent by Brother Oram. The letter was marked urgent and for the attention of Lord Garlan himself. As Lord Garlan's Adjutant was currently deployed, the letter was delivered to Master-at-Arms Roe, second on the Knight-Marshal's staff.

Roe opened the letter, and gasped. He ran to the

old Knight-Marshal's quarters and knocked on the door.

'Sir! sir! We have received a message from Brother Oram.' said Roe.

Garlan had been busy reading. He set down his book, left his private bedroom and entered the room with the long table. Master-at-Arms Roe handed the note to Garlan. He also gasped when he read the message.

Lord Garlan,

I hope this message finds you well. I met with the Abbot and we have discovered the threat is one of a supernatural nature. The Abbot has given me a tome and a potion to aid us. I am returning to Ormsby Keep at full haste and will explain to you more then. Once you see the book for yourself, I feel it will provide an explanation.

Your servant,
Brother Oram

Lord Garlan realised that the situation was now more dangerous than he first imagined.

'Sergeant Major, notify me immediately when Brother Oram arrives back at the keep.
Also have Captain Burke notified and brought here.' said Garlan.

'Yes sir, as you command.' replied Roe, saluting and leaving the Knight-Marshal reading the note once again.

****

Sebastian Le Romme arrived on horseback at Westerly Watchtower, accompanied by Master-at-Arms Lukas Zill and two other Scouts. Zill was a veteran Royal Scout and his most noticeable feature was the number of scars upon his face. The Ensign cast a critical gaze at the watchtower and was far from impressed.

This wasn't the type of post he had hoped for, and he had grown accustomed to the large private room he used to occupy at Ormsby Keep. The snow was thick in the area, and he could tell the tower would be both cold and dirty. Privacy, if indeed there were any, would be very limited. The watchtowers were not built for comfort, and the ranks would be in close proximity to himself.

Le Romme despised the lower ranks. To him, they were recruited from the dregs of society; the poor, the unwanted and most of all, the dangerous. He was repulsed by their smell, their habits, their manners and the way they talked. Westerly was a far cry away from his family home of Le Romme Hall and the elegant and scenic city of Ronnestone.

His elder brother had served on a detachment to one of these northern watchtowers in Garmer. The post had proved fruitful, as it had guaranteed his brother's promotion to Knight-Major. A friend of his brother, Knight-Captain Harbill had put a good word in for him with Lord Garlan.

Le Romme knew Harbill was *'one of his kind'*, and these types of officers always watched out for one another. They attended the same schools, moved in the same social circles and married into the same families.

One good turn deserved another, and eventually he would repay Harbill for his help in some way. For Ensign Le Romme, a quick, rapid, promotion to Lieutenant would help, and Westerly was only a means to an end.

Le Romme preferred never to address his enlisted men directly, and would instead issue his orders only through his Sergeants. For those with fewer than three stripes, their opinions, and indeed their thoughts, did not matter to him.

Outside the watchtower were two Scouts guarding the approach to the drawbridge. As he neared them, Le Romme cast his eye over the men determined to find any fault in their attire. Their leather armour was wet and their boots were damp and slightly muddy in places, but this was not unusual while in the field. The two Scouts brought themselves to attention as the Ensign came near.
Le Romme turned his head to face Zill.

'Filthy, Sergeant-Major, filthy! Have these men cleaned up. This is not the standard of dress that *I* expect!' snapped Le Romme.

Zill looked at the men, and was puzzled, as they were no more dirty than himself. The two Scouts on horseback behind Zill then quickly looked at their own attire, fearful that the Ensign would comment on them also. If anything, they were less tidy than the chastised men who stood before them.

Le Romme dismounted, then tied his horse to a post. Zill and the two Scouts dismounted, but led their animals across the drawbridge and into the tower. The stable level smelt of wet horses, straw and the pungent odour of fresh horse manure.

Le Romme's face twisted with contempt, and he carried on up the stairs. Zill secured his animal, then followed the Ensign. When he reached the main mess hall, he saw the Quartermaster and another Sergeant busy in conversation. They noticed Le Romme and both stood to attention.

'Sir!' they both said.

'I am the new commander of this garrison, Ensign Le Romme is my name.
This is Master-at-Arms Zill who will be my second in command here.' Le Romme paused to survey his new command.

'Now, your last commander is gone, and judging by the state of this post and the men within, that may not be a bad thing.
Filth, gentlemen, there is filth everywhere here. I want this post cleaned properly, and I will hold the three of you to account.
Dismissed.' said Le Romme to the Sergeants. He then went upstairs to the garrison commander's quarters and began to dread what he would find. The room was tiny, with a wooden bed, wardrobe, wash basin and a footlocker. He had a small barred window which was covered by a shabby brown curtain.   The view though from his window was of a western direction and it was impressive. He could see both The Cut and the top of the High Falls. The view, he thought, was wasted on such a foul, decrepit building, and Le

Romme longed for the comforts of his old room back at Ormsby Keep.

Downstairs, Zill approached the two Sergeants, who were noticeably shaken by Le Romme's petulant outburst of criticism.

'Lukas Zill.' he said, reaching out his hand. Zill was tall and his scars were themselves intimidating.
The two Sergeants shook his hand in turn, and introduced themselves as Quartermaster Saxby and Sergeant Andrews.

'The Ensign is a new officer, out of training no more than three weeks.' said Zill.

'That explains everything sir.' said Saxby.

'We will have to placate him for the time being, but after a few weeks, the condition of the tower will be the least of his concerns.' said Zill.

Zill had looked after many new officers like Le Romme, and had seen them come and go. Le Romme at least wasn't a bully; but he was stupid, and this, combined with a superiority complex made him dangerous. Stupid officers could get others killed, and his character would not compel him to reverse bad decisions. Zill now knew why Lord Garlan had personally requested him to accompany Le Romme.

He would have to keep close tabs on this officer, mistakes in remote locations could easily prove disastrous. The troops in the tower began to tidy the tower and themselves the best they could. They suspected though that, no matter what they did, their new commander would always find fault.

****

Old Grey-back cautiously sniffed the air, his clan had been driven from the Stone City, down to the bottom of the High Peaks and into the tundra, close to the human towers. He was nervous, as their natural instinct always told them to avoid the area if possible. The humans who rode on the backs of other animals were particularly dangerous.

The majority of his pack, and many others, had been slaughtered by the strange smelling humans who had driven them from their territory. There were only twenty-four of them in his group, including five cubs. The other, larger, group of adults had departed eastwards with White Tusk, the alpha male. They travelled over the Great High Peak and down into the eastern steppes.

There were long abandoned human buildings there, the location long overgrown with plenty of both shrub and forest for cover, not to mention food.
Old Grey-back had declined to travel with the others, as he knew the cubs could not survive the climb east at this time of year. He opted for the easier but longer route south-west along The Cut.

Once there, they could raid the settlements along the way for food, then pass beside the High Falls and into the southern side of the Great Western Wood. They could then move along the tree-line eastwards, passing the tusked humans territory, and finally, reunite with White Tusk and the rest of their clan.

For Old Grey-back, the future route was still a low

priority. His pack were starving, they had not eaten for days and they needed food desperately. Grey-back sniffed the air once more, and he detected the aroma of cooking coming from the direction of the tower.

He could see the battlements and humans moving there. He forced himself to ignore the primal urge that wanted him to follow the smell of food. Grey-back gave a low grunt, and stealthily moved along the cover of the trees, continually watching, listening and sniffing for any threats.

He detected the faint odour of wolf scent, but it was several days old. Grey-back ran to the edge of the cut, then gave a 'whoop' noise. The rest of his pack heard the call, and followed him. The Cut was one hundred feet wide from one side to the other and the ravine dropped to a depth of three hundred feet at its lowest point. On the opposite side, the roaring water from the High Falls poured down into the great stone valley below. The sound of the water was deafening, as it roared its way to the bottom.

Grey-back knew that this was impassable, even for an adult great grey troll, so he turned south into the Brokenlands. This was the home of the short humans. Despite their size, these short humans made up for this by their ingenuity. They were never seen in the High Peaks and tended to remain in their own territory, deep underground.
Troll legend had it that the first short humans had dug a tunnel all the way to the top of the Great High Peak itself. This had been the first time that Grey-back's ancestors had encountered these short humans. After

this, the slim humans arrived and built the Stone City, they eventually departed and the troll-kind inherited the ruins.

Grey-back led his pack further south, soon he detected the scent of animals. He salivated, as his hunger was now intense. He gave a short growl, and a low bark. Four of the large males followed him, and the rest of the pack lay low, motionless, hugging the contours of the ground. The male trolls moved forward slowly, with the smell of animals growing stronger.

Before them they could now see a herd of goats, the animals' collar bells made a dinging noise every time they moved. Grey-back sniffed again, and he could also smell a short human nearby. He grunted, and two members of his hunting group moved left and made their way around the flank of the goats. Grey-back and the two others moved along to the right.

The trolls were now in the perfect ambush position. The trolls on the left flank charged towards the goats. The animals started to panic and rushed in the direction of hidden Grey-back and the other two trolls. The dwarf looked around to investigate the commotion from his panicked animals. He saw the grey trolls advance towards his position and panicked, rushing desperately back to his camp to find a weapon.

The trolls roared, slashing at the goats killing the animals instantly. Grey-back and the others joined the hunt, attacking the oncoming goats, who tried desperately to change course. The trolls lashed out taking down more of the terrified animals.

There were ten dead goats now laying on the

ground, and the trolls began gathering their kills. The four big males lifted the carcases, and Grey-back lifted two dead goats. His four companions ran off with their kills, back in the direction of the waiting pack. Grey-back was about to join them, when the dwarf came running towards him with a club.

He stared at the dwarf and roared, his teeth showing, and he had no fear. The dwarf immediately stopped in his tracks, the large troll was nearly three times his size. Attacking this animal by himself would simply be suicidal. His goats were already dead, and he had no wish to join them. The dwarf felt a warm wet feeling from his trousers, as he soiled himself.

Grey-back was not interested in attacking the short human, he had achieved his aim, and feeding his pack was his only priority. He roared again, then snarled, calming his inner rage. He took off running at pace with the food.

The dwarf breathed deeply, he had never seen a troll before. He would notify his village, the warriors and hunters would best deal with it. Grey-back was aware that the short humans now knew his pack were in their territory, and they would come looking for them. The also kept animals that they used to help them hunt. The troll pack divided the kill, first feeding the cubs and the females.

The males then fed and Grey-back fed last, once the pack's hunger was sated. He 'whooped' again, and the other trolls prepared to move. The cubs were now visibly more contented. Grey-back sniffed the air, and the smell of short humans was in the wind. The pack quickly returned north to The Cut, following their tracks back to the edge of the ravine. The trolls then started moving westwards in a column, keeping to the cliff edge and out of sight. The sound of the rushing water below was deafening and also helped conceal any sounds the trolls made. Grey-back barked to his pack members and they whimpered in response to his call.

This journey he knew was going to be tough, and he looked at the stragglers at the rear of the group with concern. He barked once again and four of the large males near the front switched places to the rear. They began to support the slower trolls.

CHAPTER 13

Brother Oram arrived back at Ormsby Keep, his horse was extremely tired and panting heavily. He had maintained a gallop most of the way from Morrack, and had only stopped once, in order to give his horse water.

The soldiers on the gate recognised the monk immediately and moved back to allow his entry. Oram bowed to the men and rushed through the gates into the inner courtyard and began climbing the steps towards Lord Garlan's quarters.

The word had already reached Allun Roe that Oram had returned, as there was much excited activity amongst the soldiers outside. He could hear the soldiers shout,

'The monk has returned. Oram is back!'
Roe walked towards the Knight-Marshal's private room, and knocked upon the door.

'Sir, Brother Oram is back.' said Roe.

'Thank-you Master-at-Arms, please fetch Captain Burke and his men.' replied Garlan, entering the room with the long table.

Roe then went to the window of the courtyard and shouted down to a soldier below.

'Corporal!'
The soldier looked up and replied. 'Yes sir.'

'Corporal, fetch Captain Burke and his men and ask them to come to Lord Garlan's rooms at once.' said Roe.

'Yes sir, at once.' replied the Corporal, running

from the inner courtyard and entering one of the other doors below.

When Brother Oram entered the long table room, Garlan was seated and Roe was walking back from the window.

'Welcome back Brother Oram, I received your message, I have asked Captain Burke and his men to come here.' said Garlan.

'Thank you my Lord, my visit to the temple will aid us. I have much to show and unfortunately we have much to do.'

Lord Garlan gestured for Oram to be seated.

'Have you eaten, Oram, perhaps some refreshments?' asked Roe.

'Thank you but no. We have much to do, and I will be happier to eat later.' said Oram.

Captain Burke, Tellan and Bartack arrived at the quarters.

'Ah, good, Captain Burke and his men, please take a seat gentlemen.' said Garlan. They all sat down at the table. Oram placed an old tome onto the table in front of him, and then placed a phial of yellow liquid beside it.

'This book is the Tome of the Undying' which I was given by the Abbot in the temple of Zella.'

'The Abbot found the creature that Captain Burke encountered. Captain Darnley had been infected by and had become a vampera.' said Oram, opening the book to the exact page he was referring to. Oram turned the tome around and handed it across to Lord Garlan. As he looked at the picture the Knight-Marshal was shocked by the uncanny likeness.

'Just like the head of Captain Darnley.' muttered Garlan.

'Indeed.' said Oram.

The Knight-Marshal showed the picture to Roe and Burke, who both agreed.

'Bartack, Tellan, was this the creature you saw?' asked Garlan, showing the picture to the boys.

Bartack gave an audible gasp, and Tellan's jaw dropped open. They *had* seen similar to this creature before, and Bartack in particular had been right next to it. The teeth, the eyes, it was an accurate likeness.

Bartack read the words aloud, 'A vampera.'

'By all accounts, young Bartack here was very lucky. The reason the victims' bodies turned to dust in the daylight is because they too had been infected.' explained Oram.

'They would have risen as vampera, including the Lieutenant. Which takes me to this bottle.' Brother Oram held the bottle up for all to see, glinting in the light from the courtyard window.

'This is a phial of liquid light, it ignites and reacts if it touches the skin of a vampera.

The Abbot experimented with just one drop on Darnley's head, and it hissed and produced a small flame.

I suspect that the Lieutenant's body would have reacted similarly had it survived intact.' said Oram.

'And Darnley's head, where is it now?' asked Garlan.

'I left it with the Abbot, he was going to transport

it to the High Abbot on the Isle of Zella to study further. Perhaps they will discover more.' added Oram.

'But what to do?' asked the Knight-Marshal.

'Another vampera must have infected Darnley. Now, he wasn't like this prior to his posting at Beanoch, so it must have occurred there.
The watchtower must have been attacked by another vampera.' said Oram.

'But why only Darnley? None of the other troops from the garrison were infected.' said Burke.

'That I don't know, Captain. But Captain Darnley had become a vampera. And that means the person or persons who created him is out there somewhere.' said Oram.

'We must find that creature and destroy it quickly. We cannot afford for more of these things to spread.' said Garlan.

'The question is where *do* we begin to look, and what *do* we look for?' added Oram.

'Perhaps the increase in the grey troll sighting was as a result of this? Maybe the trolls were actually fleeing from this thing, rather than looking for food?' added Burke.

'Could be, Captain, could be. Perhaps the ruins of the Stone City require some investigation?' added Garlan.

'But that would violate our treaty with the elves.' said Roe.

'It would, at least if we did so openly.' said Garlan.

'We need to be vigilant of unusual deaths. That could lead us to the vampera itself.' said Oram.

'Agreed.' said Garlan.

'There is a herbalist outside the keep, I will see if we can produce additional phials of the liquid light.' said Oram.

'Excellent. I will inform Sir Jeffrey. He may decide to pay us a visit. In the mean time I would like all of you to remain here.' said Garlan.

'Yes sir.' replied the group in unison.

****

Night fell and Mareck prepared to return to his master at the Stone City. He knew that Gorath Marr would be impatient and expecting results. Bonna had assured him that he would find Timmis, if not through the Thieves' Guild, then using his Assassins' Guild contacts.

Mareck was impressed so far, Bonna had the makings of a wonderful ally as his knowledge of the area was extensive. After their long imprisonment in the sarcophagi, their knowledge of Dolia was now sorely outdated and lacking. Mareck found out from Bonna that the elves had long abandoned the Stone City and were now found on the Immortal Isle, Demaneer, Woodingvale and Heighgaard.

Mareck knew Gorath Marr would *never* forgive the elven nations for his treatment by their hands. Mareck wanted to leave a gift amongst the citizens of Glyvale, just as he had done at Hander. He felt it would be much more fun, and the cemetery here was much larger.

This would create a diversion and provide the first real test for his enemies. In this war of ultimate attrition, his opponents would face death on every level. Eventually their foes would have to fall back and contract, unable to hold or defend their territory. Into this vacuum would come Gorath Marr, to claim the land as his own.

Mareck, accompanied by Randarr, rode their horses in the direction that Bonna had given to him, and he found the cemetery, just north on the outskirts of Glyvale. The cemetery and its occupants reflected the life of the town, a place driven by greed, crime, violence and betrayal.

Mareck could not help but see the irony. The victims now buried here would soon turn on the very denizens who caused their demise. They would be returning to the place that killed them, but now *they* would be doing the killing.

Mareck removed his piccolo and started to play his sweet, haunting lament once again. The sound seemed even more powerful this time as the night was still. The air crackled and became loaded with static. The bard magic began to weave its way throughout the graves, the headstones, the monuments and the mausoleums. From high born to peasant, from the wealthy to the pauper, they were now all one.

Only the dead heard the music, and only the dead would appreciate it. Waking from their eternal slumber, the cemetery was alive. Mareck could feel their clawing from the earth, and he knew when they finally embraced the night air, they would have an insatiable hunger. Mareck laughed, his only regret was being unable to witness the destruction that this would bring.

Mareck pressed on and left the outskirts of Glyvale, then crossed the bridge towards Beanoch. He and Randarr had destroyed the garrison, and he wondered what had happened to Darnley and those who discovered him.

In the dark he could see many torches and fires coming from around the watchtower, and there were torches lit at the very top. He knew that the tower had been reclaimed, and judging by the number of lights, the humans had significantly reinforced it. Not wanting further delay, Mareck opted to avoid Beanoch and take a north-easterly direction past the High Peak tower.

As they got close, the only lights were two torches beside the entrance, and four torches burning high in the battlements. At the very top, he could see three men on lookout. Mareck and Randarr were too far into the darkness to be spotted.

Mareck came upon a small cemetery, that was no more than four hundred yards from the tower. The headstones were decorated with a variety of soldier's helmets, shields, old bows or swords. This, Mareck surmised, was the garrison cemetery.
These graves were probably quite shallow, and the cold, ice and snow would have helped preserve the contents.

An evil grin came across his face, and he wondered how the current residents would fair against their former comrades. Randarr looked at Mareck, and instinctively knew what the bard was thinking. He took out his piccolo, and began to play his lament, the tune travelled into the night air. Mareck smiled and they rode off.

In the watch tower, one of the Scouts looked over the battlements in the direction of the cemetery.

'Did you 'ear that?' he asked.

'Hear what? What are you talkin' about ya fool?' snapped Murrat, shivering and annoyed with both the cold and the guard's comment, and the duty he was doing.

'I thought I heard music?' replied the Scout.

'Music eh? In the middle of *fucking nowhere?* Six more months of this shit. Just go fetch me a drink!' demanded Murrat shaking his head in displeasure.

'Yes Lance-Scout!' and the guard ran downstairs, fearful of a beating from the volatile Murrat. Left alone, Murrat sniffed the air and breathed out slowly. He looked over the battlements in the direction the Scout had been facing, and heard and saw nothing. He puffed out, his warm breath clearly visible in the cold night air.

Back in the garrison cemetery, bony hands began to break through the surface staining the snow with brown patches of freshly dug earth.

****

In Glyvale the residents had fallen into their usual daily routines, none of them had predicted the events about to unfold.

At the west gate house two guards were deep in conversation, arguing about the best ale house in town, then joking about the promotion prospects of one of their colleagues. They heard a raspy groan which interrupted them. The guards turned round and staggering towards them appeared to be an old ragged man.

'Are you all right there?' asked one of the guards.

The old man made a groan and continued staggering towards them. Still in the darkness, the guards could not see his face clearly, and then the old man reached the limit of the torch light.

The guards could see the flesh on his face was rotten, the eye sockets were deep and black. His mouth began to open, and the lips were pulled back in a grotesque grin. He suddenly lunged at the closest guard, knocking him backwards onto the ground.

'Fuck!' exclaimed the guard, as he tried desperately to get back to his feet. The other guard tried to pull the old man off his friend. As he did so, a huge chuck of rotten flesh tore off in his hands. The guard was shocked at this and couldn't believe what he saw. The guard felt sick, and struggled to prevent himself vomiting.

The old man then turned to face the guard who had pulled at him and lunged, biting the guard in the throat. The old man tore, and began to happily chew.

The guard screamed in agony, grasping his throat as the blood began to pour profusely from the wound. His colleague pulled a dagger, and stabbed the old man repeatedly. This didn't seem to have any effect. The old man moved after his victim trying to grasp him. The other guard stabbed the old man once again in a downward motion striking the head and piercing the skull.

The old man fell to the ground, no longer moving. The injured guard was now lying on the ground and gasping desperately for air, as his life blood drained away. The other guard tried to nurse him, but to no avail.

'Guard Commander!' shouted the guard, desperate for support.

From behind the gate a Sergeant came running. He glanced at the old man, and the guard supporting his injured companion.

'What the hell's happening here?' asked the Sergeant.

'That...thing attacked us, he bit him.' explained the fearful guard.

His colleague started to cough violently, convulse, and then stopped moving.

'He's gone sir.' said the guard to the Sergeant.

'Listen.' said the Sergeant.

In front of them they heard a low ominous groan that seemed to echo in unison in the darkness.

'What *is* that?' asked the Guard Commander.

'Don't know sir.' replied the guard, listening to the sound.

Behind them a guard came running over to them.

'Sergeant, the Constable asked me to message you, there are disturbances reported at both the

North and South gates of the town. Dead people are consuming the living!' He has asked you to complete a full call out of your guard force and seal the gate.' shouted the messenger.

The Sergeant looked shocked and considered this for a moment, then said abruptly, 'You remain here with him, and close the gate. I'll go to the guardhouse.'

He quickly ran to a two storey wooden building that sat adjacent to the town wall. The building was not far from the gate itself. The messenger went over to the guard who was still kneeled beside his now deceased comrade.

'Help me get him inside, we have to close the gate.' he said.

They lifted the dead guard by the arms and legs and carried his corpse into the town side of the gate, setting him carefully down. The body of the old man was still lying where it had fallen. Behind the old man the groan had become louder.

'What in the name of Zella is that?' asked the messenger guard, looking round and staring down the road that led from the gate.

Before him he could see more than thirty figures approaching, staggering, dragging their legs, stepping like unsteady infants, unsure of their footing, fearful of falling over.

'Close the gate, *now!*' screamed the messenger Scout and he started to push the heavy iron gate closed.

'Help me, help me!' he pleaded and the other guard began to push too. Both men strained themselves, as the heavy gate began to finally move.

Inch by inch the gate started to close and the men were strenuously putting their backs into it. On the road, the figures were getting ever closer. The guard glanced at them and saw their clothing was similar to that of the old man he had killed.

'Quicker, quicker! There's more of them!' he shouted. The messenger Scout wasn't sure what he had meant by 'them'. Up to that point, all he had witnessed was one dead guard and an old man's body.

The gate creaked, as it continued to close and the two guards were now starting to tire. Both were breathing heavily and gasping for air to fill their lungs. Their muscles were sore and tiring, but fear drove them on.

The dead were now illuminated by the limit of the gate-house torches and the two men could see the full horror that was approaching them. Women, men, even children, rotten and decomposing, skin and bones, but all with hungry gasping mouths.

The guards continued their endeavour, and one of the men's feet slipped momentarily on the ground. He quickly steadied himself and regained balance, aiding his companion in pushing the gate once more. The dead got closer and those at the front were now fully illuminated by the torchlight. The guards could now smell their putrescence.

The shamblers completely ignored the body of the old man, stepping past it, only hungry for fresh flesh. Suddenly the guard felt a hand grasp his left shoulder, and he jumped with fear. He turned around, and there was the Sergeant. The man breathed a huge sign of relief. Behind the Sergeant stood a dozen guards.

'Lets go you lot, get these damn gates closed. Now!' screamed the Sergeant. The fresh guards began occupying vacant spots along the gate and began pushing. The gate moved rapidly now, and slammed shut with a loud clang.

A guard bolted the gate just as grasping hands began to claw between the gaps of the bars. The messenger Scout and the original gate guard, both exhausted, collapsing to their knees. The guard muttered a prayer of thanks.

One of the fresh guards removed a lit torch from the wall. He then tried to use it to force the dead back, waving it at them in a left to right motion. Immediately the dead fell back when faced with the raw flame. It was obvious that the burning torch scared them.

The guard then ignited the sleeves of one of the zombies, and it quickly became engulfed. The other dead stood back from it, desperate to avoid the same fate. The burning zombie began to stagger backwards, bumping into its neighbours, and accidentally igniting two of them. The zombie group moved back, deliberately avoiding the other three burning zombies. The first zombie on fire soon collapsed, falling onto the ground, their corpse still burning. The Sergeant looked, and realised the guard had discovered something.

'You four stay here. The rest of us will go help the other gates. While you are here try and burn the rest of those things if they get close enough.' said the Sergeant as he departed.

As the flaming corpses went out, the other dead then occupied their space beside the gates. Their hands were outstretched, and they continued to claw at the men behind the gates.

'What the hell are they?' asked a guard.

'Don't know but one killed Martin, and tried to get me.' the first guard said.

'Let's see if we can burn the bastards.' said the messenger guard.

The four men began to light fresh torches, then went to the gate bars waving the torches at the zombies, and periodically setting some alight. Once alight, the flaming zombies became only fixated on their burning clothes, losing interest in the men.

The dead behind them though, avoided the burning zombies, and were still completely fixated on their human prey. Outside the gate there was now a sizeable horde, all grasping and groaning in unison. The zombies were determined to break through the gate and feast on those inside.

CHAPTER 14

Timmis crept into the thieves' quarter of Morrack. It was a dangerous location, even during the daytime for the unwary. He entered a side alley and then arrived at the door of a tobacconist shop. Outside there were two men who eyed Timmis suspiciously through the smoke of their pipes. He entered the shop, and the owner just nodded to him.

Timmis went out the backdoor of the shop and found himself in a small courtyard. He pushed a wooden crate aside, revealing a hidden, wooden hatch. He opened the hatch and there was a tunnel containing a ladder which led downwards.

He began to climb down, reached the bottom of the ladder, and followed the tunnel. The tunnel itself was made of brick, and Timmis knew he had arrived in the city sewers. He continued on, deeper into the sewers, eventually arriving at a solid metal door.

He tapped the door twice quickly, followed by a single heavy tap, and then three short taps. Suddenly he heard several bolts drawn back and the iron door swung open. Behind the door was a tall black man wearing leather armour. He ushered Timmis in, then closed the door behind.

'Well, well, Timmis, haven't seen you in Morrack for a while.' said the man.

'No Ramone, been working around Glyvale and there about.' replied Timmis, not wanting to reveal too much.

'I need to speak to Osumain.' said Timmis.

'He's in the back.' replied the man.

'What about the hooded guy from Marandale?'

'Yea, he's with him. Must be desperate, he's been waiting several days now for you.' said Ramone.

Timmis continued walking down the corridor and then entered into a large room. There were eight men already in there all debating over loot that they had acquired, and who would receive the highest price for it. The room was bare, except for stacks of crates and small wooden boxes. Timmis approached the group of men.

'Where is Osumain?' he asked.

One of the men gave a pointing gesture in the direction of another room. The men then glanced around at Timmis as he walked towards the room. They began to snigger, then quickly resumed a straight face when Timmis looked back at them.

Inside the backroom the décor was completely different. The walls were adorned with large oil paintings, and there was a red velvet suite of furniture in one corner. At the other side of the room was a large mahogany table, and seated behind it was a bald, tanned man with a wide black moustache, wearing a purple and gold robe. Sat next to him was a man wearing a red hooded robe. Timmis could not fully see his face, but he had a black goatee beard.

'Ahh, Timmis, welcome. Your journey proved fruitful I hope?' said Osumain in a friendly, but equally threatening tone.

The hooded man bowed his head, but said nothing.

'You have...the items you wish to sell?' asked Osumain, who already knew the answer.

Timmis nodded, and from his robe produced a willow wand, the talisman and the ten inch quartz crystal. Timmis noticed the red robed man began to smile. Osumain was motionless.

'First the wand.' said Osumain.

The hooded man reached out with an open hand. Timmis handed the wand to the man. He began to mumble a chant and the wand began to glow with a yellow light.

'Magnificent.' said the hooded man, admiring the wand's workmanship. This had been the only word uttered by him up to this point.

Osumain looked at him, and could see he was pleased.

'Is it the one?' asked Osumain, but he instinctively knew the answer.

'Yes. Yes, this is it.' said the hooded man.

Timmis then produced the talisman from his pocket, and the red robed man smiled once again. He handed it over to the man who began to chant. The talisman then began to glow with a yellow light.

'Excellent.' said the red robed man, and he nodded to Osumain in approval.

The man then removed a leather purse from inside his robe, which made a chinking noise.

'Your commission fee, as agreed.' said the hooded man handing the purse to Timmis in exchange. Timmis looked inside, and it contained platinum pieces. Timmis smiled.

'What about this crystal and the other items I

found?' asked Timmis as he placed them on the table before Osumain.

'I know a man in Port-hareesh who may wish to buy these from you. It will take a few weeks though. Come back then.' said Osumain.

'Great. I'll return in two weeks then?' replied Timmis.

Osumain said nothing in response, and Timmis took this as a signal that his audience was now over. He stood up, bowed, then left the room, leaving the blue crystal, remaining elven coins and various gems with Osumain. Outside the room, only three men remained, the others were all gone. They looked at Timmis as he left and went back to the Guild entrance. Ramone was seated beside the door, and Timmis nodded to him as he left.

Osumain looked at the hooded man.

'How much will you pay for the other items?' he asked the red robed man.

'I'll pay what we agreed. Once I am happy with the items.' he replied.

The hooded man took hold of the crystal and began mumbling a chant. Just like the previous items, this too began to have a yellow glow. The hooded man's face was illuminated by the light, and he smiled in deep satisfaction.

'Here is your arrangement fee, Osumain.' and he handed him another medium sized purse.

'You can keep the elven coins and gems for yourself as a bonus. I only want the crystal.' said the robed man.

Osumain smiled, and then pocketed the purse. There was no buyer in Port-hareesh, that was just a lie, he would keep the majority of the money and give Timmis a small cut.

'So, your little thief managed to reach and then find the crypt then? I thought it was impossible.' said the hooded man.

'Don't get me wrong, Timmis is naive, we in the Guild know this. But, at gaining entry to a location, or avoiding traps of any kind, none are better than he. That I *will* give him. Plus he has visited the Stone City many times.' said Osumain.

'Plus he is expendable.' added Osumain, laughing.

The hooded man was pleased. The items proved that Timmis had gained entry to the crypt. The crystal proved, more importantly, that Gorath Marr was now free. He would return to the mages guild at Valatoch. With Marr free, he knew the chaos had already begun. Their agents in Ormsby Keep had informed them of the massacre at Beanoch watchtower. From this chaos, the Mages' Guild would once again reclaim its true position in Dolia. Soon, he thought to himself, they will be begging the mages to help. That help, however, would come with a heavy price.

The fools in the Thieves' Guild had been unsuspecting assistants to their aims. Greed is indeed a powerful weapon. No-one would suspect that the Mages' Guild at Valatoch was behind this. To everyone, it would appear that a greedy thief had unsuspectingly released the lich by accident.

With these items in their possession, Marr would not be at full power. Without the talisman he would not be able to walk in the daylight. The Mages' Guild would use this knowledge to defeat Marr. They also now had the quartz crystal binding stone. If they could not destroy him they could imprison him once again.

The red robed hooded man rose from his seat. He bowed to Osumain.

'Thank you once again. You must excuse me, I have much work to do, I have to catch a boat.' said the red robed man. He left the room and exited the door past Ramone.

Osumain then approached Ramone.

'Follow him, see where he goes. And make sure he does not see you.' Osumain ordered Ramone.

'OK boss. But is he not OK?' asked Ramone in a perplexed tone.

'Oh, he's OK. But I need to know more about him. Now go.' ordered Osumain.

Ramone exited the door of the Guild, and Osumain secured the door behind him. His instinct told him the hooded man was not what he seemed; he was not a priest, but he had used magic. Osumain did not trust the red robed man, who had told him he was only a trader from Marandale. Maybe he was a trader, but what he had witnessed proved he was *more* than a *just* a trader. Besides information was as valuable an item as gold. If anyone could find out more, Ramone was certainly capable.

****

Murrat gave a huge fart, and chuckled to himself. The two Scouts on the tower with him looked at him in disgusted bemusement.

'What you lookin' at?' he snapped.

His companions looked away, scared that he would single them out. Murrat looked over the battlements, then rubbed his eyes. He then took a huge swig of the bottle he was holding and gave a loud, contemptuous belch.

One of the Scouts looked at his companion in disgust and said nothing. He didn't need to say anything, Murrat was already despised by the troops in the watchtower. Rude, obnoxious, bad tempered and a bully, they knew his type. At a normal fortress, he would just be completely ignored. However, at a remote base, he could easily have an 'accident', a 'fall' or 'go missing' on a patrol. No-one would care, and no-one would care enough to ask why?

Death was an everyday risk for those stationed at watchtowers. If you were going to risk your life here, it wouldn't be for someone like Murrat. The troops in the watchtower already had a nickname for him, 'troll breath' was what they called him behind his back.

Murrat had another look over the battlement, then some movement caught his eye. He rubbed his eyes just to make sure that he wasn't imagining it or that his eyes were playing tricks. Approaching the tower were multiple figures, with a staggering, stumbling gait. They appeared to be dressed in the uniform of Royal Scouts.

'What the fuck's this? What's a patrol doin' out at

this time o' night?' said Murrat.

The other Scouts looked at him, then walked over to see what Murrat was referring to. They too could see the staggering figures approaching, and recognised the uniforms.

'We better let them in. They'll be freezing, probably a lost patrol from another watchtower.' said Murrat.

The other Scouts were puzzled.

'Shouldn't we report this to the watch officer?' asked one of them.

'Well *you* go and tell him, and you come with me.' said Murrat, pointing to the other man. The Scout went off to the duty officer. Murrat and the other Scout went downstairs. As they passed through the mess hall, another Scout who was seated looked up.

'What's going on?' he enquired.

'A patrol outside.' replied Murrat.

'Are you sure?' asked the Scout.

'Course I'm bloody sure, they 'ave our uniforms on.' snapped Murrat angrily.

Murrat walked down the stairs to the stable area followed by his Scout companion. He hoped by taking the initiative he would gain favour from the Quartermaster.

'Alright lower the drawbridge.' Murrat demanded of the Scout. He followed the order and went over to the controls and began turning the wooden wheel. The huge chains began to rattle and the wooden drawbridge started to lower. The Scout whom they had spoken to in the mess hall rushed down the stairs.

'Stop, wait, no!' he shouted at Murrat and the Scout.

But it was too late, the drawbridge had been fully lowered, and Murrat had opened the doors and walked outside across the bridge to meet the patrol. The figures drew nearer, then the torch light fell upon them and Murrat screamed in terror.

They wore the uniforms of the Scouts, but they were walking corpses. Derrin and Toby had been awoken by the shouts below, Markus however slept on. They got up and went downstairs to investigate. The Scout on the drawbridge controls then ran to see what was happening to Murrat. He went out the door then froze.

The other Scout then screamed, 'Close the doors, close the damn doors!'

The Scout ran back, and started to close the main doors. The mess hall Scout, Derrin and Toby ran over to help him. They started to push the door closed. Murrat was now screaming and ran back across the drawbridge. The main doors slammed shut in his face.

'Open up, *fucking open up!*' Murrat screamed. Derrin looked at Murrat through a view slit on the door. Murrat immediately recognised him.

'Let me in lad, quickly, let me in.' said Murrat to Derrin, his tone one of pleading.

'Let me in you little scum, let me *fucking in!*' Murrat shouted at Derrin, his tone now crazed, and his face red and full of rage.

Murrat glanced over his shoulder and the dead were now just a mere three feet away from him. Their arms were outstretched, and their ravenous hunger directed towards him. Murrat dashed to the edge of the drawbridge, and with no other option, jumped into the dry moat.

He landed heavily, and there was an audible cracking sound from his leg, Murrat screamed. Derrin looked through the view slit once again, and could see the bloody corpses as they touched the front doors. They could sense the living behind the doors, and began hammering with their fists.

Corporal Haynes suddenly appeared at the bottom of the stairs.

'What the hell's going on?' asked Haynes.

'Murrat, Corporal. He made us open the doors and lower the bridge. He's outside, the things nearly got in.' replied the scared Scout.

Haynes went over to where Derrin stood, he could hear Murrat screaming. He looked out the viewing slit and recognised Scout Tenby and other deceased Scouts standing before him. They had dead eyes and their wounds were just as before. Haynes gasped, then looked at the Scouts.

'Return to your posts!' shouted Haynes.

'Derrin, Toby, come with me.' added Haynes, and the others started to make their way to the top of the tower.

Outside, Murrat began to attempt to crawl away from the drawbridge and the terrifying monsters on it. His leg causing him to wince every time he pulled himself forward. The dead no longer sensed any living behind the tower's doors. Their heads turned, their attention drawn to the crawling Murrat in the moat.

The zombies began falling off the drawbridge and into the moat. Several zombies impaled themselves on the wooden spikes as they fell. The first zombie fallers into the moat shattered their bones, and were left writhing where they fell. Other zombies began falling on top of them, their impacts cushioned by their unfortunate counterparts. They fell over, and then slowly began to try and get to their feet. Their eyes were completely fixated on Murrat.

Haynes and the boys reached the tower top, and he issued each with a bow and a quiver. They began to aim and fire at the undead, the arrows just hitting them to no effect. Derrin hit one on the head and it fell over. The dead began to close in on Murrat. He turned and looked around, screaming as he realised they were approaching him. He desperately tried to speed up his crawl, but as he did so, the pain became more intense in his leg.

A zombie lunged at Murrat's leg, and he tried to kick back but to no avail. It grabbed hold of him, and bit into his injured leg. Murrat screamed, and the pain almost caused him to pass out. In the tower the defenders continued to fire at the zombies.

Haynes' arrow hit the zombie that bit Murrat with a head-shot and it fell on top of him. Murrat was now unable to move, and tried to push the dead zombie off.

Two more zombies pounced on Murrat and he screamed. They bit into his flesh and tore at him with their teeth. The blood began to pour from Murrat's legs, as he struggled to deal with the agony.

'Help!' screamed Murrat.

Those in the tower knew there was nothing they could do for him. He had endangered everyone by opening the doors. Murrat continued to scream as the zombies knelt over him and began consuming him alive. Murrat had come to the tower to gain back his lost stripe. Instead, he would now lose his life. Toby closed his eyes, and fell to the ground on his knees. He tried to block the scene of bloody carnage from his mind.

Horrified by the screams, Derrin drew an arrow in his bow, and aimed it at Murrat. He remembered the training camp, the bullying, the pain and fear for Marie, and released the arrow. The arrow struck Murrat on the chest, and he stopped screaming.

Haynes looked at Derrin, and knew Murrat's suffering had needed to end. A running Tyerose arrived at the top of the tower.

'Fill the moat with oil, and light it up!' ordered the Quartermaster.

The Scouts began to empty the oil barrels into the moat. The oil splashing on Murrat and the undead that were now eating him. The liquid began trickled around the moat. Haynes dipped an arrow into an oil barrel. Then touched the arrow to the flame of a nearby torch, it ignited. He quickly aimed and fired the arrow into the moat, and the flame ignited the oil.

The trail of flame spread, consuming the dead Murrat and the zombies feeding over him. The zombies began to writhe and stagger as they burned. All off the zombies in the moat were now on fire. The smell of burning oil and flesh began to rise into the night. Derrin sat on the ground exhausted and Haynes sat down beside him.

'They would have torn him to pieces while alive.' said Haynes.

'I would have expected you to do the same for me.' added Haynes.

His words were little consolation for Derrin, he had never killed a man before, and he felt physically ill.

After the attack the Scouts were eating in the mess. Toby and Derrin sat quietly. Quartermaster Tyerose sat down beside them.

'Corporal Haynes told me what happened. How are you lads doing?' asked Tyerose.

'A bit shocked sir.' said Toby. Derrin stayed silent, but Tyerose could see he was still trembling with shock.

'Look, I want you to know you helped save the whole watchtower. If that door hadn't been shut when it was, many more would have died.' said Tyerose.

'Murrat killed himself by his own actions, and damn well nearly everyone else too.'

Derrin hated Murrat, but he had sympathy for him. Not even Murrat deserved to die in such a terrifying, horrible way. Since he had barely survived the troll, Derrin appreciated life that much more. He realised just how quickly life can be taken, and always when we least expect it. His thoughts went back to Marie in Dollan, he wondered what she was up to.

What would she think of him if he told her what he had done to Murrat. To Marie, Derrin could not harm a fly. Now he had killed his first man, even though it was indirectly. He was, after all, a Royal Scout, and he would have to defend himself. If it hadn't been now it would be later.

Derrin realised that Haynes was right. If that had been himself instead of Murrat he would have been thankful for the mercy shown to him. After the meal, Derrin returned to his room downstairs alone and lay curled on his bed. This night had been worse than the day he had faced the troll. Despite his attempt to console himself, Derrin wept.

CHAPTER 15

The dead had arrived at the other gates of Glyvale, and the carnage had been much worse than at the west gate. The defenders had managed to close the north gate just in time, after bravely fighting back those dead that had broken through and killed some of the citizens.

The guard commander Sergeant from the west gate had saved the day, thanks to getting the guards to use flaming torches rather than swords. Those that had used swords found that unless the zombie was beheaded, stabbing weapons were ineffective. Crushing weapons such as spiked morning stars or maces had proved devastating.

The defenders then poured oil onto the zombies outside, and ignited them by throwing a lit torch onto the liquid. The south gate had got off lightly, as most of the cemetery zombies had arrived at the north and west gates. The River Dale, which ran along the east of Glyvale had actually protected the town, sweeping away any dead that tried to cross it.

The town Constable now realised that the woman they had found earlier had also survived something similar. The difference being that there had been guards here to defend the populace, unlike Hander. The Constable went to see the Regulator Captain to discuss the defence.

'Sir, we have managed to seal the gates and destroy the attackers.' said the Constable.

'Well done. It seems that woman was not mad after all. How many casualties were there?' asked the Captain.

'About fifteen civilians, we lost twenty seven guards.' said the Constable, sighing.

The Captain looked gaunt, he knew that the town could not defend another attack by itself. Glyvale did not have enough soldiers to defend it, and they could not afford to open the gates. The countryside around the town was now too dangerous.

Although they had destroyed the majority of the cemetery dead, there would still be single zombies and small scattered groups wandering the woods.

The Captain drafted another letter to go by carrier pigeon. This time he would have to inform Lord Garlan that Glyvale had been attacked and that they desperately needed reinforcements and the town was sealed except for the east gate. He added that Hander had probably already fallen. The message was sent, and the carrier pigeon flew off to Ormsby Keep.

****

Having waited for nightfall, Bonna departed through Glyvale's east gate, heading across the bridge for Morrack. He noticed ten guards had been posted to the bridge itself, and all carried burning torches. He was stopped by one of the guards.

'Where are you off to?' asked the guard.

'I have business in Morrack, but after tonight, perhaps Glyvale is not so safe, I'm thinking.' replied

Bonna smiling.

His reply had clearly rattled the guard, who now seemed more anxious than before.

'Just be careful out there.' said the anxious guard.

'I will, but I think I may be safer out there my friend, than those in here.' replied Bonna, playing with the guard's anxiety.

'You had better move along.' said the guard.

'Aye, you are right my friend. I need to be in Morrack by sunrise. Glyvale is now too dangerous.' replied Bonna, grinning to himself as he rode off.

The attack had been the perfect diversion, and he had fed once again on another victim. The victim's corpse would be blamed on the attack no doubt. Just another victim amongst many others. He knew the zombies had been Mareck's doing. To Bonna, this confirmed Mareck was mad, and extremely dangerous.

He was glad that he was an ally. He would dread to see what having the crazy bard as an enemy was like. Besides, Mareck had given him a gift few would ever possess. He would not age, he would retain his wealth for ever, he no longer felt the pain of an ageing body.

As he rode Bonna let his mind wander. With his new found power he could even end up controlling the Thieves' Guild entirely. Who would stop him, he thought. And those that tried to stop him would quickly regret it. He now had to find Timmis, and recover the items that had belonged to Gorath Marr.

Even Mareck seemed afraid of Marr, and Bonna felt getting on the wrong side of him was not advisable either. Besides, if he had followers such as Randarr or

Mareck he must be quite powerful. With Marr as an ally he would only accrue more wealth and treasure for himself.

****

Ramone followed the red robed hooded man to the docks, staying out of sight and in the shadows. The thief was an expert at this, and as far as he could tell the robed man was oblivious to him.

Ramone knew the area well, and was able to get ahead of him. He took the back alley routes and climbed through yards. The robed man stuck to the main roads leading to the docks.

Ramone got to the dockyards, and stole an old fisherman's jacket and hat that was hanging to dry over a drying net. He put the clothes on, then waited for the man to appear. He had predicted correctly; the robed man appeared out of the street and headed down to the docks.

Ramone had ambushed many unsuspecting merchants in the dock area by blending in, but this time his prize wasn't money or gold but information for his boss, Osumain. Ramone hid next to some crates, then waited.

The robed man began to walk down towards an anchored clipper, then proceeded up the gang-plank. Ramone kept slipping behind crates, edging his way along to keep the man in sight. He got as close as he could. The ship was named the 'Star of Ronnestone'. A sailor wearing a red leather jerkin approached the robed man.

'Mister Radahl, we are loaded up and ready to leave as soon as you wish, sir.' said the sailor.

'Thank you, I have completed my business, you may set sail immediately.' replied the red robed man, walking aboard and disappearing below deck.

Ramone now had the robed man's name, which was more than Osumain had. The sailor then followed Radahl below the decks.

The thief now needed to find out where the ship was heading. Shortly afterwards, three sailors appeared from below deck. One began to lower the main sail, the other went and stood behind the ship's wheel and the other began to untie the clipper from the dockside. The thief approached the sailor who was untying the ship. He remembered the vessel's name and took a chance.

'Excuse me, I was told this ship is due for Ronnestone, and it can take paid passengers?' Ramone asked the sailor.

The sailor looked up at him, while busily trying to manhandle the rope.

'No, we're sailing to Dale Bay Island, then Gunimore. But I'd have to ask Captain Volber about taking a passenger.' replied the sailor.

'Oh, I need a direct passage to Ronnestone.' replied Ramone, pretending to be disappointed.

'Sorry about that, perhaps try further along the docks.' said the sailor.

'Thanks anyway.' said Ramone.

He turned and then headed back towards where he

stole the clothing, placing them back where he found them, onto the net. They weren't worth taking and reeked of old fish. He would have to have his own clothes washed, as they now smelled of fish oil too.

Ramone began to walk back to the Thieves' Guild, and re-entered the sewers through an old drainage tunnel. He followed a maze of sub-tunnels, then arrived back at the familiar door of the Guild. He tapped it twice quickly, then a single heavy tap, and then three short taps. A few seconds later it opened and Osumain was waiting by the door himself.

'You are back then Ramone. What did you find out?' asked Osumain.

'Well the robed man got onto a clipper ship at Morrack docks which was sailing to Dale Bay Island and then Gunimore.' replied Ramone.

'Anything else?' Osumain asked.

'No. No boss. That's all that I could find out.' replied Ramone.

'Good, good, you have done well.' replied Osumain smiling.

Ramone looked at him and wasn't sure what he was really thinking. He now knew three things that his boss did not; the names of both the red robed man, the captain and his ship. He decided to keep these to himself.

There were two lessons he had quickly learned in the Thieves' Guild. Firstly, only reveal the bare minimum necessary, never too much. Secondly, only a complete fool would give away valuable information for nothing.

Osumain hadn't even asked him if he was OK. That in itself was telling. He had witnessed his boss swindle many of the other thieves behind their backs. He had probably done the same to Timmis, he thought. But Ramone would not allow Osumain to do the same to him. He returned to the store room and began checking his bag.

****

Mareck and Randarr finally arrived back at Stone City. As he approached the main road, Drusilla was seated on an old wall.

'Where have you been Mareck? We have been busy clearing this city.' said Drusilla.

'Doing the master's work, and trying to recover what was stolen.' replied Mareck in a defensive tone.

'*Trying?*' said Drusilla, seizing on that word.

'Yes, trying. Now *where* is the master?' asked Mareck losing patience.

Drusilla nodded her head, indicating for Mareck and Randarr to follow her. They walked off further down the street and then approached a building that would have once been a temple. The pillars of the temple were carved with elven writing, and had images depicting warriors and mages.

'As I said, we cleared the city of those creatures.' said Drusilla, talking as they walked.
The temple building roof was still intact, and the building, despite its age was in generally good condition. The elven builders had clearly built it to last.

They entered the empty doorway, the wooden

doors had rotted and were now long gone. Only the rusty imprints of the hinges remained. At the far end of the temple four torches were alight, and Mareck could clearly see two hooded figures; a plate mailed knight standing beside his master, seated on a throne.

Mareck didn't require the torch light, and could see quite clearly in the dark. Perhaps this was for the benefit of the others, or just for effect he thought.

As they approached Gorath Marr, Mareck, Randarr and Drusilla all bowed.

'You have returned, Mareck, Randarr.' said Marr in a raspy voice.

'Yes master, and we have news that will please you.' said Mareck. Drusilla shot a questioning glance at Mareck when he said this.

'We have found the locations of where the accursed elves fled. They are located at the Immortal Isle, Demaneer, Woodingvale and Heighgaard.' said Mareck, hoping to please his master.

'I have also attacked our enemies by raising undead foot soldiers. We now have a vampera ally by the name of Bonna.'

'And I have something else master.' said Mareck in an excited tone. From his robe, he produced Marr's ruby encrusted ring.

The lich showed no emotion whatsoever, and reached out with his bony hands grasping the ring from Mareck. He motioned to place the ring back onto his left hand little finger, then remembered his little finger had been damaged by the thief. He paused a second then put the ring onto his right hand little finger instead. Anger began to stir in Marr, as he remembered what had happened.

'And what of the thief?' exclaimed Marr.

'We could not find him, master, though we learned his name is Timmis. But our new ally Bonna will find him for us.' said Mareck in response.

'And what of my wand and my talisman!' roared Marr.

'They were in the possession of the man Timmis. He escaped us as I could not move by day.' said Mareck.

'And you said you attacked *my* enemies?' asked Marr.

'Yes master, I used my bard magic to raise the dead in two of their

towns, and we destroyed one of their watchtower garrisons.' said Mareck.

'And who gave *you* permission to do this?' said Marr in a threatening tone.

'*But master*. Was this not what *you* wanted?' asked Mareck, now afraid.

'*No!* I had asked you to recover the items, we are not ready to attack. And now *you* have alerted our enemies.' said the angry Marr.

'But master, I only did this to help you.' pleaded Mareck. The dark paladin Randarr just stood in silence.

'No! *You* did this to indulge your own inflated narcissism.' snapped back a raging Marr.

'But master.' said the scared Mareck.

'You are a *fool*, and now we will have to act quickly. I hope for your sake Mareck *your* ally finds *my* belongings.' said Gorath Marr in a threatening tone.

Drusilla smiled, she took great pleasure in seeing Mareck chastised. The master had chosen the wrong follower for the task, she thought to herself. Perhaps she or one of the other dark priests would have their opportunity now.

'Drusilla!' snapped Marr.

'Yes master.' replied Drusilla.

'Go north of the peak with Yandora and search for potential allies.'

'Amera, Hazak, go to the wastelands and find the crystal people.' commanded Marr.

'Master, what if they have gone?' asked Amera.

'They are not gone. They are elemental beings forged from within Dolia itself. Now go.' said Marr.

'Randarr. Guard the Stone City from intruders.' commanded Marr. The dark paladin bowed his head in acknowledgement. He knew his master was displeased.

'And *you* Mareck, remain here, and do *exactly* as commanded.' roared Marr to the bard.

The bard bowed his head, then wandered off, rebuked in front of his peers. Mareck went walking into the darkness, away from the light of the torches. He mumbled to himself, and was taken by an internal madness. No-one had ever rebuked him like that before, and he held his hands upon his ears.

Inside, Mareck raged, and his eyes blazed red, his canine teeth on full display. Why did the master do this to him, he thought. He had only ever wished to serve him. Now he had turned against him. Mareck then thought of Drusilla, perhaps she had poisoned Marr's mind? Drusilla had always been jealous of Mareck.

Amera, Hazak, Drusilla and Yandora bowed to the lich, and then began their journeys. Amera and Hazak took the two horses that Mareck and Randarr had left. They would be travelling further than the others. The four left together as a group, then would split up once they reached the base of the northern face of the northernmost peaks.

The north face was steep in some areas. The snow and ice made their descent much slower than they had anticipated. The three priests had been thankful that the dark paladin Hazak was with them. He had been strong enough to guide the horses by himself. This freed the hands of the others to help themselves climb down.

Two hours later, and they were finally at the bottom of the peaks. The fir trees here were thick and coated in a layer of snow. Amera and Hazak mounted their horses and rode westwards. The horses struggled through the snow, and the cold was affecting them now.

Their journey would take them north through the Great Western Wood, and travel would be much faster once they had left the snowline. Drusilla and Yandora would travel north on foot. The Emberdale River basin had previously been home to the tusked people. The trade route to Marandale had brought them into conflict with the humans.

The tusk people had been driven south, and now were forced to live in the south of the basin. The humans had taken their lands in the north and built their own settlements. The area had also been garrisoned by towers, but many of these had been long abandoned by the human populace. Tensions were always high, and the tusked people wanted to reclaim their lost land. The southern basin was for subsistence living only, and it was not suitable for crops.

As Drusilla walked, the woods were quiet, apart from a raven which could be heard calling out. The further they walked from the peaks, the less and less snow lay on the ground. Eventually the snow was patchy, then there was none. They were still in woodland, but the trees were more spread out than previously. Yandora then stopped and pointed.

'Smoke, I can see smoke from a fire.' she said.

Drusilla looked, and ahead she could just make out plumes of smoke. It was a settlement, and it wasn't too far ahead. As they got closer to the settlement, a wooden post was adorned with human skulls. She knew that this belonged to the tusk people. They would have to take care, but they would be valuable allies.

Both Drusilla and Yandora had been humans, and they prepared themselves for an unfriendly reception. They would have to gain the tusk people's trust, and would only do so by aiding them.

Ahead of Drusilla appeared four tusk people warriors. Their armour appeared to be made of bone, and they carried spears. Their faces were almost boar like, and they had two large upward facing prominent teeth coming from their mouths. It was apparent how they had received their name. The warriors pointed their spears and Drusilla and Yandora were led to the settlement.

The warriors encouraged them to move with their spear-tips. The tusk people warriors made odd snorting sounds, as they herded the priests. It was a medium sized town, built entirely from wood. On the outside it was protected by a wooden stockade which had ramparts providing excellent observation points. The town was well camouflaged inside the woods. Only the smoke had indicated its presence.

The priests were led into the centre of the settlement, where groups of the residents had begun to gather. From one of the wooden huts a tusk man approached them. He was dressed in a grey robe and carried a wooden staff that was topped by an animal skull. He was an old male and had a serious look to his face. The priest guessed this was either the elder or leader.

To have any chance of success they would have to get this grey robed man on their side. The two priests of Gorath Marr bowed, then began to chant.

CHAPTER 16

The Regulator Captain's carrier pigeon arrived at Ormsby Keep. The message was delivered straight to Lord Garlan's office, and handed to Master-at-Arms Roe. Roe then notified the Knight-Marshal who opened and read the note.

From his expression Allun Roe knew that it was a serious matter.

'Sir, what has happened?' asked Roe.

'Glyvale was attacked by the undead, and according to the Regulator Captain, Hander may have fallen already.' replied Garlan.

'Master-at-Arms, send orders to the garrison commanders at Westerly and Beanoch towers to investigate Hander. Ask Harbill to send some of his infantry to assist Glyvale.' commanded the Knight-Marshal.

'Yes sir! Right away.' replied Roe.
The old Sergeant Major then took the orders to the carrier pigeon aviary.

****

Old Grey-back's pack had continued to move west. He could smell the short humans behind him, estimating they were one to two miles behind. So far the pack had managed to stay ahead of them. To the south Grey-back could see the fires of the short human city.

It was built out of the very stone of the Brokenlands, and the towers of the city stood high for all to see. The dwarves had mined this land completely and it appeared desolate and exposed to the environment.

The land was naturally hilly, but all of the foliage and grass was long gone. Grey-back sniffed the air, there was no-one ahead of them, and pushed on. The dwarf hunter pointed to the troll tracks.

'That's a small pack, maybe around twenty or so.' he said to the warriors. It had been some time since he had trapped a troll. They rarely were found in the Brokenlands and the hunter wondered why a group this size were here. The hunters knew they would have to rely on fire weapons. Their quarry were too large and powerful to be brought down by swords or bows alone.

'How far ahead do you think they are?' asked the warrior.

The hunter then examined some scat, rubbing it in his finger tips and sniffing it.

'An hour, maybe two ahead.' said the hunter.

'Let's move.' said the warrior dwarf and they continued their pursuit.

Old Grey-back urged his pack on, the cubs were struggling the most with the pace. The environment around the trolls did not suit them. They were too large and too exposed in these bare hills. The trolls followed the contours of the valleys, making sure not to climb over the peaks. Doing so would mean that they would stand out, and potentially be spotted.

The smells of the dwarf city drifted toward the troll pack. The scent of the short humans there was very strong. The trolls could smell many fires, and this made them afraid. For nothing terrified them more than fire.

Grey-back knew that the cubs would not be able to defend themselves. The males would have no choice but to fight to protect them. There were many short humans there, far too many to fight. The pack would only survive by avoiding confrontation.

The troll cubs whined as they were beginning to tire. Grey-back gave several grunts and the large males picked up the cubs, carrying them. This would put the pack at a disadvantage if attacked, but they had no choice. To the south Grey-back noticed some dwarves, and they spotted the trolls. They began pointing and shouting. He knew very soon there would be more pursuers.

The old troll made a 'whoop' noise and the pack went into a gallop. To the east, the shouts of the dwarf hunters could be heard.

'We have our quarry ahead.' said the dwarf hunter.

'Charge!' shouted the dwarf warrior.
The dwarves could see the dust created by the rear of the troll pack. They had them in sight.

As the trolls ran, one of them at the rear noticed the dwarf hunters. He made a screech, and Grey-back looked around, then gave two barks. Two of the male trolls at the rear turned back towards the dwarves and ran towards them.

Grey-back and the others continued running away from the hunters. The dwarves saw the two large trolls galloping towards them. The dwarf warriors drew their swords, the hunters desperately tried to light the torches they were carrying instead.

'You need fire!' shouted a hunter to the warrior.

It was too late, the trolls closed in. The big males lashed at the first dwarf warrior in front of them. One dwarf was thrown through the air. Another dwarf met the full force of the troll's claw and had his head decapitated. Momentum caused one of the trolls to ram into three unfortunate dwarves.

The melee had afforded the hunters time to light their torches. The warriors lashed out at the trolls with their swords. One troll was cut on the arm, and it screamed in pain. The troll struck a dwarf with a backhanded slap knocking him down and breaking his nose. The dwarf warriors formed small circles round each troll. They lashed out, and then dodged as the trolls counter-attacked.

The dwarf hunters prepared their bows, then lit the arrows from their torches. They aimed and fired at the trolls. One troll was hit on the back and screamed in agony. The hunters missed the second troll which moved after they had fired.

The uninjured troll leapt forward pouncing on a dwarf, and then began pummelling him rapidly with each claw. The dwarf's face was bloodied and unrecognisable now. The other dwarves stabbed the troll repeatedly while he was attacking their companion. Several swords were now sticking from the troll's back.

The troll clawed at its back to try and remove the

embedded swords, but to no avail. As the troll twisted, the dwarf hunters fired on it, three flaming arrows struck home, and the troll fell over. The dwarf warriors hacked at the downed troll.

The second wounded troll had now received a leg wound and was struggling, it lost its balance and fell over, crushing two dwarves beneath it. The dwarves hacked at the troll until it stopped moving.

The battle was over and the dwarves had lost four of their number dead. Three dwarves suffered broken limbs and one had a broken nose. Both trolls were dead.

Grey-back and the others continued their gallop. Their two pack members had just sacrificed their lives to buy time for the pack to escape. The dwarf hunters pursuit would probably now be delayed, or at best ended. The hunters now would have to tend to their wounded, dying and dead.

Twenty warrior dwarves rode out from the city after the fleeing troll pack. The tracker with them took the lead, guiding them and they easily picked up the creatures' tracks. The trolls were making no attempt to conceal themselves.

The trolls were now at the end of The Cut, and they used their claws like climbing axes making their way up the ridge to the woods above. Once at the peak, on their right side, they could see the top of the High Falls.

The water was flowing downwards, and the force was producing mist which drifted onto the land. Running to the left of the falls was the start of the woods. Behind the falls, the mighty High Peak mountain range stood. This had been their home. They would keep the High Peak range on their right. Following this around would lead the pack to the north face and eventually the ruins.

The trolls disappeared into the treeline just as the twenty dwarf riders reached the end of The Cut. They looked up and Grey-back was the last troll to enter the woods. He stopped, looked at the dwarf riders and roared defiantly, then disappeared following his pack.

The trolls had now safely made it into the woods. This meant they had more cover and would be harder to spot. They now had the advantage, and their sense of smell would prove invaluable.

The dwarf riders began to climb the end of The Cut, it was a much slower affair with horses, and they were careful in case of rock falls. They reached the top, and then searched for the troll tracks. The dwarves would now be leaving their territory, but they had to deal with the trolls.

These trolls had been extremely audacious, coming so far into the Brokenlands. They couldn't allow this to happen again, and would have to hunt them down to act as a deterrent.

The dwarves began to enter the edge of the woods. They admired the great water fall next to them, as the thundering water meandered its way deep into The Cut. The dwarves would have to slow their pace in the woods. Not only would they have to be vigilant for trolls, but anything else that lived there.

****

A carrier pigeon landed at the top of Westerly watchtower. One of the Royal Scouts who was on guard saw the bird and tried to grab it.

'Come here ya' bugger.' said the Scout, struggling to get hold of the wriggling bird. The pigeon began to flap its wings and the Scout was afraid it would fly off. He finally caught the bird and took it downstairs, then removed the message pouch from its leg and placed it in a small cage. The pigeon cooed.

The letter was addressed as urgent to the garrison commander, and had the seal of Knight-Marshal Garlan himself. He would have taken the message directly to the commander, but the new Ensign expected his men to use the chain of command. Le Romme would only listen to the Sergeants, and he was only a Scout after all.

He took the message to Master-at-Arms Zill, whose scarred appearance always made others feel uneasy.

'Sir, urgent message for the garrison commander.' said the Scout, handing the note to Zill.

'Thank-you, dismissed.' replied Zill.

Zill walked to the Ensign's quarters, and knocked on the door.

Le Romme answered, 'Enter.'

Zill opened the door and Le Romme stood staring out his window.

'Yes, Sergeant-Major?' said Le Romme

'Sir, we received a message for you from Knight-Marshal Garlan.' replied Zill.

The Ensign reached out his hand and took the message, then began reading it. The Knight-Marshal had ordered him to investigate Hander village. Westerly was the closest watchtower to the village. Le Romme smiled. This would be a great opportunity to to impress the Knight-Marshal; perhaps expediting his promotion to Lieutenant.

'We have been ordered to investigate Hander village, Master-at-Arms. We will take twenty-five men, plus yourself and myself.' said Le Romme.

'Sir, that would only leave five men to defend the watchtower.' said Zill, questioning the reasoning.

'Make them ready Mister Zill.' snapped Le Romme.

'As you wish sir.' replied Zill, who was seriously concerned about the watchtower strength.

The Master-at-Arms prepared the men, and they were armed and mounted on their horses ready to leave. Le Romme was last to leave the watchtower, mounting his horse, and he joined the front of the column alongside Zill. The Ensign gave the signal to move out.

'Forward!' responded Zill, relaying the signal to the column.

****

Harbill was concluding his inspection of the tower when the pigeon arrived. Quartermaster Gant brought the message to him. Gant could see the shock on Harbill's face.

'Glyvale has been attacked. Send one full infantry detachment there immediately.
Prepare one Scout detachment, one cavalry detachment and one infantry detachment to move out. Place the watchtower on full alert.'

'Yes, sir!' replied Gant.

The troops at Beanoch were glad to be moving out, especially those quartered outside the tower. The infantry detachment set off for Glyvale. Soon the other troops were ready and they began their march.

Because the infantry was accompanying them, the column of cavalry and Scouts would be travelling at the speed of the men on foot.

Harbill set off on horseback, leading the column, accompanied by Quartermaster Gant.

****

Bonna arrived at the Thieves' Guild in Morrack. The sewers were unpleasant, but had proved an adequate protection from the sunlight. He knocked on the door using the code and the door viewing hatch slid open. A thief peered through the hatch, then opened the door beckoning him in.

'I'm here to speak to Osumain.' said Bonna.

'Come in.' replied the thief.

'Thank-you for inviting me in.' said Bonna, smiling, knowing that he was now much stronger.

'Have you seen Timmis?' asked Bonna.

'No.' replied the thief, as he closed the door.

Bonna walked through to the larger room, inside the

room were seated three thieves.

The thieves were busy playing cards and smoking. Each had a pile of coins beside them and there was a large pot of coins in the centre of the table. They were laughing and placing bets, and were heavily drunk.

'Do any of you know if Timmis came to see Osumain?' asked Bonna.

'Yes, I remember seeing him.' replied one of the thieves.

'Where is Osumain?' asked Bonna.

'Through there.' pointed the thief.

Ramone remained hidden in the backroom and watched Bonna enter Osumain's room. He then pressed his ear to the wall in the corner and listened.
He heard Bonna close the door behind him.

'Ahh, Osumain, how have you been my friend?' asked Bonna.

'Not bad, not bad, surviving as they say.' replied Osumain, surprised to see Bonna in Morrack.

'So Bonna, what brings you to our neck of the woods? Vacation? Business? Both?'
Bonna smiled, and felt that Osumain's tone was more sarcastic than mere small talk.

'Well I am on an errand my friend. I am looking for our friend Timmis. He had some items for sale. Does he still have them?' asked Bonna.

'No, the wand and talisman were sold to a trader from Marandale.' replied Osumain.

'That is *most* disappointing. Who was this trader?' asked Bonna.

'I don't know, but he caught a boat to Dale Bay Island, and the boat's destination was Gunimore. Ramone followed him to the docks, maybe he knows more?' said Osumain.

Ramone cursed, Osumain was trying to save his own face, and drag him into it.

'Ramone you say?' asked Bonna.

'Yes, he is one of our thieves here.' replied Osumain.

'Then you are no further use to me.' said Bonna, as he lunged at Osumain,

'No get off! Help!' screamed Osumain.
Bonna lifted Osumain and threw him to the wall that Ramone was listening from. His body bounced off the wall like a rag doll. Ramone heard this and started to panic, this man would soon come after him, he thought.

He ran from the backroom, into the large room and then out to the exit.

'Bye Ramone.' said the thief manning the door. Ramone didn't say anything but left.
He ran off into the sewers, then hid, observing the Thieves' Guild door.

'I don't know anything, please let me go!' screamed Osumain at Bonna.

Bonna smiled and his fangs protruded from his mouth, his eyes were like burning red embers. He lunged and tore into Osumain's throat, and drank. When he had finished with his victim, he snapped his neck.

Bonna then left the room and went to where the

three thieves were seated. He removed a dagger from his robe and stabbed the nearest thief in the back. He slumped forwards and his head came to rest on the table.

It happened so quickly the thieves thought that their friend had fallen over drunk. Bonna bit into the second man's neck. Tearing out his throat; blood spurted onto the table, and he swiftly snapped his neck.

The third thief rose from his seat and drew a knife, lashing out at Bonna. The thief cut his cheek, and Bonna hissed at him. The thief in his inebriated state saw his red eyes and teeth. For a second, he thought he was hallucinating due to the alcohol.

Bonna pounced like an animal and knocked the thief over, then began to claw and tear at his face. The thief screamed in agony, and the thief manning the door heard the ruckus and came to investigate.

He saw Bonna with his knees on top of the thief. He pulled a dagger from his sleeve, then threw it at him, striking his target accurately and squarely on the back. The dagger was embedded into his back, but he did not slump over. Instead Bonna turned to face the man, his face in a twisted angry snarl, his eyes like a roaring fire.

The man blessed himself then dashed for the door screaming in terror. Bonna killed the thief on the floor, then ran after the fleeing man. From his hiding place outside, Ramone saw the door open, and the doorman come running out screaming. He was clearly terrified and trying escape.

He started to run along the sewer, then dashing out

of the door a bald tattooed man ran after him with a dagger stuck in his back. The bald man pulled out the dagger and advanced. His speed was unnatural.

Ramone lost sight of the two men, then he heard a scream, then silence. Has heart was beating fast, what *was* that man, and what just happened inside the Guild?

Ramone waited, he was afraid to come out from where he was hiding. He maintained his position and it seemed like hours. The thief looked left and right, just hoping to catch a glimpse of the bald man. He would feel safer if he just knew where he was, but there had been no sound since the scream.

Ramone could not stay where he was, in his haste he had forgotten his belongings in the Guild. He decided he would chance going back there to recover his bag. Ramone's heart began beating intensely. He quietly left his hiding place, then slowly made his way to the open door of the Guild. He looked behind him, checking both ways, before entering the building. There was nothing there, and no sound, only that of the water dripping.

Inside the Guild, Ramone could only imagine the full horror of what had happened. At the table were two dead thieves, and a third man lying on the ground. Their winnings, and the gambling pot still lying on the table. The area was covered in blood.

Ramone went into Osumain's room, and he was lying dead slumped on the floor. Blood splattered the walls of the room and furniture.

'Damn you Osumain.' said Ramone.

He knew that he too would have ended up like the others if he had not taken his chance and ran. He also knew the bald tattooed man would now be looking for him. He quickly went into the back room and collected his bag.

Ramone heard footsteps approaching, his heart beat intensified and felt like it would burst from his chest. The steps were drawing nearer; he could hear someone going into the room containing the dead thieves.

The person then moved into Osumain's room. Ramone heard the sounds of someone searching in the room. He pulled his dagger, waiting with his back to wall. The person then left Osumain's room, and he could hear the sound of money being being moved.

Ramone crept out, and there was Timmis.

'Timmis.' whispered Ramone.
Timmis was startled, and jumped, spinning round.

'What happened here?' he said.

'Shush.' said Ramone, putting his finger to his lips.

'We have to leave. *Now!*' he added.

'Follow me Timmis, we are both in danger.'
Timmis looked shocked, and the colour left his cheeks. Despite this, the thief still tucked some of the coins into his pocket. Ramone gave him a disapproving look.

'More compensation.' said Timmis.

'Compensation for what?' asked Ramone.

'The blue crystal, money and jewels. Osumain never paid me for them. I was looking for them. I couldn't find them in his room.'

'Let's get out of here, we need to talk about those items.' said Ramone.

The two thieves left the guild, watching carefully in case anyone was waiting for them. Satisfied that the coast was clear, they exited the door and entered the sewers. Timmis was about to go in the direction the doorman had ran. Ramone grabbed him.

'No, not that way Timmis, this way, follow me.' The two thieves began to make their way through the sewers. They came to some stairs, and climbed up. They were back on the surface.

'Do you have a safe house nearby?' asked Ramone.

'Yes, this way.' replied Timmis, beckoning him to follow.
Ramone followed Timmis, and they walked off through the streets, coming to a metal shack. Timmis produced a key and unlocked the door then went inside. They entered and locked the door behind them.

'The items you gave to Osumain. You mentioned a crystal. Where did you get them?' asked Ramone.
Timmis took a deep breath, and shook his head.

'The Stone City. The robed man from Marandale gave me the map, asked me to find a wand and a talisman in a crypt. He never told me his name. I took the other items as booty, old elven currency, some jewels and a ruby ring. I still have an old dagger too.'

'If he had the map, why did he need you?' asked Ramone.

'Don't know, Osumain lined the job up for me and the red robed man commissioned me to retrieve the wand and talisman specifically. Said I could keep whatever else I found. He got the items he wanted then paid me.' replied Timmis.

'The man who just killed everyone in the Guild knew you, he was looking for the wand and talisman too. He was bald and tattooed, Osumain called him Bonna. Do you know such a man?' asked Ramone.

'Yes. Bonna. He was a buyer from Glyvale. I sold him the ring.'

'Well he is now after us both, and will kill us if he finds us. Osumain asked me to follow the man from Marandale to the docks. I found out his name was Radahl. He sailed on a ship called the 'Star of Ronnestone', captained by a man called Volber, to Dale Bay Island. The ship was destined for Gunimore.' said Ramone.

'From what I heard Osumain also sold the crystal to Radahl.'

'He told me he had a buyer in Port-hareesh and to come back in two weeks for my money.' replied Timmis.

'Well he lied, and it sounds like you had been set up by both Osumain and this Radahl.'
Timmis nodded in agreement, resigning himself to the truth.

'Why would the ship have gone to Dale Bay Island first? Asked Timmis.

'What do you mean?' enquired Ramone.

'The only things there are the Mages Guild and a portal ring.' replied Timmis.

'Perhaps this trader is a mage, or they dropped goods off there?' said Ramone.

'When Bonna chased after the doorman, he moved fast. Nothing like a normal man. He had a dagger in his back, that didn't even stop him.
Morrack is now too dangerous for us. We should go to the Guild in Tarrondale.' said Ramone. Timmis nodded in agreement.

'Lets go to the docks right now, we'll pay for passage. Take just what you need.' said Ramone. The two men cautiously left the shack, and headed for Morrack docks.

Ramone checked constantly to see if they were being followed. The men knew that there would be consequences for the murders at the Guild. Bonna would already be looking for both of them. This Bonna would have no hesitation in killing anyone who stood in his way, thought Ramone to himself. They would only be safe once they had departed Morrack.

CHAPTER 17

Derrin, Toby, Haynes and Tyerose were outside the watchtower, along with six Scouts. The clean up from the night had begun. The charred bodies of the undead filled the bottom of the moat, and there was still a smell of burning ash. The Scouts began clearing the moat of the remains, and removed zombies that had impaled themselves onto the stakes.

Under a pile of dead, lay the remains of Murrat, only the tip of the arrow remained. It was still embedded through his leather armour. Apart from this, he was now unrecognisable, his flesh black and burned.

'What do want us to do, sir?' a Scout asked Tyerose.

'Dig a pit, we'll bury them together.' replied Tyerose.

Four of the Scouts began digging a pit about thirty feet away from the stockade. Toby and Derrin helped the other Scouts gather the bodies. They began to lay them out close to where the pit was being prepared. Two Scouts were about to lift Murrat's remains, but Derrin went over to them.

'I've got this one.' he said, and the Scouts left Murrat and moved onto another corpse instead.
Derrin and Toby lifted Murrat and carried him over to the pit. It was deep enough to begin receiving the bodies for burial. They placed Murrat at the bottom. The other Scouts began moving the awaiting bodies,

lowering them alongside Murrat.

When they had finished, the remains were now in a straight row, one on top of another. It was almost like they were on parade once again. They began filling in the grave, and soon they were covered.

Tyerose walked over to Haynes.

'We need to notify Ormsby Keep of what happened, I wonder when Captain Burke will be returning?' said the Quartermaster.

'I don't know sir, I can go myself, or do you want me to send one of the men?' asked Haynes.

'Yes. Take one of the men with you. Take Derrin. After last night he looks like he could do with a change of scenery.' ordered Tyerose.

'Yes sir.' said Haynes.

Haynes approached the exhausted looking Derrin.

'We are off to Ormsby Keep. We are going to report on what happened and see the Captain. Get your horse ready.' said Haynes.

Derrin walked off into the stables. He looked at the doors and the drawbridge controls, and the memories of last night came back to him. He could not get the image of Murrat's terrified face out of his mind.

He stroked his horse, then secured the saddle and reins. It would be good to get away from the tower for a while, he thought. Then he thought of Marie, he could write to her from Ormsby, she must be worried sick. He also wondered how Bartack was fairing at the keep.

Haynes and Derrin then rode off to Ormsby Keep, waving farewell to the Scouts outside. In the watchtower Tyerose watched the two riders disappear out of sight. He then sighed.

****

'Advance!' shouted Le Romme.
His small band had reached the woods, just north of Hander. A short distance ahead, they noticed a staggering figure in front of them. The person's gait was jerky and unsteady. Previously the figure was walking away from the patrol, but the neighing of the horses attracted its attention. The figure stopped, then turned round, facing the column, it was a man.

His face was pale grey, with deep set eyes, and blood stains ran from its mouth. The man's attire was stained and unkempt, he was barefooted and the trouser legs were torn and frayed. It reached out with both arms, and began approaching the Scouts in a slow, staggered motion.
As the man got closer, it was clear his appearance was off, and this person was undead. He began to make a raspy guttural sound and lunged towards La Romme's horse. The Ensign pulled back, as his horse became spooked. Zill drew his sword and charged towards the zombie, cutting it down with a sweep of his sword.

The zombie fell, missing part of its shoulder. Its arm, now only hung from it torso by some rotten skin and muscle. Zill circled the zombie, cutting down with his sword again with force, slicing open the zombie's head. The remains of decayed brains, and maggots spilling from the skull. La Romme, became nauseous at the sight, and barely prevented himself from vomiting. He coughed violently and spat excess saliva onto the ground. He wanted to wipe his sleeve across his mouth to clean himself. Then he remembered that a gentleman should always use a handkerchief. He reached into his pocket, removed an embroidered handkerchief, then wiped his mouth. He quickly pocketed the item, hoping that this would symbolically draw a line under the incident.

The Ensign was embarrassed by his momentary show of weakness in front of the men. Spitting or wiping your mouth with one's sleeve was behaviour the enlisted would do. It did not become a gentleman, thought Le Romme. He composed himself, then looked at Zill.

'Send the troops into Hander.' said La Romme, eager for a distraction.

'But sir, shouldn't we first scout the area?' replied Zill.

'*Now* Master-at-Arms! *Send them in!*' ordered La Romme.

Zill knew this was a mistake, Royal Scouts were not infantry, and they were not cavalry either. Their skills were tracking the enemy, harassing them, ambush and using ranged attacks with bows. Melee combat was a last resort; leather did not afford the same protection as metal armour. La Romme being a Royal Guard officer, did not help.

As the patrol moved closer to Hander they could see the dead wandering around the village. In the street the remains of the unfortunate victims lay scattered about. Crows were beginning to feed on the remains, and the birds were perched on the bodies. They pecked and pulled at the exposed flesh.

'Engage the enemy. Charge!' shouted La Romme.

The Scouts in the patrol charged towards the undead, swords drawn. As they entered Hander the zombies began shambling towards the riders. The first Scouts reached their targets and cut down a few zombies as they passed them, removing hands or arms. A few riders rammed zombies over, knocking them to the ground. The Scouts became scattered. Zill noticed this and was concerned. The Scouts were not cavalry, and fighting on horseback with swords was somewhat alien to them.

'Sir, our troops are too spread out. Will I order a recall?' asked Zill.

'No, they *must* engage.' snapped Le Romme.

Those zombies not engaged in combat began a guttural groan in unison. First it started with a few undead, then they all began their groan together. The Scouts were unsure why this was happening. Then that question was quickly answered. From the houses, shops and inn came more zombies. The horses became unnerved by the noise, and the Scouts struggled to control them. One horse violently reared up, and its rider fell heavily to the ground.

Two zombies pounced on the fallen rider and another zombie attempted to bite his horse. The horse reared up, knocking the zombie over, then bolted out of the village.

A companion came to his aid, and was forced to dismount to reach him. The Scout struggled on the ground with the first zombie. The second zombie bit the man hard on the ankle and he screamed in agony. His companion slashed at the second zombie, his sword connecting with its neck. The zombie slumped over. He then pulled the first zombie of his companion, kicking it to the ground.

He helped lift his injured companion, who could barely walk. They tried to make their way out, but the dead began to close in. The two men fought back to back but to no avail. The injured man fell over and was attacked immediately.

His rescuer was forced to leave him, and then he found himself surrounded. The Scout screamed as he was pulled to the ground. The grasping decayed hands of the dead tore and pulled at him from all sides. A zombie bit into his face, tearing a lump of flesh from his cheek. The wound erupted like a red fountain of blood. He screamed, punching the zombie in retaliation. The man with the leg wound was overpowered, and the dead began to consume the screaming man, he then fell silent.

Other Scouts soon began to struggle, as the zombies, unable to reach the riders, attacked their horses. This forced the Scouts to dismount and engage in melee. The dead began to crowd in.

'Sir, we need to fall back!' said Zill.

'They stand and fight!' replied Le Romme, as he got off his own horse and joined the fray.

Zill, against his better judgement dismounted and joined his commander. Very soon all of the Scouts were unmounted and hacking at the horde. Their unsecured horses fled in terror, and scattered throughout the village, many fleeing to the woods.

It was now carnage in Hander, as the troops found themselves completely surrounded. Eight Scouts were already dead, the zombies forming little circles around the bodies as they fed on the corpses.

'Fall back!' shouted Le Romme.

But it was too late, many of the men were already wounded, and to escape they would have to fight their way through.

'Sir, we need to get inside the inn. That's our *only* chance.' said Zill.

'Retreat to the inn!' shouted Le Romme in vain.

His troops were now separated into little groups. Five men were beside Zill and Le Romme; the other men were either by themselves or in groups of three.

The zombies closed in, and quickly overpowered the smaller groups.

'Three of you, cut through with me.' shouted Zill to three of the men.

Zill and the three Scouts pushed forward, hacking at everything in their path. La Romme stayed behind them and the two other Scouts covered the rear.

The other Scout groups began to fall. Men screamed everywhere as the zombies bit, tore and clawed at them. The ground was littered with dead zombies and fallen Scouts.

Zill's group battered, slashed and kicked their way to the steps of the inn clearing a small path.

'Inside now!' shouted Zill. Le Romme and four Scouts ran into the building. Zill and the other Scout covered their exit, hacking at any dead that came onto the steps. A zombie approached him and Zill push kicked it backwards. The zombie fell, causing two other zombies behind it to fall over.

Inside the inn, two of the Scouts dispatched a zombie that had still been inside.

'Move!' shouted Zill to the Scout beside him, who then ran into the inn. Zill slashed out once more, then entered the inn closing the doors behind him and bolting it shut. There were many half eaten dead bodies and entrails littering the floor of the inn, most being from the hapless villagers.

'Barricade quickly!' shouted Zill to the men. The Scouts began to gather chairs, and drag tables to the door. Soon the doorway was blocked. From outside, the zombies began banging on the door with their fists, determined to reach the fresh food inside.

Le Romme sat down on a bench with his head bowed over. He was clearly broken by the whole experience, his eyes filled with remorse and self-reproach.

Zill looked around behind him and stared at the pitiful sight of Le Romme. Zill realised *he* would have to take command himself if they were to survive.

'Secure and search the rest of the ground floor, just in case there are more inside. Go in pairs. I'll go with you.' said Zill to the five remaining Scouts.

Le Romme said nothing to this, his head still bowed and now placing his shaking hands over his ears. He only stared at the floor in front of him.

Zill and the others began searching the building. They found the back door open, and closed it, securing the bolts. Luckily, nothing had entered the open door. The zombies inside had probably been drawn to the village square by the moans. The store rooms and the cellar were also both empty.

From the evidence, it looked like the doors had been opened from the inside. Which meant that the attackers had come from outside and had been let in. There had been a struggle, as there were also the remains of dead zombies.

Satisfied that downstairs was now secure, Zill ordered the search to commence upstairs. They checked the doors of the rooms which were closed. When they found a locked door, they shouted 'Hello?', then listened for a response. When nothing happened, they continued to the next room along.

All of the rooms had been secure except one. It contained no belongings, and the wardrobe had been pulled across the window.
Happy that the upstairs was safe, the Scouts prepared to head back downstairs.

Zill heard one of the rooms click unlocked, and a young blonde woman peered out of the doorway. She appeared dishevelled with cuts to her arms, and wore the attire of a serving woman. She ran over to Zill and hugged his chest tightly.

'Please sir, help me! Have those creatures gone yet?' asked the sobbing terrified woman.
Zill was unsure how to respond to her.

'I'm afraid they have not.' replied Zill.
The woman looked at him and was now shaking with fear.

'Martin the innkeeper answered the door. They dragged him outside, and then came in attacking people. It all happened during that bard's performance.' she said.

'What happened?' asked Zill.

'The bard had a concert in the inn. He asked for nothing, but wanted all the villagers here to see him play. He was with another man, a knight, scary looking man.' cried the woman.

'We have to head back downstairs, follow me. What is your name?' said Zill to the woman.

'Rebekah.' replied the woman.

'I am Master-at-Arms Lukas Zill.'

Zill, Rebekah and the five Scouts went downstairs. Le Romme was still seated, but he had now begun to compose himself.

'The building is secure. Or secure as it can be.' said Zill to the Ensign.

'We've lost twenty men Master-at-Arms.' said the sorrowful Ensign.

'Yes, we have sir. But we have to make sure those here don't join the others. We have also found a survivor from the village.' said Zill pointing to Rebekah.

'What should we do Mister Zill?' asked Le Romme in concessionary tone.

'There are too many at the front, and they are too close together. We'll have to wait till they spread out, or try the back exit later.' replied Zill.

'Get a fire going.' said Zill to a Scout.

They would then watch, and decide when to take their opportunity to escape.

****

On the hilltop Knight-Captain Harbill surveyed the woods that lay in front of his force. He had sent his Scouts forward and was awaiting their imminent return. A leather armoured rider approached the Knight-Captain and saluted.

'Scout, what do you have to report?' asked Harbill.

'About ten undead, mostly scattered sir. We also found six horses, all saddles from the Royal Scouts. We also found the remains of two men in Provost Regulators uniform. They had been eaten it appears.' replied the rider.

'Quartermaster Gant.' shouted Harbill.

'Sir!' replied Gant.

'Send a detachment of cavalry out, instruct them to cut down all undead they find.'

'Yes sir!' replied Gant.

The Quartermaster began issuing orders to the Corporals, who quickly began to assemble their squads. The order was given to move out and the cavalry advanced on the woods leaving the column behind.

'Yes, the cavalry should clear the woods and this will clear the way into Hander.' said Harbill.

The cavalrymen moved out as ordered, then entered the woods. Behind them the infantry and Scout detachments waited beside Harbill and Quartermaster Gant.

The twenty cavalry troops were in their element. Trained to engage infantry on foot, their sabres easily cut down the undead. The weapons were powerful, and the blade's downward cut was deadly.

Once the zombies were routed, the cavalrymen returned to the line beside the other troops. Harbill, was pleased by their performance.

'Very good Quartermaster. Send the Scouts forward to investigate Hander, also ask them to keep watch for any of our troops in the area.' commanded Harbill.

'Very good sir.' replied Gant.

The detachment of Royal Scouts rode into the woods and towards Hander. As they got closer to the village they immediately spotted nearly thirty zombies. There were many bodies lying in the middle of the village. The zombies were bent over them feeding on the remains.

The Scouts held their position, while a Scout Corporal returned to the column, and reported their findings to the Captain.

'Sir, thirty undead in the village. Lots of dead bodies lying around too. We have taken up position outside, and are ready to engage by bow.' said the Corporal.

'Very good, Corporal. Engage at range only.' ordered Harbill.

The Scout Corporal rode off back to his skirmish line and passed on the Captain's orders to the men. The Scouts began to dismount and prepared their bows.

'Infantry. Cavalry. Advance!' shouted Harbill.

The cavalry and infantry advanced to the skirmish line that the Scouts had set up. The infantry took position in front of the line of Scouts. The cavalry were split equally on the left and right flanks.

'Scouts, loose arrows.' ordered Harbill.
The Royal Scouts aimed and fired their long bows. The arrows flew through the air, and started to rain down amongst the dead. Two zombies fell dead as the arrows pierced their skulls. Other zombies now had arrows sticking from their torsos, arms or shoulders.

The dead now became aware of the troops, and the zombies groaned in unison. Those that were feeding on corpses looked around, stopped feeding and stood up. They started following the other dead in the direction of the troops.

The Scouts aimed, then loosed another salvo of arrows. The arrows rained down once again on the undead. Another was struck on the head killing it instantly. Other zombies were hit but only on their bodies. The dead continued their advance.

The Scouts aimed and fired again. Two more zombies fell, but the others were unaffected. Harbill realised the arrows were not particularly effective against these enemies. The bowmen would require head-shots to kill their targets.

'Scouts hold fire. Cavalry carry out one charge, then reform once again here.' ordered Harbill.

The horsemen charged, sabres drawn and pointed towards the advancing undead. They cut through the zombie lines, slicing downwards with their sabres as they passed. Five zombies fell in the attack, one rider was almost unseated, as his horse became spooked.

The riders circled back around the dead and returned to their own lines reforming on the flanks once again.

'Infantry, draw swords and shields and advance on the enemy. Scouts, prepare to fire, aim for the head *only*.' ordered Harbill.

The soldiers began to move forward in line. Behind them, the Scouts took aim at the zombies' heads and fired. Three of the arrows struck true, striking the dead directly on their forehead, they fell down immediately.

The infantry were now in melee range, and began hacking at the zombies. They used their shields to push the dead back, then quickly struck a blow with their swords. One soldier was pounced on by two undead and fell over. The zombies tried to bite him but his chain mail managed to protect him.

Another soldier came to his rescue and sliced the head of one zombie, and pummelled the other with his shield. Soon there was only one zombie left, and this was hacked to the ground.

Harbill ordered the Scouts and cavalry to join up with the other troops in Hander. The infantry began checking and clearing the buildings. Two soldiers went over to the inn and hammered on the door.

'Hello!' they shouted.
Inside they heard the shout and started to remove the barricades.

'Hey! Wait there!' shouted one of the Scouts from inside.
Zill opened the doors, and standing there were two

infantrymen. He noticed Zill's rank insignia.

'Hello sir. Are you all right?' asked the soldier.

'We are now thanks. Good to see you.' said Zill.

'The Captain will want to see you sir.' said the soldier pointing to Harbill.

The surviving Scouts, Le Romme, Zill and Rebekah left the inn and went over to Captain Harbill. Zill and Le Romme saluted the Captain. He returned the salute.

'Master-at-Arms Zill and Ensign Le Romme. What were *you* doing here?' asked Harbill.

'We were ordered to investigate Hander by Lord Garlan. We found undead in the area and attacked them.' explained Le Romme.

'Is this all of you?' asked Harbill, looking puzzled by their small number.

'I'm afraid so sir. We lost twenty men here.' said Le Romme.

Zill said nothing, as he knew the men were lost due to Le Romme's stupidity.

'We found one survivor from Hander sir, this young woman called Rebekah. It seems she was the only survivor and was present when they were attacked.' said Zill.

'Glyvale was also attacked. I had to send a detachment of infantry there to support them.' said Harbill.

'How many men do you have left at your outpost Ensign?'

'Just five sir, and what we have here.' replied Le Romme embarrassed.

'I'll send my infantry there to reinforce your

garrison. Quartermaster Gant will go with them, along with your remaining Scouts from here.'

'However Ensign, you, Master-at-Arms Zill and Rebekah should head to Ormsby Keep. Lord Garlan will want to speak to you. We also recovered some of your escaped horses. You can use those.' added Harbill

'Yes sir!' replied Zill and Le Romme.

'I'm going to head back to Beanoch with my Scouts and cavalry. Goodbye gentlemen.' said Harbill. Zill, Le Romme and Rebekah mounted their horses and then rode off to Ormsby Keep.

****

Derrin and Haynes arrived at Ormsby. At the front gate were two chain mailed soldiers.

'Halt.' said one soldier, and Derrin and Corporal Haynes stopped.

'We have an urgent message for Lord Garlan from High Peak watchtower.' responded Haynes.
The soldier directed Haynes through to the steps across the courtyard.

'Lord Garlan's quarters are up there. You can tie your horses in the stable area.' said the soldier.

'Thanks.' replied Haynes, as he and Derrin dismounted. They went up the steps and into the long table room. In the room was Captain Burke, Lord Garlan and Allun Roe.

'Corporal Haynes.' said Burke.
Haynes and Derrin saluted.

'Sir, High Peak was attacked by undead. We had

one casualty. It was the men from our own garrison cemetery.' said Haynes.

'This is more serious than we first thought.' said Garlan. 'I have received word from Sir Jeffrey Rolland, he has dispatched Lady Rowena to Ormsby Keep.'

'I am also awaiting word from Beanoch and Westerly on the situation around Hander.'

'Now gentlemen, please find quarters to refresh yourselves. I must speak to the Captain and Master-at-Arms alone. Thank-you.' said Garlan.

Derrin and Haynes saluted, then left Lord Garlan's quarters.

'Let's go and see if we can find Bartack. He'll be about here somewhere.' said Haynes.

They went to the quartermaster's office, and received a billet. The men's quarters in the keep was basic, but better than those at the tower. Haynes lay on his bed and had a nap.

Later in the mess, Derrin and Haynes were reunited with Bartack. He rushed over to see them.

'Derrin! Corporal Haynes! How are you both? How come you are here?' asked Bartack.

'Long story.' said Haynes.

'Yes. Murrat was posted to High Peak.' said Derrin.

Bartack's demeanour shifted at the mention of Murrat's name, which brought a grimace to his face.

'Let, me finish Bartack. He was posted there, but he was killed. We were attacked.' said Derrin.

'By trolls?' asked Bartack.

'No. We were attacked by men, well...at least they

were men…once. Dead men.

Murrat got trapped outside after opening the doors. We had to close the doors or would have all died.

Anyway, they bit him and he was wounded. They started eating him alive. There was no choice, and I had to kill him.' said Derrin.

Bartack's eyes widened and he looked shocked by the revelation. Murrat was a cruel bully, the man who had battered Derrin to a pulp, but he never imagined this would have happened.

After their meal, the boys returned to their quarters with Haynes. Derrin took the opportunity to write to Marie, explaining in the letter he was OK and what had happened. He wrote that he loved and missed her and would see her soon. Bartack meanwhile, lay on his bed taking in everything that Derrin had told him about Murrat. He was glad that he hadn't been there.

****

Much later, Zill, Le Romme and Rebekah arrived at Ormsby Keep. The gate guards recognised both men and saluted the Ensign.

'We need to see Lord Garlan right away.' said Zill to an apprehensive Le Romme.

The three began to ascend the steps to the Knight-Marshal's quarters. They entered and Garlan, Burke and Roe were present in the long table room. Zill and Le Romme saluted Lord Garlan.

'Master-at-Arms Zill and Ensign La Romme. What brings you here?' asked Garlan.

'We have bad news sir. Hander had fallen to the undead. There was only one survivor. Rebekah here.' said Zill.

'What happened?' asked Garlan.

'I received your order to investigate. We entered Hander and were attacked. I regret most of my men were lost. We simply were not equipped for such an undertaking. We then were forced to take refuge in the inn, until Knight-Captain Harbill arrived.' said Le Romme.

'We found the girl inside the inn sir. She was there when they were first attacked.' added Zill.

'Tell us what happened, Rebekah.' asked Garlan.

'Well sir, a bard turned up, accompanied a knight. He wanted to stay and perform a show. Handsome he was.'

'We hadn't had no-one there for so long. The innkeeper agreed to allow him to play. And the man did not ask for any money.'

'Most of the village were in the inn watching. During the performance there was banging at the door.'

'My boss went to open the door and then got attacked. Those corpses then came into the room and attacked everyone.'

'I fled upstairs and locked myself into a room due to be cleaned.' said Rebekah, trying to hold back her emotions.

'Where did this bard go?' asked Garlan.

'I don't know sir, but the creatures did not touch him.' replied Rebekah.

'Clearly this bard had a part to play in all of this.

We need to find him.' said Garlan.

'Do you have family elsewhere Rebekah?' asked Garlan in a concerned tone.

'My parents are dead sir. But I have a brother who lives in Gunimore.' replied Rebekah.

'We can get you safe passage to Gunimore. It's faster to sail by Morrack. We will transport you there during our next troop transfer. In the meantime, you are welcome to remain here as my guest at the keep.' said Garlan.

'Thank-you sir.' said a grateful Rebekah.

'Please get yourselves quartered. Master-at-Arms Roe will escort you to your accommodation.' said Garlan.

Roe dropped Rebekah off first, then Le Romme.

'What *really* happened Lukas?' asked Roe as soon as he was alone with Zill.

'Le Romme's stupidity got them killed Allun. He went charging in, and then had the Scouts engage in melee combat.

He wouldn't see sense.' said Zill shaking his head in regret.

Roe sighed deeply, 'Typical.' he said.

'The sooner he is posted to guarding a Royal palace the better for us all. He's a liability as a field officer.' said Zill.

'It was lucky *you* were there with him, otherwise you'd *all* be dead now.' replied Roe.

Zill knew that Roe's assessment was correct, but he found no consolation in the words.

'Come, let me get you a well earned drink.' said

Roe.

The two men then made their way to the Sergeant's quarters. Roe collected a flagon of wine and two metal goblets from a sideboard. He then filled each to the brim, handing one to Zill, and both men began to drink.

CHAPTER 18

After bidding farewell to the ship, Radahl left the docks at Dale Bay Island and made his way to the standing stones. He walked into the centre of the circle and started an inaudible chant. Before him a glimmering blue portal soon appeared, and he walked through.

Time started to warp, and yellow speeding lights dashed all around him. The movement of lights then suddenly stopped. In front of him was another blue portal and he stepped through.

Instantly he was transported and came out in the middle of some standing stones. The ground was frosty and hard. Behind him stood an intimidating grey stone fortress. The battlements and parapets were dusted in a layer of snow. Radahl walked towards its massive stone doors which opened for him, and he went inside.

He was now in a massive gallery, which had rows of tall carved pillars. At the front of the gallery was a large golden throne. Seated upon it was a white haired man, who looked no more than thirty years old. He wore a blue velvet robe, and had silver coloured bracers on his wrists.

Radahl approached him and bowed. The white haired man inclined his head a fraction in duteous acknowledgement.

'Success Lord Amorass, I have recovered the wand and talisman of Gorath Marr, and the elven binding stone.' said Radahl smiling.

'Excellent, then the thief managed to enter the

crypt. Gorath Marr must now be free.' replied Amorass.

'The ring was sold by the thief, we were unable to acquire that.' replied Radahl.

'Not to worry, we hold the most important items. Marr's spell casting will not be at full force. More importantly without his talisman of day-walking, his movements will be restricted. We also have the means to imprison him.' replied Amorass.

'My spies in Glyvale tell me that Mareck, his accursed bard, has already been up to his necromantic exploits. The settlement was attacked by zombies.' replied Radahl.

'That is good, it will get the attention of both Sir Jeffrey Rolland and King Tarnus. No doubt they will soon be begging me to help them.' said Amorass.

'What of the Dale Bay Mages' Guild?' asked Radahl.

'No, they are unaware. The southern mages are more supportive of the status quo. Since the last magi war they have been somewhat pacifistic in their approach. They are now nothing more than the dancing bears of Tarnus.' replied Amorass.

'Besides, we cannot rely on the Dale Bay fools. Only our Guild of Valatoch are loyal to our true values.' added Amorass.

'I have also cast a scrying shield over both the wand and talisman. If Marr or anyone else tries to find the items, they are been hidden by magic.' added Radahl.

'Now Radahl. We must tie up all the loose ends. The thief who found the items must be eliminated. He met you I assume?' asked Amorass.

'Yes, I met him, but he didn't see me clearly. What of those at the Thieves' Guild in Morrack?' asked Radahl.

'No need to worry about Osumain. Someone has beaten us too it. He was murdered, along with all his cronies. I guess his dealings finally caught up with him?' said Amorass smiling.

'How should we deal with Timmis the thief?' asked Radahl.

'I think the Assassin's Guild may be more beneficial to use in this instance. We take out a contract on the thief. They don't ask questions, only how much you are willing to pay. Prepare the contract.' commanded Amorass.

'At once.' said Radahl, as he bowed and left his Guild Master.

****

Old Grey-back sniffed the air, and at once he recognised the scent. He gave a low growl. It was the same smell as the strange humans who had killed and driven his people from their home. The smell of this familiar scent caused Grey-back to snarl. But why were they outside of the High Peaks he wondered? Grey-back gave a gulping sound and his pack stopped moving immediately.

As the great troll moved forward, he saw the two figures. One wore a hood and the other wore plate mail armour. These indeed were the ones who drove the trolls from the Stone City. These people were dangerous, and would be deadly to the cubs and females.

Their two horses were tied up and they were deep in conversation. They hadn't noticed Grey-back; and he knew instinctively this was his packs best opportunity to move past undetected. He made three gulping noises, and moved off to the right flank. His pack followed him and they moved quietly and steadily around the two people.

They continued on, the troll sniffed the air, he could now smell short humans, and the scent of the two strange humans had weakened. The pack moved on, deeper into the woods. He had taken them further north than he was initially going to. He had to try and lose the short humans who were obviously following.

To the north-east he could see the peaks of the Steppes of Garmer. In the woods ahead he noticed a west-east dirt road that cut through the trees. The troll pack turned sharply east, and followed the edge of the road, but staying in the treeline.

The scent of the short humans weakened. The dwarf riders advanced through the woods following the troll pack's trail. Morra Blackhammer knew they would soon be upon them. The riders each lit a torch, as attacking a troll without fire would be madness. The downside to this was that the smoke would make them detectable to others.

Morra signalled, and two of the dwarves rode forward. From no-where an arrow struck the tree next to one of them. He looked around and in front of them were five auburn haired wood-elves. The dwarves drew their weapons.

'That was a warning shot, dwarf. You are a bit out of your way aren't you?' said one of the elves.

'So what *are* you doing here dwarf?' asked the elf.

'None of your damn business, sharp ears.' replied Blackhammer in a contemptuous tone.

The elf could see the visceral hatred the dwarf held for him. Blackhammer could not believe the arrogance of the elf. They were outnumbered four to one, and this elf was playing the tough guy.

'I would leave here before you end up out of your depth. Not a great deal of a surprise for a dwarf anyway.' replied the elf, sarcastically.

The comment enraged Blackhammer further. He hated the elves' condescending self superiority. He desperately wanted to teach this one a hard lesson.

'I suggest you head back to whatever pit you came out off.' said the elf sneering.

Suddenly, the elf started to cough and choke. He placed his hands on to his throat. The elf looked at his hands, then noticed that he was starting to age rapidly. His skin began to wrinkle, and he could feel his life force draining from him. He was now an extremely old man and collapsed to the ground. He then began to wither to dust.

His four companions looked on in shock, and then realised the watching dwarves were equally as shocked. A large broadsword blade erupted from the chest of an elf. The others spun around and behind him stood a plate armoured knight.

The other three elves readied their bows and

aimed at the knight. They fired, and the knight used the elf's dead body as a shield. All three arrows struck the body of their former companion.

Hazak pulled his sword from out of the elf, kicking the body to the ground. The dark paladin advanced towards the elves, taking a high guard with his sword. They readied to fire another salvo of arrows at the knight. A red glow appeared around the elves' heads and their vision became blurred and impaired.

They could no longer see their target, and fired arrows in front of them in the hope of hitting something. From behind a tree, a black cloaked figure appeared, it was Amera. She was chanting and began making circular motions with her hands.

The three elves grasped desperately for an arrow from their quivers. Then prepared to fire again. Hazak closed in, and cut down an elf with his sword. The other elves fired, missing him completely.

Hazak carried out a spinning cut attack, slicing off the left arm of an elf and destroying the bow in the process. The elf screamed in agony as blood spurted and poured from his stump. The other elf swung in an arc with their bow, hoping to strike their opponent. The bow struck Hazak's plate mail, giving a 'clank'; but it glanced off doing no damage to the paladin.

Hazak lunged forward with his blade, parrying the bow out of the way and piercing the elf in the chest. The elf gave a gasp, then fell. Hazak performed a reverse under arm thrust with his sword, finishing off the one armed elf who was now behind him.

Amera walked over beside Hazak. The dark

paladin cleaned his blade on one of the dead elves.

'Show off.' said Amera to the dark paladin.

The stunned dwarves looked on in amazement at what they had just witnessed. They still had their weapons drawn and were prepared to engage the knight and hooded woman. Blackhammer was impressed by the pair, and glad to see the back of the arrogant elf.

'There is no need for any hostility master dwarf.' said Amera to Blackhammer. The dwarf lowered his weapon and signalled to his men to follow suit. The group of dwarves lowered their weapons.

'Who are you, why did you kill the elves?' asked Blackhammer.

'The reason we killed them is because they *are* elves. My master despises them, *all* of them.' replied Amera, in a matter of fact tone.

'Well, thank you, you saved me the trouble.' said Blackhammer.

'My name is Amera, my companion is Hazak.'

'I am Morra Blackhammer. Your master, who is that, if you don't mind my asking?' asked the dwarf.

'My master is Gorath Marr. A magic user of much renown...once.' replied Amera.

'I too, am not too fond of the elves. They still claim the High Peaks and stole Heighgaard from my ancestors.' replied Blackhammer.

'My master has reclaimed the High Peaks, and would be happy to assist you in the recovery of Heighgaard and with your revenge on the elves.' replied Amera.

Morra studied the woman for a second, and comprehended what she had said.

'What do you mean by reclaimed the High Peaks?' asked Morra.

'The elves are long gone, and so are the hairy creatures that plagued the mountains.' replied Amera.

'The trolls?' replied the dwarf.

'Yes, if that's what you call them.' Amera replied.

'I was...just chasing a pack of them.' added the dwarf warrior.

'Leave them. You have more important things ahead. My master will want to meet you in the High Peaks in order to formulate a plan.' replied Amera.

'Meet me?' asked the dwarf.

'Of course. Then you can see the Stone City for yourself.' added Amera.

'So when will I meet your master?' asked Blackhammer.

'I have to complete a mission for my master first. But then I will bring you with me upon my return. Where will I find you?' asked Amera.

'Come to Stonewold, and ask for Morra Blackhammer. You will have no problem finding me.' said the dwarf.

'I will, master dwarf, now I must bid you and your companions goodbye. We have far to travel.' replied Amera.

The dwarves bid them farewell, and then returned south heading the way they had come.

'What do you think of that pair?' said a dwarf to Blackhammer.

'Which ones?' replied Morra, laughing in a joking reference to Amera's ample bosom.

'They are dangerous, I'd rather be on their side than not, judging by what happened to those elves.' he added.

'Do you think what they said was true?' asked the dwarf.

'No idea, but I doubt we will see them again.' replied Morra.

'What about those trolls?' asked the dwarf.

'Long gone, and probably someone else's problem now. I wonder if it was our new friends who caused the trolls to enter the Brokenlands to begin with?'

'Never mind, lets get home. Beer, food and bed. Besides, the wood elves won't be too pleased when they find their dead friends. We would probably get the blame.' Blackhammer laughed and the dwarves rode on.

****

Ramone and Timmis arrived at Tarrondale docks transported by a small cargo boat. The crew had asked no questions, and were happy to earn a little extra money for a trip that was scheduled anyway. Departing the boat, they slipped through the dock area keeping a low profile.

There did not appear to be anyone watching them or following them. In the dock area, traders, ships crew and merchants were going about their business. These docks were extremely busy, and the accents suggested that the people here were from all over Dolia.

'We'll need to find somewhere to stay. Somewhere out of the way.' said Ramone.

'Why not the docks area? Many people come and go there, new faces amongst many?' suggested Timmis.

'That's not a bad idea, we should find an inn around here.' replied Ramone.

They approached a nearby fisherman, who was mending a net.

'Excuse me. Is their a decent inn nearby?' asked Ramone.

The fisherman looked up, and eyed both Ramone and Timmis. He rightly assumed they had just arrived by boat at the docks.

'Aye, just down there and on the right. It's called the Black Dog Inn. You fellas should be *right* at home there.' said the fisherman smiling.

Ramone nodded thanks to the fisherman, and he and Timmis followed his directions. A short distance on the right was the Black Dog Inn.

'What did that fisherman mean by *we should be right at home there*?' asked Timmis.

'Don't know for sure, but I guess we will soon find out.' replied Ramone.

The two men entered the inn. It was very smokey inside, and was full of punters chatting and drinking. Ramone approached the innkeeper.

'I need a room for two.' asked Ramone.

'Double bed or two singles.' asked the innkeeper smiling at his own jest.

The innkeeper could tell from Ramone's face that he

wasn't impressed by the comment.

'I mean, do you both want single beds or double beds?' said the innkeeper quickly correcting himself.

'Single beds are fine.' replied Ramone.

'What type of room do you want? The choice is budget, moderate or premium.' asked the innkeeper.

'Moderate is fine, as long as its got a decent lock and a comfy bed.' replied Ramone.

'How long will you need the room.' asked the innkeeper.

'One night...for now.' replied Ramone.

'That's one silver piece.' replied the innkeeper. Ramone handed him the coin. The innkeeper gave him a key.

'Room nineteen.' added the innkeeper.

An irritated Ramone nodded and left the bar-room followed by Timmis. They went upstairs to their room. Inside, the room was pleasant but simple, with two single beds. The room had a window, which looked out onto the rear courtyard of the inn. Ramone inspected it, and realised that they could easily escape from there if needed.

'Timmis, I am going to go to the Thieves' Guild, I'll try and find more out. Wait here till I come back, and don't go wandering off. And *don't steal* anything either.' said Ramone.

The thief left the inn and then made his way in the direction of the docks warehouse area. This was off the beaten track, and the warehouses were large. Only merchants or those storing goods would travel here, and even they would never venture here at night.

Instinct told Ramone that he was being followed. He caught a glance of movement, and then it was gone. Ramone smiled, a cutpurse looking for an easy target no doubt. Ramone turned the corner and entered a small lane between two wooden warehouses. He ducked into a deep recess, and waited. Ramone pulled his dagger out from his belt.

A short person wearing a brown cloak walked past unaware. Ramone lunged, grabbing them, and pushed them into the wall of the warehouse. He brought his dagger up to their throat, and with his other hand pulled down their hood.

It was a young brunette woman and Ramone now saw her face.

'Anitaa!' exclaimed Ramone, and he relaxed his grip and lowered his dagger.

'You always were a charmer.' replied the woman smiling.

'I could easily have *killed* you. What *were* you doing following me?' asked Ramone.

'I saw you leave the Black Dog Inn. I hadn't seen you in Tarrondale for such a long time. In fact the last time I saw you was in Morrack.' replied Anitaa.

'I'm off to the Guild now.' said Ramone.

'It's shocking what happened in Morrack wasn't it?' said Anitaa.

'What was?' asked Ramone pretending to be unaware.

'Osumain was murdered, along with some other Guild members.'

'And it was by one of our own. Timmis is his

name.' added Anitaa.

'Who told you it was Timmis?' asked Ramone.

'A new Guild leader has been appointed in Morrack, Bonna is his name. He was an old friend of Osumain from Glyvale.' replied Anitaa.

A look of shock came to Ramone's face, as he was there when Osumain was killed. Clearly Bonna wanted the Guild for himself, thought Ramone.

'Bonna had witnessed the attack, but there is now a bounty on Timmis. To attack another thief in the confines of the Guild completely breaks our rules.' said Anitaa.

'Lets go to the Guild.' said Ramone.

The two thieves backtracked out of the side lane and back onto the main path.

'So *what* are you doing here Ramone?' asked Anitaa with curiosity.

'You *always* were too nosey Anitaa. Have you forgotten what I taught you?' responded Ramone.

'Yes, yes. Only give out the minimum information and only part with information for the right price.' said Anitaa, doing a mocking impersonation of Ramone.

Although Anitaa jested with Ramone, she knew deep down he was right. He had taught her many things and was one of *the* best at tailing targets and finding people in the guild.

They carried on deeper into the warehouse sector, then entered the Thieves' Guild itself. The doorman eyed Ramone suspiciously.

'Hello Anitaa, did you have a successful day?'

asked the doorman.

Anitaa nodded laughing, 'Not bad, managed to separate a few purses from their owners.'

'And you friend. Haven't seen you before.' said the doorman.

'It's OK Owanne, he's a friend of mine.' replied Anitaa.

'We are on the look out for a wanted thief, Timmis is his name.' said the doorman.

'Have you come across this fellow, *friend*?' the doorman asked Ramone.

'No, how much is the reward?' asked Ramone.

'A thousand gold for information leading to his capture. Or five thousand gold for his capture, alive, *or dead*.' replied the doorman.

'What did he do?' asked Ramone, trying to garner more information.

'Attacking brother thieves inside the Guild. Stealing objects from a fellow thief inside the Guild. Murder of Guild brothers inside the Guild.'

'What did he steal?' asked Ramone.

'Magic items, a wand and talisman owned by Bonna.' replied the doorman.

'Owned by Bonna you say? Who is Bonna?' asked Ramone pretending not to know.

'Bonna is the new Guild leader at Morrack. He reorganised the Guild there after the killings. Luckily he was there, as he normally lives in Glyvale.' said the doorman.

'Very lucky indeed. Well I'll be sure to let you know if I come across this Timmis character.' replied

Ramone.

Ramone then spent a little time in the Guild trying to find more information. When he found out that the thieves were on the look out for Timmis across Dale Bay, he decided to leave.

'Anitaa, I have to go, I'll see you round.' said Ramone.

'You can't be going so soon?' asked Anitaa.

'I have to. Take care of yourself.' said Ramone as he left the Guild.

Ramone returned to the docks, then the Black Dog Inn. He went immediately to room nineteen, and knocked the door.

'Hey, it's me.' said Ramone.

Timmis unlocked the door, then opened it.

'I'm glad you are back, I'm bloody starving. Can we go and get food?' asked Timmis.

'No, we need to get out of Tarrondale *right* away.' replied Ramone in a serious tone.

'The Guild have put a bounty on your head, five thousand gold pieces dead or alive.'

Timmis gasped and went ashen pale.

'Bonna is the new guild leader at Morrack, and he framed you for the killings in the guild. He also told them you stole the wand and talisman from him. Right now Timmis, every thief and bounty hunter in the Dale Bay area is after your head.'

'But I...I didn't do any of that!' protested Timmis.

'I know that, *you* know that. But right now *they* don't care, and because I know the truth, Bonna will have me killed too.' replied Ramone.

'But where will we go to?' asked Timmis.

'We need to get out of Dale Bay, get a boat to Port-Stalwart, and from there a boat to either Hateem or Snowvael.

They are both a long way round, but much safer routes.'

'Plus there is no Thieves' Guild in Port-Stalwart. So if we do run into any trouble it will likely be bounty hunters only.' said Ramone.

'Ahh, *only bounty hunters*, nothing to worry about then. That's not very *reassuring*.' replied a concerned looking Timmis.

'But right now we need to get out of here. We'll head out the back way through the window.' said Ramone, pushing the window up and climbing onto the roof.

'Let's go.' said Ramone.

Timmis followed Ramone onto the roof, then both men climbed down into rear courtyard of the inn, and exited onto the street. They made their way down to Tarrondale docks, regularly checking around them, in case they were being followed.

They found a fishing boat that was about to set sail for Port-Stalwart. Initially, the Captain was loathe to take passengers, but Timmis offered him twenty gold pieces and he quickly accepted. Timmis then boarded the craft and went below deck.

Ramone sat down on the deck, staring at his feet.

'I can't believe you were planning to go *without* me.' said a female voice.

Ramone looked up and Anitaa was standing on the gangplank.

'*You* followed me?' asked Ramone.

'Yes, you and the man with you. I knew you would head out of the back of the Black Dog Inn. That's what you taught me.' said Anitaa.

'Anitaa, you can't come. It's too dangerous.' said Ramone.

'That man with you, he's Timmis isn't he? I could tell by your eyes you had seen him when you spoke to Owanne.' said Anitaa.

Ramone instantly knew that she had figured it out, she had always been clever. Lying to her now would only insult her intelligence.

'The stuff that happened in Morrack is a lie. Timmis didn't kill Osumain, Bonna did.' said Ramone. An intrigued look came to Anitaa's face.

'How do you know?' asked Anitaa.

'I was there at the time. I overheard him fighting with Osumain. I left the Guild, then hid watching the entrance. Then I saw him chase the screaming doorman out of the guild and into the sewers. Bonna even had a dagger stuck in his back.'

'Bonna moved like no man I ever saw. There was something strange about him. When I thought the coast was clear I entered the Guild and found everyone dead. Timmis wasn't even there at the time.' said Ramone.

'I believe you.' Anitaa replied sympathetically.

'I wanted to keep you out of this. Bonna framed Timmis, and he'll kill me too because I know the truth of what *really* happened. Now you are in danger too.' said Ramone.

'What do you mean I'm in danger *now*? I'm *always* in danger *every* day.' replied Anitaa laughing.

Despite everything she always managed to smile, thought Ramone.

'If you come along there is no turning back, you have to understand that. They will hunt you too.

Or you can go back to the Guild, and forget you ever ran into me.

But this boat leaves right now.' said Ramone.

Ramone looked at Anitaa, and wondered what she was thinking. She had been his apprentice seven years ago, and she had become an excellent thief since.

'What *are* we waiting for then! Let's go!' said Anitaa.

Anitaa and Ramone went below deck, the Captain then set sail, leaving Tarrondale behind.

Below deck, Timmis was drinking from a small flagon of rum. He turned round and was surprised to see Ramone and the woman beside him.

'Who is she?' asked Timmis in a concerned tone.

'This is Anitaa, Timmis, she's coming with us.' said Ramone in a calm reassuring manner.

'*You're* the guy they are after.' said Anitaa.

'How did you find us?' asked Timmis.

'I followed Ramone.' said Anitaa.

'I thought you said no-one was following us?' Timmis asked Ramone.

'I did, maybe I'm loosing my touch.' replied, Ramone laughing.

'Well I did teach her all she knows.' joked Ramone.

'I think you might have taught her *too* well.' laughed Timmis.

'We have two choices Timmis, we head back to Morrack then after Bonna, or go back to where you found those items.' said Ramone.

'What about finding the hooded man. Could we go to Dale Bay Island?' asked Timmis.

'Dale Bay is now too dangerous, plus we have no idea where he went after that.' replied Ramone.

'You would never get near Bonna, he and his men will be on high alert.' added Anitaa.

'She's right. We need to go back to the Stone City.' said Ramone.

'Do you know *how dangerous* it is there?' Timmis grimaced, as he said the words.

'Yes, but no more dangerous than going to Morrack. And you know the safest way in and out.' replied Ramone.

Timmis sighed, 'OK, Stone City it is. We should travel to Hateem, then go north.' said Timmis.

'Agreed.' said Ramone smiling.

CHAPTER 19

The Corporal escorted the young woman to the quarters of Knight-Marshal Garlan.

'This is Lord Garlan's quarters ma'am.'

The soldier knocked on the door, and listened.

'Come in.' said Roe.

The Corporal opened the doors and held it open for the woman. Through the doors walked an attractive, brown eyed blonde who appeared to be in her early twenties.

'Lady Rowena.' said Lord Garlan.

'You have arrived. Please come in and have a seat. Master-at-Arms Roe, please…some refreshments for Lady Rowena.' added Garlan.

The young woman curtsied to Garlan, and he bowed in response.

Allun Roe brought a wine jug to the table and poured a glass for Rowena.

'Thank you.' she said to Roe smiling.

'Lady Rowena, please be seated.' said Garlan.

'Sir Jeffrey received your message, and he informed King Tarnus. Both the King and Sir Jeffrey are concerned about recent events.

The attack on Glyvale was most disturbing.' said Rowena.

'I'm afraid, my lady, Hander was also attacked. There was only one survivor from the village. We have also had watchtowers attacked by these undead.' replied Garlan.

'Sir Jeffrey has requested that you investigate the Stone City.' said Rowena.

'But what about our treaty with the elves?' asked Garlan.

'This mission must be completed covertly. A small team only, and they will need to go in disguise. They cannot be linked to the army, King Tarnus or Tarrondale.' said Rowena.

'The men will be collectively known as 'the Marauders', not called Scouts or anything else, they should not even use their ranks. The men are to be kept under vows of extreme secrecy, on pain of death. They cannot mention their mission, role or purpose, even to close friends or family.'

'They will have to operate outside of our territory, their orders will come from Sir Jeffery to yourself.
Only you and Master-at-Arms Roe are to be aware.'

'The head of the Thieves' Guild in Morrack was murdered, along with several of his accomplices. We don't know if the killings were linked.' said Rowena.

'A murdered thief is hardly unusual my Lady.' added Garlan.

'In most circumstances, that would be true Lord Garlan, but they were murdered *inside* the Guild itself.' replied Rowena.

'Assassins?' added Garlan.

'Perhaps. But we are monitoring the situation closely in Morrack. They already have a new Guild leader appointed there.' replied Rowena.

'And who do you want to lead these Marauders?'

asked Garlan.

'I'll leave that entirely up to you Lord Garlan. You will need someone familiar with the area and competent. Do you have anyone in mind?' asked Rowena.

'I do, and he is here already.' replied Garlan.
Lord Garlan looked at Roe, and he nodded knowingly in agreement.

'Would you like to meet him?' asked Garlan.

'Yes my Lord, that would be a good idea.' said Rowena.

'Master-at-Arms, can you please fetch him?' said Garlan looking at Roe.

'Yes, sir. At once.' replied Roe, exiting the room.

Lord Garlan walked to the window and stared out. The courtyard was busy, several supply wagons had arrived from Tarrondale. The soldiers were unloading the goods and new troops had arrived. He saw Rebekah climbing into the wagon, and taking a seat. Beside her were some soldiers. She must be heading off now to re-unite with her brother, Garlan thought. His brief moment of contemplation was broken by a knock at the door.

Roe returned to the room accompanied by Captain Burke at his side. They approached the table, and Burke's eyes met with Rowena.

'Lady Rowena, this is Captain Evan Burke, the garrison commander at High Peak watchtower.' said Garlan.
Captain Burke saluted the Knight-Marshal and bowed to Lady Rowena.

'No need for such formality Captain. I am Lady Rowena.' said the blonde woman.

'Lord Garlan here clearly holds you in very high regard Captain. He has selected you for an important new role. Please be seated and he will explain the situation to you.'

'Captain Burke', began Garlan, 'we need you for a mission of the *utmost* importance. Complete discretion and secrecy are *critical*.'

'We will be forming a new unit, that will have no links to the Scouts, army or Tarrondale. They won't even use ranks or uniform. They have to be *completely* anonymous. The new unit will be called the Marauders.' said Garlan.

'I want *you* to lead them Captain. You will need a good second in command. I can recommend Master-at-Arms Zill. You can choose the others, but it must be a small team.' said Garlan.

'Your orders will come directly to me, and you will only answer to myself. Just another thing; to help you, I will assign Brother Oram, my cleric, and Keesha, one of our magi here to the Marauders.' added Garlan.

'You views Captain?'

'Well sir, I...of course I will accept.' said Burke. The Knight-Marshal laughed.

'You have volunteered and I haven't even told you where you will be going. That's certainly dedication on your part Captain.'

'Your first mission is to investigate Stone City. We will then assign other missions as required.' said Garlan.

'*Now* I understand why the need for secrecy, the elves would be most upset.' said Burke.

'Indeed Captain, we need you to scout the area and report back to Lord Garlan.' added Rowena.

'Captain, who else do you want in your team?' asked Garlan.

'Well sir, it would make sense to use those who have experience in the High Peaks. Corporal Haynes, Bartack, Derrin and Tellan.' said Burke.

'You have them. Master-at-Arms Roe, can you please bring all of them here, and ask Brother Oram and Keesha to attend? Thank you.' commanded Garlan.
The old Sergeant-Major left the room.

'Major Burke, this is of the utmost importance to Sir Jeffrey and King Tarnus, please understand that.' said Rowena.

'My Lady, with respect, I'm only a Captain.' replied Burke.

'You mean you *were* a Captain, Major. This role comes with a promotion.' replied Rowena.

'*Thank-you my Lady.*' replied Burke.
Burke was pleasantly surprised; then realised that even though he had gained the rank, he wouldn't even be using it.

'Well done Evan.' said the Knight-Marshal congratulating him.

'Thank-you sir. But what about the High Peaks watch tower? Who will take command of the garrison there?' asked Burke.

'Who do you think would make a good commander there?' asked Garlan.

'Quartermaster Tyerose has done an excellent job, both when I was there and during my absence, as Corporal Haynes will attest.' said Burke.

'Then the Quartermaster will be promoted to the rank of Ensign. Here, take this letter of commission. You will be able to deliver it to him in person.' said Garlan.

There was a knock at the door, and Master-at-Arms Roe entered accompanied by Haynes, Bartack, Tellan and Brother Oram. Behind them walked a half-elf female who was wearing a yellow robe. Her features were petite and attractive; she had light brown hair and intense emerald coloured eyes.

'Ahh, welcome everyone. And thank-you Keesha.' said Garlan.

The half-elf female bowed to Lord Garlan.

'My Lord.' said Keesha.

'Now everyone, please be seated, we have much to discuss.'

****

The enchantment had succeeded, and the grey robed tusk-man was now pacified and under her control. He indicated to the warriors to lower their weapons, and brought Drusilla and Yandora into his hut.

'My name is Drusilla and this is Yandora my companion.' said Marr's priestess.

'My name is Barotar. You are humans, you took our lands.' said the grey robed tusk-man.

Drusilla had to hold in a laugh at this comment.

'Well, we may look human, but really we are not. My master has asked me to find allies to help him. Naturally I think you and your people would make ideal allies.' said Drusilla.

'But what do you want from us?' asked the tuskman.

'You have warriors, and priests?' said Drusilla.

'Of course. But why should I risk my people for your cause?' asked Barotar.

'Your people were driven from their lands in the Emberdale basin. My master will help your people reclaim your lands once again.' said Drusilla.

'You come here to our settlement and tell me your master cares for us? I'm sorry. But I will need much more than the word of a stranger.' replied Barotar.

'We understand that this may be difficult for you to accept. All we ask is that we be given the opportunity to prove ourselves. Now what can *we* do for you?' asked Drusilla.

'Very well stranger. A chance for you to prove yourself then. Nearby there is a human settlement, a small village. Can you assist my warriors when we raid it?' asked Barotar.

'We will do more than assist, we will raise the village to the ground. There can be no survivors though, none. *That* is the price.' replied Drusilla.

'Very well, my warriors will lead you to the village on a raiding party. Once you have been successful, return to see me.' said Barotar.

Barotar, Drusilla and Yandora left the hut. Outside the

tusk-people were impatiently waiting for an answer from Barotar.

'My people. These strangers want to be friends, and help us regain our land stolen from us. First though, they must prove themselves worthy. They will help our warriors on a raid. There must be no survivors there.' replied Barotar.

'Damaak, you and your men go with the strangers and lead them to the human village north of here.' commanded Barotar.

Damaak gathered his men, and left northwards followed by Drusilla and Yandora.

The tusk people watched the war party leave with anticipation of victory.

****

Amera and Hazak had made their way through the Great Western Wood, sticking closely to the edge of Steppes of Garmer. They had not seen any wood elves since their previous encounter. Before them was the famous Pass of Garmer, which linked the western trade route to the east.

Once the area had been heavily defended, but now the old watchtower there was in ruins. Travellers to this area had to rely on their own fortitude to protect themselves.

They travelled into the pass, the wastelands were to the north-west, while the settlement of Hopeley lay to the south-east, just past the ruins of Old Garmer tower.

Amera and Hazak rode into the wastelands, the soil became grey and cracked. No longer was there vegetation. The land was pock marked, and the only features were tall mounds of rock that looked like termite mounds. To the north were the calderas, and the fire mountains.

Pockets of steam periodically rose from fissures in the ground, as they exuded an acrid, sulphurous smell into the air. Few living beings ventured here, and for good reason. The air was toxic and burned the throat. For Amera and Hazak this was not an issue.

Their horses began to struggle, and the animals snorted frequently, trying their best to inhale fresh air. This was practically impossible, and only exacerbated the mounts' desperation.

They pushed on, then Hazak, as a former knight, noticed his horse was nervous.
He looked about him, but could see nothing. In the distance, to the right of them, they heard a roar. He drew his broadsword, readying himself.

Amera began to speak a protection prayer. They listened carefully, then heard shouts and the roar once again. Hazak dismounted, giving Amera the reins of his horse. He crept up to the top of a small hillock and peered over.

He could see four men with a horse drawn cart battling desperately with a saurian creature. The horse had been killed by the creature. The beast was ten foot tall and stood on two legs with a long thick tail. It had four small arms and a sizeable head with large white protruding teeth. The men slashed and stabbed at the creature trying to force it backwards.

The saurian roared, circled and snapped at the men. The whole scene amused Hazak and he wondered who would be the victor from this encounter. What these men were doing in the area was anyone's guess. However to be here, you would either have to be incredibly brave or extremely foolish.

The saurian beast bit at one of the men, tearing off his left arm and shoulder. The man screamed in agony and fell to the ground, blood poured from the wound. His companions battled with the beast to try and force it back. One of the men tried to aid his wounded companion.

The saurian beast roared once again and advanced on the men.
It bit at the companion of the injured man, removing his head in one bite. The two uninjured men broke and ran, leaving their injured companion and the remains of the other man. The beast roared and came in for the kill, mercilessly tearing the injured man apart. The creature hungrily gulped down its victim's remains.

The creature began to feed on the remains of the headless human and the dead horse. Hazak smiled, it certainly was entertaining, the beast was indeed fearsome, and he admired its power and aggression. He returned to Amera, remounted his horse and indicated the safe direction to take.

'Some men were being attacked by a creature, we need to avoid these animals.' said Hazak to Amera.

There would no doubt be more of these creatures about and they would need to avoid them. Hazak knew he could use the horses to detect them as the animals would smell the beasts first. The dark paladin began to chant and he cast a protection prayer over himself and Amera.

As they got closer to the calderas, they could see grey smoke rising. At the base of the caldera were cave entrances. The riders dismounted and secured their horses as best they could. The caves were wide and tall, and on either side the cave walls were covered in blue and green crystals. The crystals seemed to glow by themselves, but there was no apparent light source.

The crystals at least, Amera thought, would partially light their way. Amera chanted and a yellow sphere appeared three feet above her head. The sphere illuminated a circle of light twenty feet around her in every direction.

They continued through the cave tunnels; on the cave ceiling the crystals were larger than before. Eventually the tunnel began to widen, and they entered a massive chamber. The crystals in the ceiling sparkled like stars in the night sky.

In the middle of the chamber stood ten sky blue crystal dolmens in a circle. Amera and Hazak approached the crystal circle, and they began to shimmer. There was also a notable humming noise, then the crystals in the entire chamber shimmered too in unison.

Blue light from all the crystals in the chamber travelled towards the centre of the circle forming together. The blue light began to take the shape of a humanoid, the light solidified into a blue stone-like figure.

'Welcome, followers of Gorath Marr.' said the blue stone humanoid.

Amera and Hazak bowed to the figure.

'I have felt the power of your master awaken, something I have not felt for a very long time.

Your master's heart rages like the great volcanoes here. Now why do you come here?' asked the blue stone humanoid.

'Our master has woken from his long slumber, and he commanded that we find you. He has need of your help.' said Amera.

'What does Gorath Marr ask of us?' asked the blue stone humanoid.

'We need your assistance against the elves. What is your price?' replied Amera.

'We earth elementals lived on the Immortal Isle when the elves first arrived there. They found our crystals and used us as slaves to do their bidding to build their cities.'

'We helped them move the rocks and stones. We were the architects of their very buildings, draining our own life force in the process.'

'Then, when our toil was completed, instead of returning us to the earth, they imprisoned us inside their weapons and wands. Each time these were used it drained us more and more. Until nothing was left, but a husk.'

'The husk that was left became a prize jewel for the elves. Upon the very crowns of the elf lords sits the remains of my people.'

'So I will join you, and my people will join you. The price will be freeing my people who are trapped and returning the Immortal Isle to us for perpetuity.' said the blue stone elemental.

'Agreed.' said Amera.

'Now where do you wish us to go.' asked the blue stone elemental.

'My master is trying to build an army. Come to the Stone City and meet Gorath Marr. Will you travel with us?' asked Amera.

'We are elementals, and can travel the earth and through the core of Dolia.' replied the blue stone elemental.

'I shall go to your master with some of my people.' said the blue stone elemental.

The elemental's form began to dissipate, and the blue light that formed him returned to the crystals on the chamber's ceiling.

Amera looked at Hazak, and smiled. She knew that Gorath Marr would be pleased. He had been angry with Mareck's carelessness. This would go a long way to placating her master and increase his favour.

'Where do we go now? Do we return to Marr?' asked Hazak.

'Not yet Hazak. We have to visit Morra Blackhammer at Stonewold. When we move against the elves we will need their warriors.' said Amera.

Hazak and Amera returned to the entrance of the cave. Their horses were still tied where they left them. The pair mounted their steeds, and began the journey back towards the Pass of Garmer.

****

The human village was now in ruins, the bodies of the villagers littered the area. The tusk-men had been merciless, and had slain any person who had been there. Drusilla and Yandora had assisted the tusk-men by casting curses upon the inhabitants as they were being attacked.

The tusk-men burned the village, setting fire to the thatch of the huts. They also herded any livestock and looted any items of significance. Damaak walked over to Drusilla.

'Thanks to you and your friend for your help. If your master is as powerful as you, I predict a great victory ahead. Your help will not go unnoticed by Barotar and our clans. He will spread the word that the re-conquest will soon begin.' said Damaak.

The raiding group left the smouldering village, then returned to the tusk-men settlement. The people ran out to greet them and standing at the front was Barotar.

Damaak and his men gave a victorious yell, and the crowd cheered. Barotar raised his hands aloft, and the tusk-men roared louder in approval. The tusk-men herded the captured animals into their own corrals. Damaak approached Barotar, who blessed the warrior with his staff.

'Barotar, these strangers were powerful in battle. We swept the humans aside. With these people, the re-conquest of Emberdale is assured.' said Damaak.

'I will send word to the clans that we will soon be returning to our homeland.' said Barotar.

Drusilla and Yandora approached Barotar.

'I hope we have proven our worth. Now will you assist us?' asked Drusilla.

'Yes. I will gather the clans. But I wish to meet your master. Myself, Damaak, and some of my men will travel with you to meet him.' said Barotar.

Drusilla smiled, she had secured a useful ally.

'Excellent. We shall leave at once. We will be climbing to the Stone City, so please prepare your men for the climb. My master will be most pleased to see you.' said Drusilla smiling.

Barotar signalled to Damaak to prepare his men. Damaak bowed and the tusk-men warriors started to put on warm clothing, gather rope and weapons, pack food supplies and torches in preparation of the ascent.

They knew that the climb would not be easy, but they were already fully acclimatised to the cold conditions. They had regularly hunted above the snowline around the north face of the High Peaks.

Drusilla, Yandora, Barotar, Damaak and twenty tusk-men warriors left the village and began the journey towards the north face. They looked up, and could see the clouds caressing the great mountain tops in front of them.

Drusilla was both impatient and excited, she would once again return to her master. She was certain that the alliance with these tusk-men would prove favourable, and Gorath Marr would be pleased.

CHAPTER 20

Old Grey-back and his troll pack began to cautiously approach the human ruins. They had avoided the tusk-men settlements, sticking closely to the slopes of the Great High Peak's north face. He sniffed the air, checking for threats.

He could smell the faint scent of trolls, and for the first time Grey-back began to feel relaxed. The ruins themselves were an old stone keep, one of the outer walls had completely collapsed. In its day, it would have been an impressive sight, but it had become redundant after the tusk-men clearances from Emberdale.

Surplus to requirements, the keep was long abandoned, and was now reclaimed by nature. Now only huge vines of ivy covered the keep's missing wall. The wall stones themselves were scattered across the ground, moss covered, and lying where they came to rest many years before.

Grey-back listened, and he could hear movement from within the tower. Suddenly there was a loud 'whoop' and a huge, grey troll burst through the ivy vines and began running towards the pack.
Grey-back immediately recognised the troll's scent, it was the mighty White-Tusk!

Grey-back barked in response, and the pack moved forward to greet their leader. White-Tusk was relieved to see his pack members arrive.

The cubs were physically exhausted, and one was

critically ill. The dwarf pursuit of the group had been relentless, and they all desperately needed food and rest. Grey-back let out a sad whimper to White-Tusk, and the huge grey troll knew that some of the pack had been lost in the exodus.

The group entered the old keep through the vines. Inside they excitedly reunited with the other members of the pack. The females tended to the cubs, but the ill cub finally succumbed. The fear, trauma and exhaustion of the flight had been too much for him.

Grey-back sniffed and gently nudged the dead cub with his nose. He began to whimper and whine. A fiery rage then filled the belly of the great troll, and he let out an enormous roar of anger.

The pack heard this, and they all responded to this anguished howl. The creatures all began to give a melancholy howl in unison.

The dwarves had taken Old Grey-back's child, and the strange smelling humans had taken his home. He would not forget this great wrong. His people were now safe, at least for a short time. They would have to hunt food, rest and grow strong again.

Grey-back walked outside alone to console himself after the loss, and then looked southwards. He saw the cloud covered Great High Peak towering in the distance, and his heart longed for his home in the Stone City.

****

Gorath Marr was now much calmer, he knew his followers were busy finding him allies. He felt he had chastised Mareck too much. After all, he thought, Mareck was child-like in his quest for his master's favour. He had only wanted to please Marr.

Mareck's fear of both losing his looks and old age had originally driven the bard into the arms of Marr. The lich had given him the gift of eternal life and he would also never physically age. The price was high, as Mareck had become a vampera, and his soul was bound to Marr. His bard music, once a thing of admiration and joy, had become utterly corrupted and malignant.

Marr hadn't necessarily disliked what Mareck had done to the human settlements, he only disapproved of the timing. When the time *was* right, he fully intended to unleash Mareck and his piccolo.

Marr had noticed that the elven crypts contained many full skeletons. This had given him an idea. He would ask Mareck to play his piccolo and animate the elven skeletons as guards.

Marr gave a twisted, rasping laugh at this thought. Not only had he claimed the city of his former enemies, he would use the remains of their own dead to do his bidding.

'Mareck. Mareck.' rasped the lich.
From the corner shadows of the throne room, Mareck appeared into the flame-light.

'Yes master, you called for me.' said Mareck, almost like a dog being summoned by its owner.

'The elf skeletons. Play your piccolo, raise them and let them hear the beauty of your music.' said Gorath Marr.

The words were a joy to the bard's ears, his master

had forgiven him. Mareck brought out his piccolo and began to play. The sound echoed through the old building and into the ruins.

Marr sat and listened to the music, despite his age and decay the tune brought back a memory of his youth. Perhaps the music was his last link to the living world, he pondered? This memory was quickly buried, and Marr's thoughts returned to the present.

He could hear stirring below and around the crypt. Mareck finished his tune.

'Come forward and pay homage to your new master.' said Mareck.

Entering through the doors of the old building walked scores of reanimated elf skeletons. They continued to wear the armour and carry the weapons that they owned while alive.

'Guard the Stone City and attack any enemies that you find. No survivors and no mercy.' commanded Gorath Marr.

The elf skeletons began to chatter their teeth in approval and they quickly left the room, spreading out within the city. Marr knew that these were only temporary guards, and little more than a deterrent against intruders.

Despite the elf skeletons' weakness, they were plentiful and willing volunteers to his cause. When his followers returned, things would be much clearer. Marr's wand and talisman were still missing, and this troubled him.

He had tried to scry for the items earlier, but for some reason his vision had been blocked. He suspected that someone was using magic to hide them. This troubled him even more, and he would need to find the source of this.

****

Amera and Hazak had finally reached the end of the Great Western Wood, and on their left lay the mighty High Falls. They carefully left the slopes of The Cut and entered the Brokenlands below, it was a strange contrast from abundant vegetation to none.

The great dwarf city of Stonewold lay to the south, and the pair of riders made haste. The terrain was difficult, as it was both stony and hilly. Many large boulders covered the area, and these were the only realistic places you could hide. The area had no real cover, and the horses kicked up dust as they moved.

Riders in this location would be easy to spot, but that did not discourage Marr's disciples. In the distance Amera could see a small cloud of dust approaching them. As she got closer, she could see the cloud was created by four dwarven riders. Amera and Hazak reigned in their tired horses and waited for the dwarves to approach.

'Lost are we? Not often we get humans travelling through these parts any more.' said the dwarf warrior.

'We are here to visit a friend. Morra Blackhammer asked me to call on him the next time I passed.' said Amera.

'Well its not for me to interfere with any of Blackhammer's friends. If you are the kind of company he keeps, you're probably best avoided anyway.' replied the dwarf in a wary tone.

Amera smiled, by the sound of it this Blackhammer would be a fine ally.

'Just head into the city, you don't need to find Blackhammer, he'll find you.' said the dwarf.

Amera and Hazak continued on towards the city. The buildings were built from stone blocks, the colour matching the hills perfectly. A large number of dwarves filled the streets going about their business. There was a small market which had stalls, selling armour, weapons, food and clothes.

Amera approached one of the traders.

'I am looking for Morra Blackhammer.' said Amera to an old dwarf trader.

'I think you have found him.' said a voice coming from behind her.

Amera turned around and Morra was standing there with a dozen of his warriors.

'Glad to see you made it back Amera.' said Morra.

'I have considered your offer, we will help you providing you can help us drive the dark elves out of Heighgaard.' added the dwarf.

'My master will help you.' replied Amera.

'Now, before my people aid you against the elves, I would like to visit the Stone City with you. Meet your master. *Then*, I will decide.' said Morra.

'Very well, master dwarf. I welcome you to accompany me and Hazak back to Stone City.
You may bring as many of your men with you as you see fit…if that makes you feel safer.' said Amera teasing

the dwarf.

Blackhammer was surprised by the comment, it was almost as if Amera was challenging him to go alone. For a second, he almost agreed, but then he let the comment go.

'Well Amera, we better be off then. Which way do you intend to head to the Stone City?' asked Morra.

'We will take the south face of the High Peaks. Past the humans. Does that concern you?' asked Amera. Blackhammer now began to feel that she was in some way testing his resolve.

'Humans don't concern me Amera. Do they worry *you*?' said Morra in a riposte.

Amera smiled, she knew she had touched a nerve, but the dwarf would never admit to it.

'If our alliance is successful I will recommend to King Ironforge that we join your side.' said Morra.

Morra's comment put Amera on the back foot, after all she was the one who had to find allies. Having the dwarves on their side would be critical against any war with the elves.

Morra signalled to his men to mount their horses and prepare to leave.

'We ride to the Stone City! Dwarves once again return to the High Peaks!' shouted Morra aloud.

The watching dwarves gave a loud cheer. This was a significant event, as his people had not been there since the elves claimed the area for themselves.

'Should we not travel by the tunnel to the High Peaks?' one of his men asked Morra.

'No. But we should find the entrance to the great

tunnel once we are there. We will follow our allies here above ground. *For now.*' said Morra.

The crowd was still cheering loudly as Amera and Hazak rode their horses east, followed by Morra and his men. The dwarf crowds waved and cheered them goodbye as they rode out. If this alliance was successful, it was guaranteed that the King would name Blackhammer as his future heir of the dwarf lands. Morra smiled to himself, and urged his men on.

****

The eight Marauders - Major Burke, Zill, Haynes, Derrin, Tellan, Brother Oram, Keesha and Bartack - prepared to leave Ormsby Keep.
Lord Garlan, Rowena and Roe watched as the men exited the gates of the fortress.

Their uniforms were absent and they wore the clothes of fur trappers. Thankfully, the fur trade in the village around the keep was brisk, and they easily acquired the clothing.

Keesha found the appearance of Brother Oram amusing, as the monk had worn nothing but a habit since a boy. Oram himself felt rather awkward about his new appearance.

Burke and Haynes were on horseback, but Zill drove the wagon. In the back were the three boys, Oram and Keesha. The wagon was full of supplies, an oil barrel, rope, torches and animal traps of varying sizes. There was no indication that they were in the Royal Scouts.

Each of the Scouts were armed with a cross bow and short sword. They also had a small hand axe tucked into their belts. Oram only had a staff and Keesha had a small dagger.

To the casual observer they looked like any other party of trappers who were heading out on a hunt. That was exactly the image that they wanted to portray.

'We return to High Peak watchtower first, stay overnight there and then head into the mountains.' said Burke.

'Remember we don't mention any of this mission to anyone. Not a thing.' he added.

'Sir, how should we address you?' asked Zill.

'Certainly not as sir once we leave the keep. You can call me Evan or Burke, but nothing else. The same goes for the rest of you. If our disguise is to succeed we have to appear as we are not.' said Burke in reply.

The wagon headed north following Haynes and Burke who were acting as outriders. The wagon made the speed of the journey much slower, and it bumped frequently as it rolled along the stone road.

Derrin remembered the last time he had travelled there in a wagon. He wondered how the wagon driver Michael was fairing and if he had been at Beanoch when it had been attacked. Bartack, who had been to the tower, had never mentioned seeing Michael there, so he assumed he had left before anything had happened. Besides, Michael was very savvy. There are not many people who would be brave enough to drive a wagon alone around here.

Oram began to meditate, Derrin thought he had

gone asleep, and he laughed at this. The monk had his eyes closed and appeared motionless. Bartack was impressed by this, as remaining still and undistracted on a moving cart took some doing.

Keesha became bored and tired, the furs she wore still smelled of animals. The Mages' Guild would be aghast if they saw her dressed like this, she thought to herself. She expected this trip to be uncomfortable, and she rolled over onto her side, then drifted off to sleep.

In the distance, they could see the mountain tops of the mighty High Peaks. For Derrin it was like deja vu once again. His apprehension though, was much less, as now he knew what to expect.

The wagon and riders wound their way through the steppes and into the snow covered tundra. Around them the fir trees were covered in a layer of snow. Eventually the party arrived at the watchtower. They had been long spotted by the tower guards, and outside the keep two Scouts approached.

'It's the Captain and the others!' shouted the excited Scout.

The wagon rolled up and those in the back climbed out. Keesha was abruptly woken by Bartack. Brother Oram ended his meditation, it was almost like he had been fully aware of his surroundings the whole time. Zill started to untie the horses from the wagon and led them into the stables.

Quartermaster Tyerose and Sergeant O'Rourke came outside to see Major Burke.

'Welcome back sir, I'm glad to see you return.' said Tyerose.

'Glad to be back, but it will be only for a short time. I have a new assignment, along with the others, starting tomorrow. We will only be here for the night.' replied Burke.

'So you won't *be* back sir?' said the concerned Quartermaster.

Burke opened his saddle bag and removed a parchment.

'I have something for you Quartermaster.' said Burke as he handed it to Tyerose.

Tyerose opened the letter and he began reading, his eyes lit up.

'Sir. This is *great* news. Thank-you.' said Tyerose.

'This is your commission signed by Lord Garlan himself. No-one deserves it more. Congratulations *Ensign* Tyerose.' replied Burke.

Tyerose saluted to Burke.

'*Ensign* Tyerose! If that's true, I'll be a Master-at-Arms by the time I leave here.' joked O'Rourke. The others laughed.

'Let's get inside and have a good meal to celebrate.' said Tyerose, and they all headed into the watchtower to dine.

Derrin and Bartack caught up with Toby and Markus who had missed them since they had been away. Burke allowed Keesha to use his private quarters, and he slept downstairs with the Sergeants.

The Marauders lay down for the night. They would be leaving at dawn, and then climb into the High Peaks. Although they were familiar with the climate, none of them had ever ventured into the Stone City before, nor knew what awaited them there.

****

Ramone, Timmis and Anitaa disembarked from the boat. Before them was the bustling harbour of Port-Stalwart. There was every kind of boat at the docks. Fishing boats, clippers, galleons, carracks to schooners all lining the quays.

Ramone had never seen as many craft before, and the port even dwarfed Tarrondale docks for its size. This is a place where you could easily get lost. It was also a place, he thought, you could get lost in and never be seen again too.

They had to be careful here; there was no Thieves' Guild in Port-Stalwart, but that didn't mean it was safe either, or that no thieves operated in this location. Corsairs, smugglers and pirates would frequent such a place in order to sell off their booty. There were also slave markets here, and slavers were particularly brutal and savage.

Any thief that did operate here would also be brutal, and actively breaking Thieves' Guild rules. All in all, the denizens of Port-Stalwart were not the most pleasant people. However, they did not ask questions, and for Ramone and Timmis, that would be critical for their escape.

They searched the docks for a craft that was bound for Hateem. The craft they selected was perfect, a small grain ship carrying flour and wheat.
They paid their passage to the Captain. The ship's Captain was a merchant from Port-hareesh, and

Hateem was their first stop en route to Portdarmass and the rich farming lands of the Plains of Woodingvale.

A flour and grain ship, more importantly, would also be less attractive to pirates. There was very little sell on profit for stolen grain, and pirates preferred high value cargo, such as jewellery, coinage or precious metals.

'We set off now. We must must be gone by noon from this port.' said the Captain.

The crew made ready with the sails, and cast off the lines. The ship began to move and quickly exited the mouth of the harbour. Around them other ships were arriving and departing the port.

'Why the hurry?' Ramone asked the Captain.

'Less chance of pirates. See that man fishing at the harbour mouth wall?' said the Captain pointing.

Ramone looked and sure enough, there was an old man fishing.

'That's a pirate lookout. If he sees a high value ship he'll signal by smoke or lamp to pirates awaiting offshore.' added the Captain.

Ramone smiled, he wasn't so sure, and the whole thing sounded very far fetched to be true. The Captain sounded gripped by paranoia, thought Ramone to himself. Still, at least he was cautious, and that isn't always a bad thing.

Timmis stood nervously on the deck watching the harbour get further and further away. Anitaa lay down on the deck to enjoy the afternoon sun.

'Did I ever tell you that I hate boats.' said Timmis

to Ramone.

'No.' replied Ramone.

'Hate them, I get terrible sea sickness.' replied Timmis.

'Well *now* you tell me. It's a bit late to be telling me that.' replied Ramone laughing.

Anitaa heard this and laughed too.

'I think this could be a stormy trip.' said Anitaa to Timmis, teasing him.

Timmis groaned, and his face looked pale and colourless.

'I think I'll go to my cabin and lie down for a bit.' said the nauseous Timmis, as he walked inside the ship. Ramone looked at Anitaa and they both laughed at this. The little ship was now under full sail, and cut through the sea calmly on its course for Hateem.

'I hope you weren't tempting fate about having a stormy trip.' said Ramone.

'I hope not either.' said Anitaa laughing.

'These sailors are a superstitious lot, you'll scare them.' said Ramone.

'Scare *them*? Would you like me to start talking about sea monsters next then?' jested Anitaa.

'No. We'll end up being set adrift by the ship's crew for wishing bad luck; and I don't fancy rowing all the way to Hateem.

Besides, sharing a rowing boat with a sea sick Timmis doesn't appeal to me either.' replied Ramone laughing.

Anitaa smiled, and nodded her head in agreement.

Anitaa now knew why she had decided to come along with Ramone and Timmis. When she was Ramone's apprentice, she was always guaranteed excitement and adventure. Picking pockets in Tarrondale could never match that previous high, and she missed it very much.

EPILOGUE

Radahl sat down at the table in front of the bearded man who was wearing red leather armour. The room was in darkness and only a small candle illuminated the area around the table.

Radahl appraised the bearded man, who had dark, piercing eyes and a scar across his right eye. The mage could tell he was a ruthless, cold blooded man.

'I need you to get rid of someone for me. He stole items of a most sensitive nature and was less than discrete about it.' said the mage.

'Look my friend, what this person did or didn't do, is of no interest to me.
Many people die everywhere each day, for what they did or didn't do.
Guilty or innocent, it makes no difference to me or my Guild.
I only need to know their name, and if you are you are willing to pay my price.' said Scar.

'His name is Timmis. I will pay you eight hundred gold. There can be no witnesses; and that includes anyone that you find with him.' said the mage.

'Well *that*, will cost you more than eight hundred gold my friend. Two thousand platinum. No less.' replied Scar, who remained straight faced and serious.

The mage decided not to negotiate the price; and nodded his approval of the contract. He knew that the task needed both discretion and ruthlessness, two qualities that fetched a high price. Besides,

Lord Amorass expected the task to be successfully completed, and cheapness was not a guarantee of any success, Radahl thought to himself.

'Now, where was the last place he was located?' asked Scar.

'The Thieves' Guild at Morrack.' replied Radahl.

'This will be easier than I thought. The Assassin's Guild *will* find him.' said Scar smirking confidently.

'Will you be seeking your quarry alone?' asked the mage, reluctantly.

'No, not this time. I will be accompanied by my associate Juleanna.' said Scar, making a hand gesture.

From the shadows, a slim, athletic, brown haired woman came forward towards the table. She wore tight black leather armour. She had a thin, chiselled, entrancing face, with sky blue, unfathomable eyes. She stared at Radahl, and for the first time, he felt an actual chill. Rarely was the mage afraid, but his inner sense told him to be wary.

The mage had been completely unaware that she had been in the room. There had been no sound from her, not even any breathing.

Radahl could tell Scar enjoyed the hunt the most; he lived for the hunt. But for this woman, it wasn't the hunt, it wasn't even the money, it was the kill. She would kill you in less than a heart beat; and would have forgotten about it a second later.

Radahl placed the leather purse on the table before Scar.

'Here is the deposit, and the remainder will be paid once the contract has been completed. You can

find me at my residence in Marandale.' said Radahl.
Scar lifted the purse, and took it off the table.

'Thank you, and now business is concluded.' said Scar bowing.

Radahl left, but then glanced back, and the woman was *still* watching him. He composed himself, but he could still almost feel her stare as he walked away. Timmis, he knew, was as good as dead.

ACKNOWLEDGEMENT

Special thanks to Gary Conway for all his help, advice and encouragement.

Printed in Great Britain
by Amazon

46273575R00169